THE ROAD TO WOLFE

BOOK 4 OF THE SANCTUARY SERIES

NIKITA SLATER

AUTHOR'S NOTE

Warning: Given current events happening in the world around us and due to the nature of this book some readers may find the content disturbing. I delve deep into the nature of the zombie virus, *Necrotitis Primeval*, as well as a more common but deadly flu. Both are dangerous threats to my post-apocalyptic Sanctuary world. If you think you might be triggered by similarities to the coronavirus, then please read with caution.

Thank you and take care,
Nikita Slater

You know that that old motto, life is a bitch and then you die? Yeah, that about sums it up. This is my life, in my words... and sometimes Wolfe's words. If you don't like it, you can walk away now. If you think you can handle my most-of-the-time bad attitude, then stick around, because this is going to be a wild ride.

I was born on August 15th, 2045. Twenty-three years after the Great Fall. I lived a happy life in Old Canada with my family until I was eleven. Then mom, dad and my little brother died from the flu. Not *Necrotitis Primeval* but something else. Something just as deadly but with less zombification. After the death of my parents, our home was no longer viable and I travelled with my sister, Taran, and my grandparents to the Nevada Sanctuary. We tried to build a new life, but flu and the fucking zombies killed that idea. When Nevada fell, I was unfortunately still inside. I got separated from my family and had to find my own way in the world.

Fast forward about twelve years and I finally set eyes on

my sister again. Life was much different. She was married to a Warlord and I was living in a harem, married to my own reclusive Warlord. I got to live in a palace, eat until my belly was full, wear beautiful clothes and bend the ear of the most powerful man in the city. Things should've been awesome, right?

Wrong.

Awesome turned to ashes when the fucking zombies figured out how to make nuclear meltdowns happen. I mean, how much shit needs to go wrong before we all just give up, lie down and die? I was forced to flee my Sanctuary and my husband by our head of security, the badass warrior and zombie hunter known as Wolfe. A man who terrorizes anyone and anything that comes near him. Except me. He took me back to my sister, where we would have had a joyful reunion if it weren't for the massive horde of Primitives that followed us into the Tucson Sanctuary.

If you think more shit couldn't possibly go down, you'd be wrong. Again.

We fought that horde for months, pushing them back over and over, only to be confronted with even more waves of them coming in from the east, chasing and picking off survivors searching for Sanctuary. Eventually we were able to come up with a solution; use my sister's and my magic virus-immune blood to kill the horde and vaccinate the survivors.

It worked!

The year is now 2075. Wolfe left, and I continued to live in the Tucson Sanctuary. Along with a group of warriors, I've been deployed to distribute the vaccine as far and as wide as we can get it, in an effort to eventually eradicate the disease that brought our civilization to the brink of destruction.

And we lived happily ever after....
Ha! Kidding.
Buckle up babes, this story is just getting started.

ONE

SKYE

Year: 2068, *7 years earlier*

LOCATION: Somewhere in the Mojave Desert

BOOM!

I flinch as a gun goes off over my head. Adrenaline surges through me and I have to fight the urge to climb out of the hole where I'm hiding and help. I've been tasked with keeping the children safe. I curl as tightly as I can, wrap my arms around the four terrified, clinging children and pray for the attack to be over.

I'm hidden beneath the floorboards of an old farmhouse we'd been using as a temporary shelter on our way to Sanctuary. I've been travelling with the same group of people for the past several months. There is a war happening above me, human versus zombie. The same fight we've been engaged in since the dawn of a virus that turns people into Primitives, terrifying zombie-like creatures. I long to sink my own blade into the enemy, to take my revenge for every loss I've been forced to endure, but I don't have the skills necessary to fight like a warrior.

As I hear the screams above me, I wonder if anyone is skilled enough to fight them off. Zombies move fast and attack without thought. No one is immune.

Except me.

Six years ago, when I was living in the Las Vegas Sanctuary I discovered that I was in fact immune. I found out in the worst possible way, at sixteen years of age, with a zombie's teeth buried deep in my throat. I'd closed my eyes, relaxed my muscles and waited for death. When I finally opened them again, the zombie was gone, my family was gone, and I was lying on a deserted road. I was terrified and confused, but I wasn't a Primitive.

Now, I am one of several survivors travelling from Sanctuary to Sanctuary. Searching for my family, I've been travelling for six long years. Every time I reach a Sanctuary, search the city and come up empty-handed, I leave with the next group of travelers as they head out. Most people who leave Sanctuary are in the same boat as me, searching for lost family members.

We travel together, occasionally mixing up our group as people discover their families or give up the search. Right now, we are between Sanctuaries, in a dangerous no man's land, where hordes of Primitives can easily get to us. We thought we'd be safe in this town. There's no gas here, no people, no reason for the Primitives to be hanging around. Yet, here we are, under attack.

I cringe as I hear another high-pitched scream that cuts off abruptly, probably because the screamer's throat was just ripped out. Another of our group has gone down. This horde is big, with far more zombies than I've ever seen in one place. At first, they were taking us out one at a time as we headed down to the creek for water or hunted for food. Then, as our defenses became weakened, they attacked en masse, swarming over us like a cloud of mosquitos. Now here I am, hidden away under the loose floorboards of an old abandoned house, with four children.

I squeeze my eyes shut tightly and wrap my arms around the little bodies clinging tightly to me, their frail arms gripping my clothes as we wait for the verdict above. It doesn't take long, maybe five more minutes, then an eerie silence falls. The battle is over.

I know without looking that we've lost. If the humans had won, we would hear them mourning the dead and calling out to each other. We emerge slowly from our hiding place, looking for any signs of life, but the humans are either dead or turned. I'm forced to comfort the little ones as they cry against me. What are we going to do now?

I try to organize the children, calm them down so they don't attract any straggling zombies, but I'm battling my own grief. Not over the people we've lost here. I don't let myself get close to anyone anymore. No, I'm battling my grief because once more my path back to my sister and my grandparents has been destroyed. Without the protection of other people, I won't be able to travel. We're sitting ducks out here.

My last thought is confirmed when I hear a growling sound from behind me. The tiny hairs on the back of my neck stand up and I slowly turn my head to the side, looking out of the corner of my eye.

Just inside the broken door of the broken house is a Primitive lurching drunkenly inside and sniffing the air. I silently beg the children to keep quiet, to stand still. While some Primitive senses are sharpened, sight it is not one of them. If we don't move, the Primitives might not see us.

"Run!" Lisa screams, untangling her hands from my skirt and rushing to the opposite side of the room. The other children scatter while I remain frozen to the spot.

Stupid, I think to myself with numb dismay as I watch helplessly while the zombie takes down an eight-year-old girl. I look away, squeezing my eyes shit tight while my stomach lurches painfully. There's nothing I can do for her. Children don't survive the Turn, so this one will die a bloody heap in the corner. I want to feel something, anything, but I feel nothing. Only anger. My sorrow died many years ago, along with any sense of contentment I might have been able to find. Everything died when I realized we can't win this fight. There's no way to find any semblance of peace in this world we've been forced to endure.

I hope the other children are running away as fast as they can. Once the zombie finishes, he'll start looking for his next meal. Of course, there's a good chance the Primitive's brethren are just outside the door where the children ran. I won't be able to help them any more than I could help Lisa. As soon as the zombie is done with her, I'm next.

I hope he tears out my throat, kills me. Death is more common than turning anyway. And since I can't turn, I want my death to be a quick one.

This is as close as I've ever come to killing myself, just standing and waiting to die. Truthfully, I think about it all the time. It would be a release from the daily hardships and the constant pain of losing my family. So, instead of running, I close my eyes and brace myself, waiting for death in the form of sharp teeth and claws as they sink into my flesh. I've earned this. I have travelled for too long, lost too much, and now I'm done. I want to go to sleep and never wake up.

Eventually, the god-awful sounds coming from the corner stop and I know that the Primitive has finished his meal. Which means I'm next.

I feel a shift in the room, the air rushing around me as the zombie launches itself at me. I hold still, though the instinct to run is still strong. There's no point in running now. I can't outrun a zombie and there's no one left to save me.

Something whistles through the air and I hear the dull, wet thunk of something sharp sinking into flesh and bone. I frown, feeling nothing. Is this death? Should death feel this empty and painless?

I open my eyes and the sight before me makes me gasp out loud and stumble back a step. Standing between me and the zombie is a huge man with dark, bushy hair, an unkept beard and piercing aqua eyes. An Outsider. At his feet is the body of the Primitive, its head severed from its body.

My heart speeds up in trepidation and gratitude. This man saved my life, but he's also an Outsider. Outsiders can be nearly as dangerous as Primitives. They take what they want, even if it means killing a settlement of people to get it. I've been in groups that were attacked by Outsiders, and it's never a pretty sight. We have enough problems with Primitives, without adding human on human violence.

I try a conciliatory approach, assuming he's helping out of kindness. "Th-thank you," I stammer.

He turns swiftly, facing me directly. He's a large muscular man with icy dead eyes. His gaze travels up and down my body in an impersonal survey that makes me want to sink back beneath the floorboards.

He jerks his head to the doorway and grunts, "Come on."

He leaves and I don't have much choice but to follow him out. There's nothing left in the room except for the body of a child and the body of the Primitive. Outside I see the other three children safe and well. I attempt to walk over to them where they sit huddled in a group together, but the Outsider catches my arm and forces me to his side.

I look up at him, my brow furrowing in question.

"You're coming with me." His voice is cold and impersonal.

I spot a car on the road and assume it must be his. Excitement blossoms inside me at the possibilities. Having a vehicle is so rare that I've only been inside one a few times in my life. My family never owned one, and the groups of travelers that I've gone with have only ever managed to get their hands on a few. Vehicles make travel so much faster and safer, but they're extremely hard to come by and they break down easily. Very few people know how to fix them anymore.

"I'll get the children," I say hopefully.

I know better though. What would an Outsider want with three traumatized children? Still, I have to try. If they're left here unprotected, they won't live through the night. Though I'm a long way from feeling empathy for anything anymore, my conscience still pricks me. If there's something I can do for them, I will.

"No children." He opens the passenger side door and shoves me in then slams it shut.

My heart starts pounding in fear and another adrenaline spike hits me. I'm about to be kidnapped by an Outsider and there's nothing I can do. In the space of one day I've been attacked by a horde of zombies, watched a young child die, nearly died myself by zombie attack and now I'm being kidnapped.

Still, this isn't the worst day I've ever had.

I throw the door open and try to climb out, but he's faster. He gets in the driver's side and reaches over to yank me back. Without a word, he reaches into the dash box, pulls out a pair of metal handcuffs, loops them through a bar in the dash and snaps them over my wrists.

I frown at him. What does he want with me? I'm not completely naive. At twenty-two I've had my fair share of male attention, violent and otherwise, but this man doesn't seem interested in me in a physical sense. He hasn't touched me more than absolutely necessary. Maybe he's taking me somewhere more private, away from the children and any straggling zombies, before he rapes me.

I watch with regret as he turns the ignition, reverses the car and heads out of the town. I twist in my seat to watch the frightened faces of the three children as they fade into the distance. Even with rape on the horizon, I'm in safer hands than they are.

Maybe I should have fought harder, but this is reality and I'm weary of fighting the inevitable. If this Outsider hadn't come along to pick me up, I'd either be dead or grabbed by someone else. The odds of a friendly group of people finding us was slim anyway. At this point, the best hope those children have is going to be a swift death, similar to Lisa's. Such is the horror of life, and death, in the Primitives' world. A grim thought, but truthful.

"Where are we going?" I ask him, assuming he must have a camp nearby. Outsiders are nomadic, but they do often set up camp for weeks or months at a time as they travel.

He doesn't say anything, so I settle back into the seat

and watch the passing scenery. Though I haven't been in a vehicle in ages, I think he's driving way too fast. The car bounces wildly as it hits holes and ruts in the road, but I don't say anything. I don't know this man; he could be quick to anger. I'll save my bad attitude until I get a better sense of who he is.

Two days later, mile after endless mile, it becomes quite apparent that this Outsider has no intention of stopping. Not even to rape me. He's on a mission and I am his captive. He hasn't spoken to me other than to grunt rude commands. Sit down, stand up, get out of the car, eat, go to the bathroom, get back in the car. This has been my life for the past 48 hours and I'm getting sick of it.

Familiarity has made me feel less afraid of this man. He hasn't touched me other than to put the cuffs on or off. I've gotten the feeling that he sees me as more of a commodity than a woman. Originally, I'd thought that he was taking me because I was old enough to be a companion to him. Now, I think otherwise.

Finally, I ask the same question that I tried two days ago. "Where are you taking me?"

This time, he answers. "Sanctuary."

My heart leaps in anticipation. My odds of survival go up exponentially inside of a Sanctuary. "Which one?"

"Santa Fe."

Santa Fe. I've never been there, but I've heard it's a thriving Sanctuary. I wonder why an Outsider would want to go to a Sanctuary. They usually avoid them like the plague (Ha! Zombie reference) since city security forces are just as willing to kill Outsiders as they are Primitives. Outsiders are notorious for attacking Sanctuaries, or convoys headed in and out of Sanctuaries, in search of food and supplies.

"What's your name?" I ask, pushing my luck now that I've finally got him talking.

He lifts his shaggy head and gives me the same icy stare he's been treating me to for two days.

"Talon."

TWO

WOLFE

Location: Santa Fe Sanctuary

"I'LL TAKE HER," the Warlord says, his lascivious eyes glued to our new arrival. "How much?"

I can tell from the look on the woman's face that she had no idea she was being brought into Sanctuary as a slave. About to be sold into our Warlord's harem.

As I watch the shadows cross her face it becomes clear that this news has crushed her. I can actually see her spirit shrink as sadness eclipses the look of hope that she'd walked in with. A naïve woman if she thought she was being taken to safety by an Outsider. Sanctuary will come at a price for this one.

And that price is...

"I want twelve months of supplies, including food, bedding, clothes, the usual. You can throw in a coin purse of a few hundred dollars too, in case I find a Sanctuary willing to trade in currency."

"Six months supplies," Silas counters.

"Eight months."

Silas looks at the woman critically, taking in her lovely features and beautifully sculpted body, before nodding his head. "Done."

Of course, it could be much worse. She could have been sold to another Warlord, one who's far more brutal. Though I don't like or respect my Warlord, he's not a cruel man. He likes women and fills his harem with them. Every shape and size, every temperament. The only requirement is that they be beautiful. And this one is no exception.

Once more my gaze strays to her. If her face wasn't twisted in misery it would be a work of art. High cheekbones, long nose, perfect lips. Her face is surrounded by a cloud of dark brown hair with reddish hints. She's tall, with hints of curves in all the right places, though it's clear that she hasn't eaten well in a long time.

The harem women will fatten her up, show her that she's safe and help her settle down. Eventually, like the others, she'll learn to enjoy her time here. And if she's lucky, the Warlord will take her as a wife. Given her stunning beauty, I can't imagine he would pass on this one.

I turn to the guard standing nearest to me. "When the sale is finished, take her to the harem. Have Hannah take care of her."

"Yes, sir," he says, his eyes on the woman.

"You will remove your eyes from the Warlord's new slave before I do it for you," I promise him.

He swiftly drops his eyes and takes a couple of steps away in the guise of doing as I say, though I suspect I make him uncomfortable. Most of the palace guard have learned that I will follow-up threat with action. It's best to follow my orders immediately without question.

The sale finishes and Silas turns to speak to his guards. "Take her to the harem."

As the guard reaches for her, she moves suddenly, plunging her hand into his belt. The startled palace guard stumbles back while she drags his knife from the sheath. She spins on the spot and lunges forward, pointing the knife at Silas and the Outsider. It's clear from the way she's standing and holding the knife that she has no idea what she's doing. Though I'm not worried that she'll do much damage, I have no choice but to step in. Our Warlord prefers not to have threats on his life.

She raises the knife high and slashes it in a downward arc toward the Outsider's belly, clearly intent on disemboweling him. I snap my hand over her wrist before she can make contact and swing her around. Her startled grey eyes lift to mine and I'm struck by the passion and fury within. When she was first brought to the throne room I thought I was seeing a woman defeated. I dismissed her as just another harem girl. Frightened and alone, but a woman who would settle easily into her new home. Instead, I'm seeing something else, something more to this woman. A fight I did not anticipate.

She opens her mouth to say something to me and I would have given up my food rations for a week if she'd been able to finish the sentence, but before she can speak the Outsider slams his fist into the side of her head. She drops like a stone at my feet.

"Bitch," he snarls, spitting on her unconscious form.

I drag my pistol from the holster and hold it on the Outsider. "You insult the Warlord's woman?" My stance and the ice in my words must alert the other man to the danger surrounding him. All of my palace guards are now on full alert, their hands on their weapons, their gazes on me.

They're awaiting instructions from their commander. If I tell them to kill this Outsider, he will be dead within seconds.

But in an unusual move, the Warlord steps in. He places his hand on my arm and when I stiffen, he drops it and takes a step back. Though I am technically his subordinate, we both know if I wanted him dead, he would be dead. I tolerate him as Warlord because it suits me.

Silas once asked me why I never became a Warlord. I didn't answer the question because he didn't need to know. Instead, I commented, "When I want the position, you'll be the first to know."

From that day, Silas's gaze became sharper whenever it landed on me, more guarded. Silas is a man who understands his strengths and his weaknesses. He's a thinker, not a fighter. He surrounds himself with loyal and talented people who are willing to help fight for Sanctuary. What he fails to understand is that I have no respect for him. I am here out of purely selfish reasons. By creating a place for myself within the Sanctuary, in a security position, I'm ensuring a long-term home for myself. I have food, equipment, and men at my back. In this shithole of a world we live in now, a man can't ask for much more than basic comfort and safety.

As I look down at the beautiful woman sprawled across the floor, her fiery attitude contained by a punch to the head, I wonder if my solitary existence is at risk. There's something about her, something that has made a tiny crack in a heart turned to ice long ago. In those few seconds when she fought for her freedom, thought to avenge herself, I saw a kindred spirit.

Silas finishes paying the Outsider, sends him on his way and turns to one of the guards. "Take her to the harem. Tell Hannah to take special care of her." Silas kneels next to the woman, brushing the hair off her forehead and looking down at her flawless features. "Stunning, isn't she? Her name is Skye."

Skye. Stormy and deceptively beautiful.

He looks up at me as he says it, something in his gaze telling me that he sees in her what I see. Jealousy rips through me and for the first time in a long time I consider cutting him down right now and taking his place.

We stare at each other for long, tension filled seconds and I wonder if he can read my mind. He's calm, not calling out to the guards to protect him. Even if he did, they'd be confused. Protect him from his second-in-command? I've never made a move against him and I'm not about to start now. Besides, if I wanted him dead, there would be nothing the palace guards could do to stop me. I am second-in-command for a reason.

I have no intention of harming my Warlord though. No one is worth the pain in the ass of having to run a Sanctuary, not even this woman. She'll take her place in the harem, settle down and learn to accept life in the palace. I will assign her a guard, same as the other harem women, and I will likely not see her often. As the Warlord's second, I run security in the palace and on the wall. I work with the police force in the city to maintain order. Our paths won't cross often. She'll be just another pretty face, like any other. She will likely cross the room when she sees me coming, and avoid me in the hall, like the other women.

Yet, as the guard reaches for her, to do Silas's bidding and take her to the harem, I push him out of the way. "I'll take her." There's no room for argument in my tone as I scoop the unconscious woman into my arms.

I try to ignore the way her body feels against mine as I stride through the halls toward the harem. She's thin from lack of food, but I can feel the definition of muscles beneath her skin. I wish her eyes were open. I want to see if they're as stormy grey as I remember them from those few seconds when she looked up at me with such passionate fury.

The harem doors open in front of me and I stride through, guided by Hannah to an empty room. I set the woman on the bed and step away. A sensation sweeps through me, something I've never felt before. Regret. I don't want to let her go.

I decide I better leave the harem before I do something stupid. It's time to forget this woman exists.

Before I leave, I say to Hannah, "Take good care of this one." I pause and then add, "Watch yourself, she's a fighter."

With one last look at the woman, I turn and walk away, determined to put her out of my mind. She belongs to the Warlord and I am not the Warlord.

THREE

SKYE

7 years later

SOME CALL THEM PRIMITIVES, people who see them as once being relatives and friends. I call them zombies, because until a cure is developed the only real cure is my blade. They aren't human, they are the walking dead.

I don't know what wakes me up but over the past several years I've learned to trust my instincts. I tense, slowly reaching one hand for my revolver and the other for my long deadly knife. Both items are resting on the seat next to me and easily reachable. I barely breathe, a weapon in each hand, as I listen intently for whatever woke me up.

Along with several members of my team I'm sheltering inside a downed passenger airplane. Two of my men are supposed to be outside the airplane patrolling, watching for Primitives.

As I blink the sleep from my eyes, I realize the airplane is filled with some kind of smoke. It takes me a couple of heart stopping seconds to realize that it's not smoke from a fire but mist. The plane had gone down near the Rio Grande river, around the time of the Great Fall, and it's a particularly humid evening, creating an atmosphere of fog.

I reach an arm out, using the edge of my knife to tap the man sprawled out in the seat across the aisle. He wakes up with a start, his hand immediately going to the holster at his side. Consciousness comes to him quickly, and he looks silently over at me, his brow furrowing. I lift a finger to my lips indicating that he shouldn't speak. My entire team is trained to keep as silent as possible. Primitives are attracted to noise, which means humans have had to become wraiths when working and moving in a world dominated by the diseased.

"We're not alone," I whisper to Deacon, my second-in-command for this mission.

Like me, Deacon slowly reaches for his weapons, hefting them in his hands and squinting through the fog. The gaping hole on the top right side of the airplane allows the outside atmosphere in. The hole is high enough up that it should keep out any lurking Primitives, but that won't stop them from surrounding the airplane or attacking my lookouts.

I don't know how and I don't know why, but I know to the marrow of my bones that they're out there. I always know. Like a sixth sense. I was born with it. It developed over the years, particularly after the death of my husband, Silas. Survival has become my single objective.

Deacon doesn't question me. He's learned that I'm always right when I predict a zombie attack. I point my knife toward the back of the airplane indicating that he should move to the rear, wake up the rest of our team.

To their credit, the team is completely noiseless as each one is woken up from a deep sleep. They've had to learn the hard way, with the loss of several of our team close to the beginning of the mission. Primitive attacks can be sudden, brutal and are often predicated by how much noise we make.

We've been travelling this region for weeks with little to no sleep. It's a barren desert region that shouldn't have been a breeding ground for Primitives. They should be closer to the cities, where they can find food. I don't know why they're all the way out here, but they are.

My core mission is to take a vaccination that was created in the New Tucson Sanctuary and spread it as far and as wide as I can. The mission hasn't been an easy one, given the scarcity of working vehicles and fuel. But so far, over the past eight months of travelling, we've managed to take the vaccination to half a dozen Sanctuaries, hitting all of the major West Coast cities. Now, we're making our way east.

As my team wakes, they move into formation, each member taking their place. I use hand signals to inform them that they'll be leaving the airplane at various exits.

I whisper just loud enough for all of them to hear, "Attack first, kill them all, no mercy, no remorse."

This has become our battle mantra over the long months of travelling. We can't show pity, though the Primitives could easily be our friends or family. We can't hesitate, even if the vaccination has shown some signs of reversing the virus. We have a mission and we can't allow compassion to get in the way.

Each member of my team nods back, their eyes grave. Though they've all been vaccinated, they could still be killed if the Primitives get hold of them. Even if they can no longer turn, they can still die by dismemberment or being eaten alive.

They are loyal to me and every member of my team will follow me into hell. I've built this team, earned their trust and fought by their sides. Each member knows that I would fight to the death for them if necessary.

With the fluidity of a well-oiled machine we split up into teams, hitting each of the exits. Two in the rear, two in the front and two at each of the emergency exits in the middle of the plane. I wrap my hand around the emergency exit pull on the right side of the plane. This is the most dangerous exit. Deacon and I will be alone on this side of the airplane, fighting whatever enemy is outside.

I look back at him, my eyes burning hatred in the darkness. I remind myself that these are the creatures that destroyed almost all of my family and killed my husband. I want them all dead.

Deacon nods, silently telling me that he has my back.

"Attack!" I yell.

All of the exits are opened at once, Deacon and I jump out onto the wing of the airplane. As soon as my feet hit, I begin to slide because the airplane is tilted with the end of the wing resting on the ground. My knees to buckle and I lie flat on the wing, allowing gravity to take me down to the ground. The second my feet touch I swing my blade out into the foggy darkness, making contact.

FOUR

"They're getting more organized every time we see them."

I don't look at Deacon when he speaks to me, my eyes continuing to rove over the tree line searching for movement. He's right. The Primitives have been exhibiting growth. Now that there's a vaccine, it seems as though their brain functions are increasing and adapting at a much faster rate. I don't know if the two concepts are related or if it's purely coincidental.

"Well then," I look over, my expression cold, "it's that much more important that we get the vaccine distributed."

I glance around the space outside the airplane. It's now littered with Primitive bodies. I feel no sadness for them, nor any shame at having killed them. Maybe my heart is dead. Maybe I can no longer feel. I don't know and I don't care. I have a job to do and I'm going to do it.

There's no sign of our two lookouts. They were either turned or killed. A depressing reality that has hammered away at our collective morale. We've grown close as a group, watching each other's backs, learning about each other. Almost as if we each want our legacy known before we become the next victim. It breaks my heart to see my team behaving this way: weary, sad, resigned, scared. Especially because I'm both their leader and the one who must be protected above all else, since my blood is needed for the vaccine.

"Do we continue in the same direction, into New Mexico?" Deacon questions.

I want to snap at him that of course we will continue on. One brief Primitive attack won't set us back. We've gone through dozens of similar attacks over the months, pushing through each one and moving on to our next destination, distributing the vaccine as we go.

That's not why Deacon's asking the question though. It's because the next Sanctuary on our list is Santa Fe. The place where I loved and lost my husband. Rumor has reached us that there are survivors and that they're rebuilding with a new Warlord at the helm. I've been hesitant to go back, to show my face. I feel guilty at having left survivors behind when we fled the massacre a year ago. Yet, I'm also eager to go back to the place I called home. To see if there's anything left.

I stifle my annoyance at Deacon. It's not his fault the apocalypse has put me in a permanently bitchy mood. "Of course. We continue until we've reached every Sanctuary. No matter what happens, no matter who dies, our mission remains the same. Spread the vaccine."

I stride away from him, my mood dark. Not that my mood could ever be described as pleasant. But this trip, being the leader of this small group of warriors, is beginning to try my patience.

Wolfe had been my only real companion. The only man I was able to stand for longer than a few minutes. Maybe because he was silent most of the time. Or maybe because he's just as bad tempered as me.

My anger begins to rise again as I think of him. He abandoned me to this. He abandoned me after I lost my husband, my friends and my Sanctuary. I want to hate him for it, call him selfish, but I can't. I was the one who drove him away. I was the selfish one. And this... maybe this is my punishment.

I walk through the tree line and into the scrub brush, searching for more Primitive victims to take out my mood on. Killing them is both my reward and my penance. It gives me purpose. As I wander it becomes clear that the only Primitives in the area were the ones to attack my crew at the airplane.

As Deacon pointed out, they're becoming more and more organized. They're not just blindly attacking anymore but using some kind of strategy. Their strategies are still juvenile and ineffective, but if they continue on their current path, they might soon become a real threat to skilled warriors like us.

It's become my purpose in life to not just distribute the vaccine but to kill as many Primitives as I can get my knives and guns on. Once the vaccine has spread across the world and the last of the Primitives are killed, civilization can rise up again.

When I return to the crash site, I tell my men to pack up. We'll continue on, away from the airplane. Primitives are drawn to any signs of civilization, even dead civilization.

I ride in the lead vehicle with Deacon at my side and Hugo, our map reader, in the back with Scarlett. Behind us is another car filled with five more team members. In total there are nine of us left. Yesterday we were eleven.

As if sensing my mood, my companions fall silent, not speaking as we drive through what remains of the night.

"How long until Santa Fe?" I twist in my seat to look at Hugo.

He unfolds a map and looks at it, tracing his finger from our approximate position toward the Santa Fe Sanctuary.

"Two days," he tells me.

I don't respond. Two days. Two days until we find ourselves in the one Sanctuary city I've been dreading. The one I've been avoiding for a year.

---

1 YEAR EARLIER...

Wolfe speaks, his voice calm and level despite the swirling emotion sizzling all around us. "You're lying to yourself, woman. And as long as you lie to yourself, you lie to me, which I am now done with. I will leave here and you will come to find me when you are ready for the truth between us." He walks away from the tent, letting the flap fall into place behind him.

"I don't understand," I whisper to myself.

But I'm lying.

FIVE
WOLFE

"She's coming, Warlord."

Without turning, I continue to look out the window across the landscape. I'm standing on top of one of the only tall buildings left intact after the Primitives razed the city one year ago, surveying my domain. The rebuild is coming along frustratingly slow.

I told my people to watch for Skye, to tell me when she's headed our way. I've been tracking her progress across the western part of the continent for the past several months as she distributes her vaccine. I knew eventually she would come here. So, I've waited.

My hackles rise as the man behind me waits for an answer. I'm not sure what he's waiting for as he's already imparted the necessary information.

I don't like people. I don't have the patience for small talk. I'm no diplomat, which is why I've avoided any kind of position that might put me in a Warlord's shoes. There had been plenty of opportunity in Santa Fe for me to depose warlord Silas and take his place. I hadn't. I preferred to be the muscle behind the throne.

Until Skye.

She'd arrived in Santa Fe as a young wide-eyed slave. At that point I finally questioned my position in life. As I was forced to watch Warlord Silas take the woman and add her to his harem, I had stood angrily by, questioning every decision that led up to that point. Had I been Warlord, the stunning brunette with the piercing grey eyes and the bad attitude would have belonged to me.

But I'm not one to linger over lost opportunities. I play the long game. I'm an ugly motherfucker with an air of deadly violence that tends to put women off. So, I watched from a distance, protecting her back and allowing her to get to know me better as the Warlord's second. At least if she didn't like me, she'd know who I was. She'd be ready when I finally stepped up to stake my claim, stealing her from beneath the nose of her degenerate husband.

But instead of taking over as I'd planned, I'd watched as Warlord Silas had become ill and it had seemed unsporting to contemplate deposing him when he only had a few short months left. At that point I'd decided to wait the other man out, allow him a dignified death that could only make me look better in the eyes of his prized wife. When the throne was finally free, I would step into it and made Skye my queen.

That hadn't happened. Instead, Primitives had figured out how to cause nuclear power plants to meltdown across the continent. The Primitives had caused mass confusion among the humans, killing them and chasing them across the country. Santa Fe had suffered the same fate as every other Sanctuary east of us. I'd been forced to take Skye and as many citizens as we could and run, begging for Sanctuary in New Tucson.

Now, I wait.

She's coming to me. She'll find her way back home.
Without turning, I say to my man, "Leave."

SIX

SKYE

"We're almost there," Deacon says from beside me.

I nod and pull my sawed-off shotgun out of its holster against my leg. "Everyone check your weapons."

The car fills with the sound of shuffling and clicking as everyone checks their weapons. Fueling is one of the most dangerous things a human can do in a Primitive dominated world. Primitives figured out long ago that humans need fuel in order to travel. Thus, they often stake out fueling stations for attacks.

Our team is getting close to the Santa Fe Sanctuary, less than a day out from our destination. The fuel station we chose is a relatively new one. After the Fall, fuel had been one commodity that'd been in abundance. Now that's changing. Fuel has a shelf life; the older stuff has gone bad. This particular fuel station was built about 30 years after the Fall and is periodically restocked with new reserves coming in from fuel rich Sanctuaries.

We heard a rumour that it's been replenished recently, which makes it perfect for filling our vehicles, but a breeding ground for Primitives. I radio to the car behind us, instructing them to prepare for battle.

"There they are." Deacon points out the window of the vehicle, his other hand gripping the steering wheel. There are three Primitives racing toward our vehicle, a gruesome and awkward herd of predators racing after its prey.

"For a species that're supposedly evolving some kind of smarts, they're still pretty stupid for running at us like that," Scarlett comments from the back seat, craning her neck to see them.

"Don't underestimate them," I admonish her grumpily.

I don't need my team getting lazy, deciding they can take down the Primitives with ease. Through skill and the vaccination, battling Primitives has indeed gotten easier, but that doesn't mean they won't tear a person apart if they get their hands on us.

Scarlett decided to join our team when she realized that one of her Santa Fe harem sisters was leading it. When we lived together in the Santa Fe harem, I was informally in charge. Scarlett is used to taking orders from me and she trusts me as a mentor. I might be cold and difficult to be around at times, but I will never lead my team wrong. When I was in Santa Fe, I was an advocate for the harem. Now, I'm an advocate for survivors everywhere.

"Should I hit them?" Deacon asks.

I think about it then nod. "Do it."

Taking out Primitives with a vehicle can be dangerous. Depending on the speed at which we hit them, we could damage the car irreparably. But if we hit going too slow then they might just go under the vehicle and cling to the bottom, or grab hold of the grill until we stop. On one memorable occasion we managed to pick up a Primitive and continue on to our next destination without ever realizing the danger lurking under the car. When we stopped for the night, we got a nasty surprise.

"Brace," Deacon instructs everyone in the vehicle.

I'm sitting next to Deacon, so only I can see the satisfied twist to his lips as the car impacts the first Primitive, his bloodlust rising as he closes in on the kill.

I grip the door handle as the car shudders at the impact. Deacon turns the wheel sharply, takes aim and hits another. Blood sprays across the windshield as the Primitive is killed instantly. The body rolls off the vehicle just as Deacon hits the third. We feel the bump as it goes underneath the tires.

Scarlett turns to look and points when she sees it far behind the car lying on the ground in the dust. The vehicle behind us hits it, ensuring its death if it hadn't died when the first car got it.

"We're here."

Sure enough, the pumps have become visible through the dirt thrown up by our wild driving. Without turning, I address the occupants of my car. "Deacon, cover us from the car, but keep your ass in that seat. I need you driving if we have to get out of here quickly. Hugo, you pump the gas while the rest of us cover you."

The second the car slides to a halt in the dirt next to the pumps, everyone moves. I jump onto the hood and then climb onto the roof, bracing myself as I lift my rifle and take aim at a rapidly approaching Primitive. As the others take their places surrounding the vehicle, I shoot the Primitive in the head. It hits the dirt and rolls, not getting up when it stops.

Silence reigns for a few seconds and I can hear the click and whoosh of gas as it enters the tank. Then all hell breaks loose, Primitives come at us from every direction. We shoot as though our lives depend on it, because they do.

We pause only long enough to allow the other car to swing around us and slide to a halt at the pump on the other side. In unison the car empties and everyone takes up position, same as us, while one member of their team starts pumping.

We've had so much practice at dealing with Primitive attacks that not a single one manages to break the line and get within ten yards of our vehicles. Every bullet counts and every bullet strikes its target. Primitives drop to the ground all around us, creating a grim pile of death that we will drive away from and forget.

"Cars!"

The shout comes from Scarlett.

At first, I have no idea what she's talking about. Cars? In a year of touring the western side of the North American continent, we haven't once come across another vehicle. Travel is dangerous and working vehicles are rare.

My gaze follows to where Scarlett is pointing and I see that she is correct, puffs of dust on the horizon announces the arrival of several vehicles heading our way. Probably looking for gas, same as us. I have no choice but to ignore them for now as I focus on the problem at hand; killing every Primitive that has staked out the fueling station as a good place to pick off humans. By the time we're done, not a single one will be left alive.

"Do you think they're hostile?" Scarlett calls up to me from her position at the rear of the vehicle.

I let out an annoyed huff and roll my eyes. "How exactly am I supposed to tell that from here?"

No one says anything as we pick off the last few Primitives. I had hoped that we would have enough time to jump back into the vehicles and leave the site before the other cars arrive, but we're too late. One by one, six vehicles line up facing us, clouds of dust surrounding them and obscuring the faces inside. If the number of cars facing us is any indication of the number of occupants inside, we are sadly outnumbered.

"Be ready, but not aggressive. Guns down. No shooting unless I say." The last thing I need is for one of my people to get jumpy and kill someone innocent.

Before the dust can clear, a man emerges. He's tall, broad, with wild dark hair hanging down his shoulders and a beard obscuring half his face. It's not the bottom half of his face that tells me who he is though. It's the one amber eye fixed on me that tells me exactly who's approaching.

Deacon twists to look up at me from the driver's window, his brow raised in question. He wants to know if he should be covering me, but I'm incapable of speaking. Not one single word. That one eye has pinned me to the roof of my car.

He stops right below me, the dust swirling around the cuffs of his leather pants and his heavy, dirt encrusted boots. He tips his head back and glares. "Skye." That one single word, my name, is filled with meaning. He's come for me.

"Wolfe," I answer.

"You," I snarl, bending down to place my hand on the edge of the car and leaping off.

As my feet hit the dirt, Wolfe reaches out to take hold of me, steadying me. The touch of his hand to my arm is so fraught with sensation that it almost burns. I jerk my arm away from him and take a step back, my ass pressed against the car.

"I didn't expect to see you again." My words come out with a harsh edge. I don't want him to know how much his leaving the Tucson Sanctuary affected me, but I can't keep the pain and anger from my voice.

"Told you I'd see you again." His voice is a dark drawl that sends shivers racing up and down my spine.

"You here for fuel?" I ask him, jerking my head back toward the pumps. "We're finished. We'll move our cars so you can get in here."

Wolfe steps toward me, backing me into the vehicle and crowding me with his big body. I suck in a sharp breath as my breasts touch his leather-clad chest. It's been a year since I last saw him, but everything rushes back as though it was only yesterday. The way he smells, the way he talks, everything about him.

"We're here for you."

"Thanks," I say, deliberately misunderstanding him. "But we don't need any help."

He doesn't answer back right away. He looks around, his gaze settling on the two vehicles that belong to my team, and the people surrounding them. His eye is assessing, cold and calculating as he contemplates my people.

"You heading to Santa Fe Sanctuary?" he asks.

I wonder if he's been keeping tabs on me or if he's just making an assumption based on how close we are to Santa Fe. I try not to let a thrill of excitement go through me at the thought that Wolfe might be tracking us. There aren't that many usable roads to Santa Fe. He could easily make the assessment that Santa Fe is our destination based on our tracks, the road that we're travelling and the lack of destinations hereabouts.

"Yes," I confirm. "I have a vaccine to distribute."

"Heard about that," he says, his gaze is still on everything except me.

"We're travelling from Sanctuary to Sanctuary, spreading the vaccine. It seems to be working. We're hearing rumours as we travel that the Sanctuaries we've visited are gradually becoming more and more Primitive free." I speak nervously, giving him information as though he requested it. This is what Wolfe does to me; I can be in perfect control, but the moment he's around I become either tongue-tied or the opposite.

"Heard about that too."

Wolfe's 'man of few words' thing is starting to irritate me.

"We'll be on our way then," I say, attempting to turn away from him to organize my people.

"We'll escort you." Wolfe makes it clear that there's no room for argument in his words.

Still, I argue. "We don't need an escort."

"Come." He takes my arm and gives me a tug, turning back toward the lineup of cars he came with, as if fully expecting me to follow.

I dig my heels into the dirt, but he still drags me. Wolfe is a big man, even bigger than I remember. His shoulders are incredibly broad, stretching his shirt until the seams look as though they'll split. His leather pants are also tight, the muscles of his thighs bulging. He was always a big man, but he seems somehow more massive than the last time I'd seen him. He must've spent time over the past year doing intense physical labour. I'm curious about what he was doing, but not enough to ask.

I grab hold of the hand that's wrapped around my bicep and yank on his finger in an attempt to get him to release me. He lets go of my arm for a second, readjusts his hold and continues pulling me.

"Hold up!" Deacon shouts from the car behind us. I hear the click of his gun cocking.

A cold sweat settles over me. I know Wolfe. He won't stand for anyone pointing a gun at him, whether they're an enemy or an ally.

"Put your gun down," I call quickly to Deacon. "He's not an enemy."

I don't know if this is true exactly. I don't know what's happened to Wolfe over the past year. He seems to know what's been happening with me. What if he's become an Outsider? He always had it in him. Back in Santa Fe, when I was married to Warlord Silas, I always got the feeling that

Wolfe merely paid lip service to the people around him. He was so completely his own man, he could walk out of the palace, out of the Sanctuary, and into the desert and be completely fine.

In fact, that's exactly what he did after the fall of Santa Fe. He travelled with me to Tucson, helped me reunite with my sister and her husband, then he walked out of my life, leaving only a cryptic message behind. "Come find me when you're ready." The words that would haunt me for an entire year.

Was I ready? He had been the one to leave me behind, not the other way around. He told me to come find him, yet here he is. He's the one to find me.

When Wolfe continues walking, dragging me toward his car, I twist around to shout at my people, "Follow us!"

Wolfe opens the passenger side of his car and shoves me inside. I'm so shocked by the entire exchange that I don't do anything but stare at him as he strides back around to the driver's side, opening the door and climbing in.

"Seatbelts." Wolfe says it like it should be automatic, but seatbelts in vehicles rarely work, so most people don't use them. Collisions aren't common anymore. It's more likely that a vehicle will just break down.

I stare at him in consternation and he reaches over to pull the belt from a spot just above my shoulder, tugs it across my chest and buckles me in. I'm amazed when I hear the click. Even the seatbelts that do work are rarely used. There's just no point anymore. We live in a dangerous world; car accidents are the least of our difficulties. I wiggle experimentally, pulling at it where it sits on my chest.

"I don't like it, it's uncomfortable."

He doesn't respond to my complaint but buckles himself in and turns the key in the ignition, starting the car.

Vehicles all around us come to life, their engines rumbling in the desert. I turn my gaze to the car next to us, focusing on the young man driving. I don't recognize him. I don't recognize anyone. Who are these people?

"Where are we going?" I ask Wolfe as he hits the gas and turns the car back on to the road.

"Sanctuary," he says cryptically.

"Any specific Sanctuary?" I ask him sarcastically.

"Santa Fe."

"Well that's convenient." When he doesn't say anything back, I fall silent. There's so much I want to say, to ask him, but pride keeps me silent. He left me. I'm not sure what he's doing back in my life now. I don't even know if we're on the same side. Is he kidnapping me or is he helping me get to the next Sanctuary on my list?

I turn in my seat, staring out behind us. Looking for the cars that belong to my team. With the dirt being thrown up as the cars race away from the fueling station, I can't pick them out. I hope they're following close behind. I don't know what this is, don't know why it took Wolfe six cars and one year to find me, but I want my people for backup. Even just for emotional support. These are the people who have fought at my side and my back. People that I trust, and who trust me. People who will defend me in a heartbeat, if I ask.

Wolfe is driving an early century car, one I don't recognize, but some kind of sports car, I think. As the world fell to the Primitives, luxury items such as sports vehicles were some of the first to go. Anything built for looks over durability didn't sustain. This one seems to be doing okay as it flies over the rutted road.

"Nice car."

He grunts. "I found it in the Tijuana Sanctuary."

I raise an eyebrow. "I thought Tijuana fell thirty years ago."

"Thirty-four," he corrects me. "They rebuilt. I went there after I left Tucson."

I look at him, my eyes drifting down his arms to land on his knuckles where they rest on the steering wheel. I forgot how scarred his hands are, some of the fingers twisted at the knuckles, clearly having been broken at some point. Despite that, his hands look capable. Capable of building, capable of destroying. Capable of touching a woman.

"What happened in Tijuana 34 years ago?" I'm not sure if I care, but Santa Fe is at least half a day away and sitting in complete silence for the entire trip will be boring.

"The city fell."

"Why'd the city fall?" Jesus, this is going to be a long ass conversation if he doesn't start volunteering more information.

Finally, he glances at me and speaks. "I was five. We were warring with neighbouring Sanctuaries, including Tucson. We didn't have enough resources and went after others for food, water and medical supplies. We weren't prepared to defend ourselves against the fallout."

I shiver at his short but brutal explanation. War. It's almost better when cities topple from things outside the hands of humans, like flu and Primitives. It's worse when we're the cause of our own downfall. It breaks my heart imagining the five-year-old Wolfe getting caught up and displaced in the war.

"So you're originally from Mexico... or where Mexico used to be?"

When cities, regions and nations fell, borders became meaningless. The only borders that matter anymore are the ones staked out around Sanctuaries. Everything else in between is a lawless no man's land, where Primitives roam and Outsiders take refuge. Still, there are enough surviving people who remember the time of the Great Fall. They keep the memory of our former geography alive.

I'm originally from what used to be Canada, from somewhere in the west. We lived in a secluded wooded area with many natural resources, but the winters were harsh and the area was lonely, mostly devoid of other people. When everything fell to shit, what was left of my family travelled south.

He shrugs. "I guess. Never knew where my parents came from."

"What about your family? What happened to them?" I'm almost afraid to ask. If his story ended happily, his parents would be alive and well, and he would know about his heritage. If his family had survived, I suspect he wouldn't be the hardened killer that he is today. Our pasts have shaped us, his and mine. We're both killers now.

"Dead. They fell when Tijuana went down."

"I'm so sorry," I murmur, lifting my hand to touch him. I drop it to the seat between us. He doesn't want my sympathy.

Then he surprises me. He reaches out and takes my hand in his, giving it a squeeze. As though he knows I wanted to touch him and aborted. I can feel my face flushing with emotion.

"Don't be sorry for me," he says. "I don't remember them. I was lucky enough to be picked up by a group of refugees heading north, toward Santa Fe. They could've easily left me behind as dead weight, but they took pity on a filthy, starving, injured child."

"Is that how you lost your eye?" I want to call the question back immediately. It's personal and I'm crossing a line.

Wolfe never talks about his eye. Yet from the day I met him, I've always been curious.

"Yes," he says simply.

In the space of just half an hour I've learned more about Wolfe than I had in the years I lived with him in the Santa Fe Warlord's palace.

EIGHT

The New Santa Fe Sanctuary is located at the foot of the Sangre de Cristo Mountains in the Rio Grande Valley. When the original Santa Fe fell, the remaining inhabitants and refugees rebuilt closer to the mountain range, creating a natural fortress. The wall held for fifty years, until the second fall of the Santa Fe Sanctuary, one year ago.

It's gut wrenching to be home again... or the place I used to call home. Regrowth and rebuild is happening along the wall. From what I can tell, it's being built stronger than ever, able to withstand entire armies of Primitives. I shudder as the thought enters my brain. Armies. That's what we've come to. Primitives have organized themselves. They've always travelled in packs, but the groupings used to be smaller, more easily managed. Now, they travel in hordes. Great big massive hordes.

As we approach the main gates, I tip my head back to stare up at the wall, a wall just as high as the Tucson Sanctuary wall. I frown and wrinkle my nose in disgust. "Are those... are those bodies up there?"

Displayed across much of the face of the wall is what

looks like rotting corpses. My stomach heaves in protest and I look away.

"They're a deterrence to the enemy," Wolfe explains. "Primitives don't like coming across their dead any more than we do."

I stare at him. "How can you tell?"

He doesn't speak right away and I wonder if he won't answer me. This is Wolfe. He speaks sparingly and in his own time. He never explains himself, definitely not to me. Not even to the Warlord, when Silas was still alive.

Finally, he answers, "Noticed after I left the Tucson Sanctuary. I hammered one of them to the hood of my car, a statement to the others. Fuck with me and die."

"And it worked?" I ask skeptically.

His eyes remain on the gates as they swing open and we're both distracted for a moment as he drives through. The last time I was here we were rushing in the opposite direction through the gates, taking as many vehicles and refugees as we could manage. Out of the 70,000 people residing in Santa Fe at the time, we'd only been able to take a few hundred. And out of that few hundred only a few dozen, including Wolfe and myself, made it to the Tucson Sanctuary alive.

But now, I see a bustling city, people moving through the streets with purpose. As we drive, I realize that there are far more than the handful that should have survived being left behind to survive a zombie attack.

I say as much to Wolfe.

"Some survived the initial attack; managed to hide and wait out the Primitives. Others are refugees from the eastern Sanctuaries. They heard we were rebuilding here in Santa Fe and asked for asylum."

I see an older woman making her way slowly across the

road, a cane clutched in her hand for balance. She's well past childbearing age and at first glance doesn't appear to be in the best of health. This woman would never have been given Sanctuary under Silas's regime, or in most other Sanctuaries. How has she managed to get into Santa Fe?

Following my gaze, Wolfe understands my silent question and explains, "We accept anyone who begs for Sanctuary. The only exceptions are those that were turned away from the city for crimes."

I'm surprised. Both at this amendment to the old law and at the way Wolfe is making it sound like he's a decision-maker for the city. In his old role as head of security and right hand to the Warlord, he'd helped make decisions, but he mostly kept to himself. Perhaps he's taken up his old position again. I know I'm wrong, though. My gut is trying to tell me he's something more to the Santa Fe Sanctuary.

Finally, I ask the question that's been burning from the moment I found out I would be coming here. "Who... who is Warlord now?" I need to know who took my husband's position.

This time, though, Wolfe doesn't answer. He maneuvers the vehicle through the city, driving it into the underground garage beneath what used to be the palace. I get a quick glimpse of the tall building before we drive into the underground. I'm blinded by darkness for a moment until my eyes can adjust. By the time I'm ready, Wolfe has parked the vehicle.

We get out and I join him as he strides toward the stairs leading up. I'm reminded of the effort it takes to climb the stairs as we go up and up and up at a dizzying pace. Wolfe is clearly in top physical condition, not that he ever wasn't. The man's body is made out of rock, probably the same rock as his heart.

I'm huffing and puffing by the time we arrive at our destination: the Warlord's throne room.

As we enter, I see that not much has changed and a stab of pain takes my breath away as I picture Silas in his role as Warlord, sitting in his big ornate chair on a dais, elevated above the rest of the room. Now, of course, it's empty of his frail dying body.

I'm about to insist once more that Wolfe tell me who the new Warlord is. I have my suspicions, but I want him to confirm. Before I can ask, though, several soldiers come through the door, lining up next to Wolfe. In unison, they bow their heads, a habit left over from Silas's days. He loved his pomp and ceremony. These men must've belonged to him. Must've somehow survived the attack.

"Warlord," one of them begins. "We're situating your guests."

"Good," Wolfe acknowledges. "Leave us now."

Without another word the soldiers file out, their eyes anywhere but on me. The averted gaze of the soldiers is reminiscent of my time in the harem. They weren't allowed to look directly at me or any of the harem women. Only Wolfe had repeatedly broken that rule, looking at me often. The Warlord hadn't cared though; he believed that Wolfe's coldness toward me indicated his lack of interest. I'd believed the same thing.

I have trouble keeping the edge of bitterness from my voice. "Warlord Wolfe. It has a nice ring to it, doesn't it?"

He says nothing, but his one-eyed stare says it all.

NINE

"So you're the new Warlord of the Santa Fe Sanctuary."
Scorn drips from my words.

Wolfe would make a good Warlord; he's a good choice
for securing a city that has fallen to the Primitives. He's
strong, decisive and brutally efficient. But there's something
about him, about the situation, that angers me. He's stepping into the role that belonged to my husband, and I hate
the reminder of how much my life has changed.

Wolfe shrugs. "Temporarily."

"What's that supposed to mean?" I demand.

Before Wolfe can answer, if he was going to answer,
we're interrupted by an approaching woman. "The
requested rooms have been prepared for your guest."

Before Wolfe can acknowledge her, she turns and starts
to walk away.

I'm shocked and say out loud, "Hannah?"

Could it be possible? Is this the woman who took my
place at Silas's side one year ago? The last time I saw her,
she was standing next to our husband, her hand on his
shoulder as I was dragged away kicking and screaming.

The woman stiffens and turns her head slightly. "Skye." She says my name in cool acknowledgement and then continues walking.

"Wait, Hannah..." I take a few steps after her, but Wolfe catches my arm and holds me in place.

I look sharply down at his hand, but he doesn't remove it. He tightens his grip until I tilt my head back to look up into his eye.

"Let her go," he says quietly. "She's not the same woman you used to know."

"What's that supposed to mean?" I say, letting the frustration leak through in my voice. "What's going on around here? What happened when we left? How could she possibly have survived?"

Wolfe begins walking, giving me no choice but to follow him or fall, since he still has hold of my arm. I hurry to keep up with his longer strides.

"She can answer all of your questions, but you need to give her time. She's not the same woman."

I growl my frustration. "Yeah, you said that. What kind of a woman is she now? Half zombie?"

Wolfe doesn't say anything, but I see a slight shake to his shoulders telling me he's laughing. He'd better be laughing at my joke and not at me.

I realize that I need to calm down, process what's happening. I'm standing in a place that used to be my home, but everything has changed. My husband, the man who I shared this palace with, is now dead. Even if he somehow managed to survive the Primitive attacks, like Hannah did, he wouldn't have survived the neuroblastoma in his brain.

I try to relax my shoulders and follow Wolfe willingly. I know I can trust him with my safety. He might be frustrating as hell, a soldier to the core, but he would never willingly leave me in danger. As long as I'm under his roof, I should be safe.

I'm surprised when he shows me to the harem. "This is where you plan on keeping me?"

"For now." He nods at one of the guards who opens the door.

Nostalgia hits me hard as I step through the opening and into another world. I can't help but look at everything with new eyes.

The large common room is tidy, everything put in its place, as though the women of the harem hadn't fled in a panic, leaving everything where it fell. I suspect Hannah must've had the place cleaned up. Where it used to be bustling with a dozen women and servants, it's now devoid of people.

Bolts of fabric line one of the walls where seamstresses used to measure us and create beautiful outfits. Next door is the kitchen, where our chef created amazing meals out of limited resources. The bedrooms are in the back. Each wife had her own room, privacy being a prized commodity at the time. We were among the lucky few. We hadn't been turned out to starve, to fight for our livelihood, to endure the hardships that other citizens would've had to endure. The only expectation was that we please the Warlord when summoned.

"Thought you'd be more comfortable in a familiar place," Wolfe says from behind me.

I raise a skeptical brow and turn to look at him. "Since when do you care about anyone's comfort? No, I think there's another reason for putting me in the most secure room in the palace."

Wolfe's expression is hard, his gaze icy as he looks me over, his eye drifting down my body. "Indeed."

Anger begins to rise at his one-word response. "Since you wish to secure me separate from my people," I say, swinging my hand around to indicate that my people are not with me, "I must assume that you have a reason. Are you trying to lock me in, or lock someone out?"

Again, he pauses before answering. "Both."

"Can you give me more?" I ask in frustration, pacing away from him. "Why am I here? I have a mission to complete. We can stay for a maximum of a few days, long enough to teach your doctor how to replicate and administer the vaccine, then we must move on."

"No." He says it simply, as though that one word explains everything.

I'm beginning to have an inkling of what's going on in that big, brutal brain.

"Wolfe," I say slowly, "you can't keep me here. I have to leave with my team. I have to move on to the next Sanctuary, and then the next one after that. You understand that, don't you?"

He shakes his head. "No, you're needed here. You stay."

Horror begins to rise up, making me feel dizzy. If Wolfe has a strong hold on the city and he wants to keep me here, then I'm not going to be able to fight him. My team is too small to face Wolfe and his army. They won't be able to help.

This isn't the first time a Sanctuary has attempted to separate me from my team and keep me. Other cities had thought to leverage me for control of the vaccination. I learned quickly not to tell them about the origins of the vaccine. Not to tell them it was created using my blood. Warlords can't be trusted with that kind of information.

Of course, Wolfe already knows about my blood.

"You plan to use me to control the vaccine?" I ask him, wanting to be completely clear on what's happening.

"No, I don't care about the vaccine. It's a Band-Aid solution. It'll stop the rapid growth of Primitives, but it won't fix the world we now live in."

"There's more to it than that," I say angrily, pacing away from him, my arms wrapped protectively around my waist. "The vaccine doesn't just stop people from turning into Primitives. It's showing promising signs of turning Primitives back into people."

I can tell right away that Wolfe didn't know this piece of information. He seems to be turning it over in his mind.

"Does it work?" he asks skeptically. "Is it capable of turning zombies into humans again?"

I give my head a slight shake. "Not so far, but I'm confident that it will."

"Who's doing the research?"

"Dr. Bishop, from the Tucson sanctuary." There's no point in keeping the information from him. The more I talk, the more likely it is he'll let me go if I say the right thing. "After Emery was bitten, Taran's blood was able to turn Emery back. She died three months later from massive organ shutdown, but the possibilities inherent in this vaccine are massive. If we can just get it to work on the Primitives, we could eradicate the virus entirely."

A pang rushes through me as I remember Emery, my sister's caretaker for many years, a kind woman who'd treated me with the love she'd shown my sister. Her death was extremely hard on Taran and surprisingly difficult on myself as well, considering we hadn't had time to forge a close bond.

"The vaccine and a cure are two very different things.

Vaccines can be created and distributed quickly. A cure can take years to create, if it's possible at all, and often has undesirable side effects. As your friend no doubt learned." His words are hard, but not untrue.

Emery had suffered right to the end, her organs failing one at a time a time. We did everything we could to keep her alive, but her body was just too severely injured from the Turn to recover.

After Emery's death, Dr. Bishop began experimenting with different versions of the vaccine in the hopes of finding a way to turn Primitives back into humans without damaging them too badly. They'd managed to test the vaccine on a few live Primitives. The younger the Primitive, the better its chances of surviving for longer. None of them actually survived though.

"Maybe so, but there's hope, and I'm part of that hope. You can't keep me here, Wolfe. This isn't where I belong anymore." I plead with him, hoping I'll get through.

He shakes his head. "This is exactly where you belong."

I throw my hands up in frustration. "What about the rest of the world? Do you not give a fuck about them? They'll die without the vaccine."

Wolfe takes a step closer to me until I'm forced to back away. He stares down at me, his single golden eye piercing. "I don't care about the rest of the world. Only you." He takes another step forward, gripping my arm as I try to step away from him. "You will stay."

I shake my head. "No, I won't. I have to leave. Why do you want to keep me here anyway? You left me, not the other way around. You don't need me."

He doesn't answer my question. He doesn't tell me why he wants me here so badly. He turns on his heel and strides through the open door, closing it behind him. It's a great big thick steel door that closes into a concrete wall. The entire harem is built to withstand anything from fire to a bomb blast. I hear the echo of the bolt slamming into place as Wolfe locks me inside.

TEN

At first, I just pace back and forth in front of the door, determined to wait Wolfe and the guards out until someone opens it. Once they do, I'm going to disable them with the weapons they were stupid enough to leave on me, find my team and escape Sanctuary.

When no one enters the harem within the first half hour, curiosity drives me to explore my old home. It's been more than a year since I've been here. Since I've lived, loved and laughed here. Silas was my husband, but the women of the harem were my roommates, sisters and confidants.

Everything is the same, yet different somehow. All of our stuff is spotless and unmoved. Each room, belonging to one of Silas's wives, is exactly how I remember it. We had become a family, a group of women from all different backgrounds who befriended each other and lived together in this insulated dormitory.

Over the years, I became Silas's favourite, and as such was allowed to roam more freely through the palace. Silas trusted me and used me as his advisor. Wolfe and I had formed a wary partnership to protect the Warlord's dignity as his health deteriorated. No one knew how sick Silas was except for me, Wolfe, Hannah and a few of his personal guards. As far as the city was concerned, Silas was strong and healthy, running the Sanctuary smoothly until the day the Primitives came. Then he'd gone down with his ship.

Even back then, I'd wondered about Wolfe's motives. He was definitely the strong silent type, but there was something calculating about him. Though he served Silas, I never got the feeling that he actually cared about the Warlord as a person. He did his job and he did it well, but he had been cold, professional and detached. Perhaps the perfect ingredients for our security master, but he was no friend to any of us.

I had become everything to Silas. His best friend, his confidant, and his head wife. In a way, I shared the role with Hannah. While I worked at Silas's side, helping him run the city, Hannah had ensured harmony in the harem and in the palace. We worked together like a well-oiled machine and forged a close bond. Which is why I don't understand her distance now. The old Hannah would have been thrilled to see me, not distant and standoffish. It makes no sense.

I get an opportunity to talk to her several hours later, when she enters the harem with a tray filled with food and drink. She sets it down on the table, but instead of moving away and leaving she remains, her shuttered gaze on me, her face set in weary lines.

I don't bother to beat around the bush, I ask her the topmost question in my mind. "How did you survive the attack?"

Hannah had stood with Silas during the fall of the city, taking the position I'd wanted. I'm a natural fighter, I should have been by his side defending him until the last. Instead,

Wolfe had saved my life and left Hannah behind with our husband. She should be dead.

She waves her hand around the room and says, "The harem."

Of course, she must've been shut in the harem during the attack. It's the only part of the palace secure enough to withstand the kind of attack the Primitives would've thrown at them. But she would've had to come out eventually, and if she'd survived, why hadn't Silas?

As if sensing the barrage of questions coming her way, Hannah begins to talk, her voice strained. "Silas used the last of his strength to shut me in here, along with anyone else left in the palace who didn't have time to leave with you and Wolfe." Bitterness creeps back into her voice as she mentions our narrow escape. "I begged him to follow me in, to lock himself in here with us. He refused, insisted that he would protect us when the Primitives came. I don't know exactly what happened, he closed us inside and that was the last I saw of him."

I cover my mouth with my hand as I imagine what Silas had gone through as he tried to protect his remaining wife. He had been so weak. Physically, he'd been mostly unable to get out of his chair. Mentally, he had been drifting, forgetting things. It would've been a last act of bravery that would've ultimately proved useless, given his condition at the time. He probably died instantly when the Primitives got to him. Or so I hope.

"What happened after that? You wouldn't have had enough food to stay in here for a long period. This place was only ever meant to be a short-term shelter in case of attack."

"We were forced to leave the harem before the last of the Primitives finally left the city. They were still finding people hiding out, biting them, eating them, turning them.

It was so horrible." She squeezes her eyes shut as the memories assail her. I want to reach out and touch her, to hug and hold her in her moment of pain, but Hannah is a different person now and so am I. Where once we were sisters to each other, now we're... I actually don't know what we are.

"Yet you managed to survive," I say softly, trying to pull her from her memories. Her dull eyes meet mine.

"Yes, some of us survived, along with some people in the city. Maybe 500."

I flinch. There had been thousands of people in the Santa Fe sanctuary when it fell. Only a few hundred escaped with me and Wolfe. That meant less than a thousand survived the Primitive attacks. The thought makes me feel nauseous.

"I'm glad you survived." I blink rapidly as tears rush to my eyes, remembering Hannah the way she used to be. Soft, pretty, motherly.

She gives me a tight smile. "Some days I wonder if I actually did survive."

I know what she means. After a lifetime of running from the Primitives, begging Sanctuary in city after city, I wonder if I'm still the same person I used to be.

I slide onto one of the seats at the table and reach for the tray. The last time I ate was yesterday, not having had time between the attack at the gas station and Wolfe picking me up and bringing me to Sanctuary. I suddenly feel as though I'm starving. I pick up the fork, pierce a cooked piece of potato and shove it into my mouth. I chew and swallow, then ask, "Are you staying here? In the harem?"

She shakes her head. "After the attacks, after the Primitives left and we were able to move more freely, I chose a house in the city. It was either abandoned or the occupants killed. It's several blocks away, so I'm still able to walk to the palace each day."

"Was there a new Warlord? What happened? How did you rebuild?" The questions spill from my lips now that Hannah seems to be willing to speak to me.

She hesitantly touches the back of a chair and then with a sigh pulls it out and sits down. I push the tray toward her a little, indicating that she can help herself. There's enough food on the tray to feed five grown men, more than enough food for two women to share.

"None of the survivors wanted to take on the responsibility of Warlord. Not at first. We debated whether or not to stay or to go find Sanctuary somewhere else, but we were hearing rumours from other Sanctuaries, as refugees started to drift in, that most other Sanctuaries had fallen as well. We didn't know where to go with so many people, so we decided to stay and rebuild. A few weeks after the city had fallen, thousands of refugees showed up from other Sanctuaries, from eastern cities that took far more damage than ours."

She reaches out and picks at the edge of a piece of lettuce, then snatches it up and starts nibbling on it. I smother a smile. Hannah always did prefer rabbit food over meat or bread. If I were to hazard a guess, I would say that this lettuce, and the other vegetables on the tray, probably come from a garden that Hannah herself grew.

"How did you manage to rebuild Sanctuary without a Warlord?" I ask.

She blushes and takes a big bite out of the lettuce. "Many of the people that were left behind trusted me and convinced the refugees that they should trust me too. It was only a temporary solution, since a woman can't be Warlord. We worked quickly to repair the wall, to reorganize the city so that we were clustered closer to each other instead of spread out and more vulnerable. We rallied around the palace. It worked, for the most part, until the second wave."

Her voice drops in pain as she mentions this.

"Second wave?" I hadn't heard of a second wave.

"Yes, a second wave of Primitives swept through the area. Only these ones seemed smarter. They strategized and trapped us, taking us out one at a time as we did things like leave the city on hunting parties, or attempt to fix the water plant. It was a terrifying time, and I was completely incapable of dealing with it."

"You were never trained to handle security situations," I say, reaching out to touch her. At first, she jerks her hand away, but then she hesitates and reaches out to take mine, squeezing.

"Thank you," she says softly. "It was hard watching so many people, so many refugees that came to us begging for Sanctuary, taken out by the second wave. And me, helpless to contain it or do anything about it. I'm simply not a soldier, I can't cope with attacks."

Even though I suspect I already know the answer, I ask anyway. "What happened? How did you stop the second wave?"

"Wolfe," she says simply. "He showed up just in time to save us. He was completely ruthless, but effective. He came in, brutally stamped out any Primitive stragglers roaming the city, and then eradicated them from the area. It was amazing, and he did it almost single-handedly. Like a machine."

I nod, understanding. I've seen Wolfe in action many times. He is exactly like a machine. He kills without thought, without remorse, without compassion. He's effective and terrifying. By himself he can do as much damage as an entire army.

"I'm so sorry it's been tough for you here, Hannah," I say to her. "But it's not much better anywhere else. I didn't want to leave you behind. In fact, I wanted to be the one who stayed and fought. I was better equipped for it. I was devastated when you stayed behind."

Tears fill her eyes and she keeps them fixed on the table.

"I know," she says. "And I'm sorry I was so cold to you when you arrived. It's just... I've been so angry for so long, I don't know what to do with myself, or how to direct the pain. When Silas died... it killed a part of me."

I nod my understanding. "Me too."

She lifts her eyes and we look at each other. Silas's two favourite wives, once more together, sharing a moment. Only we can understand what the other is going through, the pain of losing a husband who had become our everything.

Without warning a stab of jealousy hits me. Not for Silas. I had never been jealous of his other wives. Perhaps it was because I'd had to share him from the start. I'd never questioned my place in his life, nor, after we got to know each other, had I questioned his love for me. He'd loved all of his wives and he'd loved us differently, so there was no need for jealousy.

No, I'm jealous of the new Warlord, and the realization hits me like a punch to the gut.

"What about Wolfe?" I demand, so suddenly and so sharply that Hannah flinches back in her chair and stares at me with a frown, not comprehending what I want to know. I shake my head and clarify, "Does Wolfe have a harem here?" I wave my hand around the room. "Does he have any wives? Are you his wife?"

She raises an eyebrow in surprise. "Of course I'm not Wolfe's wife. He's never wanted anything to do with me and that certainly hasn't changed now that he's become Warlord."

I take a deep breath and attempt to calm down. What's wrong with me? Why do I even care what Wolfe is doing with the harem? I ignore the answering voice inside of me that tells me I cared from the first moment that I took notice of the giant warrior. I've cared for years. I've just never been in a position to do anything about it before now.

"I'm sorry," I say, giving my head a shake. "So much has changed. It's jarring. I just assumed... since the conquering Warlord gets the prizes of the previous Warlord, that Wolfe would have taken the harem."

She shrugs and shakes her head. "Maybe, but as far as I know there haven't been any women in here. Not since the day we left it, moving out into the city. The only people allowed to enter now are cleaning staff."

I continue eating and we chat more about the state of the city. I ask Hannah question after question until I'm positive that she's sick of answering. Still, she answers, calmly talking through everything I want to know. I'm not finished with our discussion when, a few hours later, the door to the harem opens and Wolfe enters.

I turn to look at him, my eyes meeting his, and everything else fades away. I barely notice as Hannah picks up the tray and leaves, inclining her head toward Wolfe as she passes him. The door closes behind her and I hear the bolt sliding into place.

ELEVEN

"What do you want?" I ask sharply, crossing my arms over my chest and glaring. "Have you come to your senses? Are you going to let me go?"

Wolfe stares at me, his expression unmoving. "My plans remain unchanged."

I throw my arms up in annoyance. "What plans? What exactly are you planning? Why do you want to keep me here?"

He walks farther into the room and then stops, looking at me silently. That's one personality trait of Wolfe's that can be both good and immensely frustrating. He doesn't say or do anything without purpose. Every move he makes is economical and purposeful. He's not one to just wander around, touching things, making idle conversation. He has reasons for everything he does, including being here with me now and keeping me here in the palace.

At first, he doesn't answer, as though he's gathering his thoughts. Then, he says, "You don't need to know that now. It will suffice that you will remain here. I'll let you know as things progress."

My eyebrows go up with my temper. "Excuse me? You'll let me know? Not good enough, Wolfe. I want to know what the fuck you're planning, and I want to know right now."

"No."

I grit my teeth and force myself to remain still so I don't storm over to him and throw a punch. Despite a year of training, fighting Primitives and sharpening my skills, I know that I'm still no match for Wolfe. He's spent a lifetime killing. Still, it might be worth it to see his face as I drive my fist into his stomach.

"You don't get to say no to me," I say furiously, pacing the room. "You don't get to take me away from my mission, tell me that I'm stuck here, and not give a reason. Try again."

"You don't need to know yet," he repeats himself.

"If that's as good as you're going to give me, then I'm telling you right now, I won't rest until I've made it out of this room, out of this palace and out of your damn city. I'm done with Santa Fe. I didn't want to come back, and I sure as hell don't want to be here now. This place holds nothing but rotten memories for me."

"That's not true." His voice is quiet, almost uncaring.

He's like a stone statue in the face of other people's emotions, including mine. A fact that has infuriated me from the moment I met him. Wolfe is as much my nemesis as he has been a soldier and friend at my side when I needed him.

He's right though. I'm lying to him and I'm lying to myself when I say that the city holds only bad memories. Some of the best moments of my life have happened here. But I don't want to think about them, I don't want to remember. It's too painful.

"You're still hung up on him, aren't you?" he growls,

taking a step toward me. "It's time to let him go. Time to live your life without his shadow hanging over you."

"What do you know about that?" I demand sharply. "You didn't care about him. You stood aside, like some kind of unfeeling statue while he slowly died. You watched and did nothing. Then you left him here during the attack."

"You know as well as I, there was nothing to be done. His tumor was a death sentence."

"You could've made his life easier though." I know I'm not being reasonable, but I can't seem to stop. It's easier to blame Wolfe for everything. It's always been easier and I almost hate myself for doing it. "You just watched, you stood aside and watched, and I hate you for that."

"I know," he says, his voice warming ever so slightly as he steps toward me. "But you're smarter than that, smarter than to blame me for something that was inevitable." He steps up to me, not touching, but close enough to grab me if he wants to. "It wasn't him I was watching and I think you know that."

I tip my head back to glare at him, my grey eyes clashing with his single amber one. His face is a battleground of scars. I wonder if he grew the beard to make his visage more palatable for others to look at. I've never had a problem with the way he looks. In fact, his wrecked face matches his black heart. My own heart beats faster and my palms grow damp as his scent hits me. Wild, masculine, Wolfe.

He's an ugly murderous soldier, not someone I should be attracted to, but for some reason every part of me notices every part of him when he occupies the same room as me. It doesn't matter where we are or how many people separate us, I will always notice him first. It's always been this way. As much as I want it otherwise, our mutual attraction has been simmering below the surface for years, waiting to explode.

"Is that why I'm here?" I ask softly, stepping back from him. My ass hits the edge of the table and I'm forced to stop. I reach down to grip the wooden edge. "Now that you're Warlord, do you intend to keep me as your prize?"

He stares at me, that eye drilling into me, the scars on his face standing out in livid relief. His long hair is a wild mess of tangles around his shoulders.

"No."

That single word is like a bucket of cold water to the face. Though I should be relieved, I'm not. I'm the opposite. I'm so angered that my hand swings almost independently of my thoughts. Wolfe has the reflexes to stop me, but he doesn't bother. I slap him so hard that his head snaps to the side and his torso twists, just a fraction. He straightens slowly and looks down at me.

He takes a moment before he speaks, a moment for me to watch as my livid handprint makes its way across his cheek and grizzled jaw.

"You hit harder than you did a year ago," he says conversationally, as though I hadn't just hit him with all my strength. "That one was free. Don't hit me again."

I grit my teeth. "Then let me go."

"No." His answer is swift and uncompromising.

I send my fist slamming into his stomach, using every ounce of strength I have behind it. The air whooshes from him, but he doesn't move otherwise. He continues to stare at me, his body thrumming with an energy that mine answers. The air crackles around us and I can sense his intention before he acts. I try to escape, lunging to the side and hurtling away from the table.

He grabs the hair at the back of my head and yanks me

into his chest. I gasp in pain and reach up to take hold of his wrist, digging my nails into the skin. He whirls me around, picks me up and slams me down on the table. My back hits hard and the breath rushes out of me in a whoosh.

I open my mouth to shout, but the sound is swallowed as he bends over me and slams his lips over mine. His kiss is fierce and painful, but intensely electric. Every nerve ending in my body stands up and screams as he kisses me, taking my jaw in his fist and forcing my mouth open before thrusting his tongue inside. It hurts, it dominates, it calls to me.

The moment he breaks the kiss, I slam my forehead into his nose. There isn't enough space between us for me to break his face, but I'm sure I got my point across. He grips me by the neck, slams me back down onto the table and covers my mouth with his. Blood is now flowing from his nose, trickling down his face and onto mine. I struggle to get away from him, trying to roll to the side, but his strength is so much greater than mine, I'm practically immobilized by his big body.

I choke as he thrusts his tongue back into my mouth. I try to snap my teeth shut, but again he grips my jaw and forces it open. I push on his chest and arms, but it's like a rabbit trying to escape a snare. Impossible. I'd have to chew off my own foot to get out.

After what feels like an eternity, he releases me and steps back. I roll off the table and fall to my knees. I only take a second to recover though, before I lunge to my feet and jump away from him. Using my sleeve, I swipe at the blood that dripped from his face onto mine. Wolfe stands staring at me passively, blood dripping slowly from his nose, over his lips and onto his chest. He doesn't try to stop the flow.

"You done?" His voice sounds gravelly and bored.

I don't bother answering verbally; he gets the hint when I yank a dagger out of the sheath on my thigh and run at him. When he reaches for me, I grab his wrist and fly underneath his arm, whirling against his back. I lift the dagger, intending to sink it into his side. It'll hurt like a bitch, but it won't kill him. He needs to understand that he can't fuck with me.

As I attempt to drive the knife home, he whips around and shoves me back, then slams his fist into my wrist, forcing me to drop the knife.

I stumble backward, about to go down when he catches me, lifts me against his chest – one hand around my waist and one at the back of my head – and brings his face down to mine.

"No, no, no!"

I try to twist my head away, but the hand at the back of my neck grips so tightly that I can't move. I'm forced to take yet another brutal assault as his lips cover mine in the simulation of a kiss. It's not a real kiss, because kisses don't feel this way. Kisses shouldn't hurt.

I wait him out and the moment he lifts his head, I attempt to slam my forehead into his nose again. But he's learned, he grips me by the back of the hair and drags my head back. He leans down and sinks his teeth into my neck, biting hard enough to leave a mark, but not breaking the skin. I shriek in anger and slam my fist into his shoulder. He doesn't let me go so I reach up and take hold of his hair, yanking.

He lets go of me, but only for a second. Only long enough for me to let go of his hair. Then he takes my hands in his and shackles my wrists behind my back in one of his huge paws. He uses his other arm to grip me underneath my breasts and lift me off the ground against his chest, my back pressed to his body. He drops his head into my neck and licks me.

"Let me go!" I shriek, struggling in his arms.

He lifts his head and presses his lips against the shell of my ear. His breathing hitches a little as he whispers, "That will never happen."

"Then I will never stop fighting you." I kick back at him, but he shifts and my leg flies past him.

He drops me and steps away. I whirl around, bringing my hand up with a gun in it. If he so much as sneezes at me I'm going to fill him with holes.

"Do it," he says quietly, stepping toward me.

I wipe my face with the back of my arm, trying to catch the blood he keeps smearing on my skin. "Don't think I won't."

He continues to walk toward me, his honey gaze now heated. I want to look away, but I know he'll use the opportunity to take me down again.

"Every time you try to fight me, I will kiss you." Even though he's spent the past ten minutes proving this statement, I almost don't believe him. Wolfe is a fighter, not a lover. He'd as soon kill a person as kiss them.

"But why?" I demand. "You've never shown any interest in me before."

"We both know that isn't true." There's a slight curl to his lips as though he's annoyed by my lie. His gaze drops to my weapon. "Put it away or I'll take it away, Skye. You aren't going to shoot me."

I growl and shove it back into my holster, whirling away from him and crossing my arms. I don't want him to see my face right now as I struggle with the truth. I hate him, but he's right. Wolfe was interested in me from the moment I called this palace home. His sharp gaze followed my every movement for years. He never acted on whatever was going on in that brain, but it was obvious that he held me in some kind of regard. Which is why I don't understand why he left me a year ago. I don't want to admit it, but that moment, when he walked away from me, was even more painful than the death of my husband.

"Where is my team?" I abruptly change the subject, trying to blink away the tears that have formed.

"They're my guests... for now."

"What does that mean?" I demand, turning back around to look at him.

"They're safe for now but will soon be asked to leave the city. I have offered them Sanctuary for the night and explained to them that you will no longer be a member of their party. Tomorrow, they will continue their journey and you will remain here."

"No," I gasp in dismay, then straighten my shoulders and add with conviction. "They won't leave without me."

He nods, unconcerned. "That seems to be the consensus among them. Regardless, they will leave tomorrow, and I will escort them personally. If they refuse to leave, then I'll make an example of their most belligerent member, a man who demands to know your whereabouts with annoying frequency."

"Deacon?"

Wolfe's thick brows lower into a frown, as though he's irritated by my uttering the other man's name. "Yes."

Fear punches me hard in the chest, taking my breath. It's a moment before I can speak again. "Please don't do this. They need me and they need Deacon. I'm their leader, they can't do this without me. And Deacon protects the team. If you keep me and kill him, you'll be dismantling our biggest hope of surviving the Primitives. The world needs that vaccine."

I allow him to see every emotion in my eyes, my earnestness, my belief in what I'm saying. But I already know his answer. I can see my future in the stony set of his features. I'm not going anywhere.

True to his personality, Wolfe says nothing more. He's already said it all and he won't repeat himself. He doesn't care about the vaccine; he doesn't care about the world.

"Can you please leave?" I whisper, my voice brittle with the tears that are now welling up and threatening to drip down my cheeks. The last thing I need is for Wolfe to see any weakness.

Without another word he turns and leaves.

TWELVE

I never had a problem with the harem before. When I was brought to the Santa Fe Sanctuary seven years ago and told that I would be part of the harem, I had felt some trepidation, but the women quickly put me at ease. Gradually I came to accept and then love the warmth and relaxing atmosphere of the harem.

Now, the longer I'm locked behind the harem walls, the more I find to dislike about my former home.

Two days have passed since I was brought here. I have nothing to do but wait, my only company Hannah when she brings food and briefly chats with me. I have tried summoning Wolfe several times, but the guards simply look at me, shake their heads and lock me back inside.

I'm completely ready for a change in scenery by the time Wolfe finally presents himself. I practically jump on him when the door opens to reveal his big scarred body.

"I want out," I demand. "Tell me what I have to do to get out."

Wolfe approaches me where I stand and looks down at me thoughtfully. Finally, he answers, "Time."

"What the hell does that mean?" I frown at him.

"It means," he drawls, "that you need time before you'll be allowed to leave. I need to know that you can be trusted."

I scoff at him. "Then I guess I'm stuck in here until hell freezes over. I'd rather fuck a Primitive than remain in this city with you."

Wolfe remains unfazed. He's always been this way. It takes a lot to excite him, either good or bad. He's like a walking Grim Reaper, constantly waiting for death to come. I swear sometimes he lives just to die.

"The doctor is coming in to see you. You will allow Dr. Summers to take some of your blood so the vaccine can be re-created."

I glare at him. "Get it from Deacon; he has plenty of my blood and plenty of the vaccine to go around."

"I already have what I need from your team, but the doctor wants a clearer understanding of how to re-create the vaccine. Your people have indicated that you're the one to talk to."

"I'm not talking to you or anyone until I've talked to my people," I insist stubbornly.

"Your people are being ejected from the city within the hour."

Fury rips through me like a razor blade. "You're sending my people away? Without letting me talk to them?"

Wolfe's eyes drop to my clenched fists and he raises a brow as though daring me to take a swing at him. Of course, I don't, because I know what'll happen. If I touch him, he'll kiss me, and I can't cope with that right now. I can't have the man that I kind of want dead kissing me and stirring up feelings.

"As long as they remain in this city, you will hold out

hope that you can escape with them. I can't have that. They'll be heading to the next Sanctuary without you."

I cross my arms over my chest and work on regulating my breathing, so I don't start screaming. "You're lying. Deacon won't leave without at least seeing me first."

"I don't lie." He says it simply, but there's an underlying steel to his words.

Wolfe is right, he never lies.

"They won't leave without me, especially not Deacon," I stubbornly insist.

He inclines his head. "It might take some convincing to get them out of the city, but they'll leave." Seeing the look on my face he continues, "They haven't been harmed."

"Your definition of harm and my definition of harm are quite different, Wolfe," I growl at him. "I want to talk to Deacon."

Wolfe narrows his eyes at me and crosses his arms over his chest, imitating my stance. "You're very interested in the welfare of your team. You've mentioned Deacon's name more than once."

I throw up my hands. "I'm their leader! Of course I'm interested in their welfare. I'm responsible for them, I'm responsible for bringing them here and putting them in your path."

"I've told you that they're fine, now let the matter rest."

Wolfe is becoming clearly frustrated. Even in the face of a Primitive attack I've never seen him anything less than unflappable, yet something about my concern for my team bothers him.

"I won't drop it until you let me talk to Deacon."

Wolfe takes a threatening step toward me but stops short of touching me. "You will not say his name again."

"Do you mean Deacon?" I narrow my eyes at him.

"You just signed his death warrant. If he enters my territory again, he's a dead man."

"Very mature, especially since you just told me my team will be unharmed. I thought you didn't lie. Do you mind telling me why you're threatening my second-in-command?"

Wolfe reaches out to take my arms in a painful grip and gives me a small shake. I stiffen and try to push away, but he continues to hold me.

"He is not your second-in-command. He never was. That's my job. No one else will get that close to you."

I'm shocked by his words. What does he mean? Wolfe is my second-in-command? The idea that Wolfe might bow down to anyone, let alone a woman, is ludicrous. But before I can question him, he continues, "I will not listen to the name of another man on your lips. You will forget him."

Again, his demands surprise me. Wolfe is always so in control of himself. He almost sounds... jealous. But that can't be right. Though we were partners when we defended Tucson Sanctuary a year ago, he never hinted at anything more. At least nothing that I caught on to. He was my shadow, my protector, but nothing more.

I tilt my face to look up into his. "What are you saying?"

"I'm saying, I don't want my wife talking about another man."

A long time ago my grandmother read the story of Alice in Wonderland to me and my younger sister. We'd been under attack by a rogue Primitive who was beating at the walls of our cabin, trying to get in, trying to kill us all. Grandma distracted us with a story. To this day I've never forgotten the tale of Alice in Wonderland. At this very moment I feel much like how Alice must've felt when she fell through the rabbit hole and found herself in a strange land and a strange situation meeting strange people. Of course, the comparison can only go so far. This isn't a harm-less children's tale that will end in the defeat of the Jabber-wocky. This is our lives, and in the time of the pandemic all lives are lost, no matter who we are. To die of old age is unheard of in this time.

"Please, Wolfe," I beg. "I don't understand. You don't want me to speak the name of another man because it'll upset your wife?"

His grip on my arms gentles and his face softens. "I don't want the woman who will become my wife to speak the names of other men, especially men that she has worked and fought alongside."

"It almost sounds like you're saying that I will be your wife." I laugh nervously. "But that can't be possible."

He doesn't answer but drops my arms and steps away from me. I can tell by the shutter settling over his features that he's done talking. I'm lucky I got as much as I did.

"Please let me talk to my team before you eject them from the city." He ignores me and heads for the door. I call after him. "Wolfe!" He stops but doesn't turn around. "I promise you, they are very loyal to me. If you don't let me talk to them then they won't leave. They might leave the city on your orders, but they won't leave the area. Not until they get me back."

He half turns, his gaze still not touching mine. "Then they will be killed."

I take a few steps toward him, my mind racing. I believe he'll do exactly as he says. He won't hesitate to kill anything that gets in his way. This is the strange dichotomy that is the new Santa Fe Warlord. He will grant Sanctuary to old women, incapable of having babies, yet he'll remorselessly kill my team if they defy him.

Finally, I use a weapon that I've been hesitant to use,

because it means admitting that Wolfe has feelings for me. "If you kill any member of my team, then I will never soften toward you." His eyes rise to meet mine, as if trying to read the truth there. "I will not condone the murder of innocents."

"You will do as I say," he says simply, and then leaves.

Once again, I'm left alone in the harem with more questions than answers.

THIRTEEN

I'm completely taken off guard when, less than an hour later, Wolfe strides through the door of the harem with Deacon in tow.

"Deacon!" I exclaim, taking several steps toward him.

The look on Wolfe's face stops me in my tracks. His stare is hard and filled with violent promise. Without a single word he's warning me away from touching the other man.

As if sensing the same thing, Deacon keeps his distance. I'm relieved to note that he looks completely fine, not a single mark on him. This helps ease some of the anxiety of being separated from my team – a group of people I've spent every single day with over the past several months.

"The Warlord says you have something to say to me," Deacon says, his voice hard with dislike.

I glance at Wolfe, but he remains silent. I realize he's brought Deacon here so I can convince him to take the team and leave. I'll have to choose my words carefully, so I don't accidentally risk the other man's life.

"Wolfe has informed me that you'll be leaving the city

without me." I try to keep the bitterness from my voice so as not to antagonize the big Warlord listening to every word.

Deacon nods. "He's told me the same. We have your back though, we're not leaving without you."

I give him a half smile and shake my head. "I knew you would say that, and I really appreciate it. It's good to know that my team doesn't want to leave without me."

"We won't have it any other way," he says, narrowing his eyes in Wolfe's direction before continuing. "We need our leader if we're going to continue this mission."

Though it pains me to say it, I give him the words I know he needs to hear to move on without me. "No, you don't. You never really needed me. You're the strength behind the team, the protector."

"But your blood – "

I cut him off before he can continue. "You have my blood. You have everything you need to continue. If anything, I've been more of a hindrance to you. Now, you can move easier, go to the next Sanctuary. Spread the vaccine as far as you can."

"You know that's not true!" Deacon explodes, taking another step toward me. He ignores Wolfe who shadows him, prepared to intervene if Deacon gets too close. "You are our leader. You hold us together. You convince us to keep moving every time we lose someone, every time we're attacked. We can't do this without you."

Tears rush to my eyes and I look down at the floor. I'm going to have to change tactics or I'm never going to convince Deacon to leave, and I know that Wolfe is deadly serious when he says he'll take them out if he has to.

"Well that's too bad." I keep my eyes on the floor and try to harden my voice, to keep the ache from it. "Because I'm not going with you." I raise my eyes to his, trying to convince him in a single cool look that I'm serious. "Wolfe has offered me the position of wife to the Warlord. This position will come with the kind of privileges that I was used to having before the fall of my Sanctuary. I want them back. I don't want to travel anymore. I'm done pretending that I'm some kind of warrior woman. This is where I want to be."

At first, Deacon looks taken aback, like I just slapped him in the face. He searches my face as though looking for answers, but not finding what he's looking for. Finally, he shakes his head.

"I don't believe this."

"I'm sorry. You're going to have to leave without me." I can barely raise my voice above a whisper. Pain is blossoming in my chest, stealing my breath and my words. It's strange; I knew leaving the team would be emotional, but it feels like leaving my family behind.

I'm always leaving my family behind.

Deacon shakes his head again. "No, what I'm saying is, I don't believe you. I think you're saying what you think you need to say to get rid of us. And I think you're doing it because of him." He turns to stare at Wolfe with hatred.

Wolfe's hand drops to the dagger on his belt, a clear warning that Deacon should back down. Of course, my second-in-command does not back down. He's as bad as Wolfe when it comes to arrogant pride.

"You got a problem with us you take it up with me," Deacon says belligerently. "Leave Skye alone."

Even I can see the problem in Deacon's words. He has no one and nothing to back him up. There are eight people left on the vaccine team, not nearly enough to take on the security forces within this Sanctuary. As this is an obvious point, Wolfe doesn't bother to answer him.

"He's not going to let me go." I don't know what else to

say. I pace away from him, my feet tapping against the stone floor in frustration. Finally, I turn back to them. I tried a lie, now I'll try the truth. "If you don't leave, he'll kill you."

Deacon opens his mouth to speak, probably to tell me that he doesn't care. I interrupt him, "He won't just kill you; he'll take out the whole team if he thinks they're a threat. You need to take him seriously. Wolfe always follows through on his threats."

Hands on his hips, Deacon stares at the floor, his mind working as he tries to decide what to do. Finally, he nods. "Fine, we'll leave. We'll continue the mission." He lifts his head and pins me with a look. "We won't forget you. We'll be back."

I give him a tremulous half smile. "Be sure that you do. I'll be expecting you."

"Good enough," Deacon says and turns back to the door, ready to leave. There's no point in prolonging an already painful conversation.

Wolfe opens the door and instructs his people to take Deacon back to his room. I realize that he and the rest of the team must be on one of the guest floors several levels below mine. At least they're being kept in comfort, and not a prison.

The door closes on Deacon and I realize this will probably be the last time I see him for months, if not years. I swipe at my eyes and glare at Wolfe.

"Are you happy now?" I snap childishly.

"That was for you." His simple words anger me, and I want to lash out.

"Yeah, if it were up to you, they'd be dead."

Wolfe holds my gaze, letting me see everything I need to see. Even though my words were spoken sarcastically, they are the truth. Wolfe would have taken out my entire team because it would be more convenient to him. He's allowing them to live because I want them to live.

"Please leave." My words are an echo of the words I spoke to him earlier.

Wolfe straightens and bows his head, as if bowing to my plea. We both know that's not true. He leaves when he wants to leave, and he stays when he wants to stay. I have no control over his desires.

He crosses the room and pauses in the doorway, pinning me with his stare. "Eventually, you will ask me to stay." Then he leaves.

FOURTEEN

I'm left to my own devices for the next several hours, which is a good thing. I need to process what Wolfe said to me. He's so damn cryptic all the time, he should probably cart around an interpreter just so people understand what he's saying.

I think he was trying to say that he expects me to enjoy his company one day. But that can't be right. It would be like enjoying the companionship of a rabid dog. Wolfe never does what I expect him to do. He's unpredictable, violent, cranky and rude. Who would want to actually spend time with him?

I quickly stomp down on the voice in my head jumping up and down and screaming, *I do, I do, I do.*

"I don't!" I snap out loud as I pace the common room.

I'm still thinking about Wolfe and our strange relationship when Hannah enters the harem with another woman. I turn to look at them, my gaze roving over the woman trailing behind Hannah.

They approach and Hannah introduces the stranger. "This is Dr. Sheela Summers."

I looked her up and down in surprise. "Doctor of what?"

Sheela Summers is an attractive blond woman with a regal bearing. Her shoulders are straight and she has a slight tilt to her chin. Her blue eyes have an openness to them that puts a person immediately at ease. She's probably in her mid thirties.

The doctor laughs and holds out her hand. "Medical doctor," she clarifies.

I look at her hand then take it with hesitation. She's young, looks healthy, perfectly capable of bearing children. Women her age don't become doctors. Though there were definitely female doctors at the beginning of the century, many of them have died and few are allowed to carry on the tradition. According to most Warlords, population survival is far more important than career choices for women.

"How are you allowed to be a doctor?" I ask boldly. I'm curious and there's no point beating around the bush.

She looks at me seriously. "I was part of an underground organization of women on the east coast. We called ourselves the Apocalypse Posse. We created laws of our own, a society of our own. We worked for and with people who became even more marginalized by the Great Fall than they were before. Many of us women had jobs beyond babies." There's a slight curl to her lip indicating her distaste at the idea of becoming a childbearing machine. My respect for her rises.

"I've never heard of an organization like that. It must've been difficult to sustain. Didn't your Warlord come after you?"

She nods and waves her hand toward one of the couches, indicating I should sit down with her. I think about refusing, since I don't like the idea of a complete stranger telling me what to do, but I'm curious about this woman. I want to know more, and if knowing more means following her directions, then I'm game. For a little while.

I sink onto the couch, and when she reaches for my wrist, I let her take it. She lightly lifts my arm and places it across her knees. Then she reaches into her bag and pulls out several glass tubes. I sigh deeply. Getting my blood drawn is not my favourite pastime, but it's something that has become more and more common over the past several months as I moved from Sanctuary to Sanctuary. She ties an elastic tightly around my bicep.

"Yes, when he found out about us, he did his best to dismantle the Apocalypse Posse. He would send out soldiers to round us up. But we had a solid base of loyal followers who benefited from our expertise and who would hide us when the soldiers came. We did a good job of staying underground, of hiding in plain sight. I practiced medicine out of a seamstress's shop, using her back rooms. My clients were mostly other women, but sometimes I would see men and children who were too poor to see the official Sanctuary medical staff."

It never made sense to me that women ended up becoming so oppressed after the Great Fall. Even once male warriors decided that women needed to start producing more babies, why were women's talents not utilized in other ways? Why take away any aspirations toward a career? The nearest I can come to an answer is that in order to force women into a child-bearing situation, they needed to be thoroughly subjugated. Stripped of everything that could elevate them to higher thinking where they might become disgruntled and try to buck the proposed system.

"What Sanctuary are you from?" It sounds like paradise. Maybe if I can somehow escape Wolfe, I can go there.

She gives me a tight smile and her expression becomes

more closed off. This is definitely a topic she doesn't want to talk about, but she answers anyway. "I'm originally from the Detroit Sanctuary, but when that fell, I moved to the New York Sanctuary. Turned out to be a bad mistake when the Primitives took out a powerplant and drove us out of the city. Unfortunately, there are only a few ways out of New York, and they were waiting for us."

I can only imagine the horror of her experience. Primitives have no mercy. They are hardwired without feelings. If the New York survivors had the vaccine, then things might've been different. The Primitives still would have attacked, still would've killed many people, but they wouldn't have been able to turn anyone.

"You escaped?" I prod her as she swabs my skin, then pushes a needle into my vein.

She nods. "Me and several others managed to get our hands on a boat. Though the Primitives were all along the shoreline, none of them could reach us."

Primitives can't swim. Long ago, after the Great Fall, some people were able to survive the Primitive attacks by going out to sea. It hadn't been easy living, according to the descendants, but it did save many families.

"Eventually we were able to find a place to land the boat. Then we followed other refugees out west, going from city to city until we found one that was capable of offering Sanctuary."

She injects a tube into the needle and I watch with disinterest as it fills with my rich red blood. I'm far more interested in the conversation Dr. Summers is providing.

"There are others?" I ask excitedly. "Are they here?"

Her face softens and she gives me a genuine smile. "Yes, there are more from our group of underground women. They're eager to meet you, if you're interested. They love the idea of a woman becoming a warrior and travelling the outlands to distribute a vaccination. You've become a legend around here, the hope for our survival."

I laugh out loud, unable to help myself. "I'm nobody," I say with scorn. "I'm just the lady with the lucky blood."

She doesn't laugh but gives me a serious look. "No true leader wants the position. Any who do are usually power greedy. People who reluctantly end up in positions of power are the ones who feel the weight of responsibility. I would far rather have a leader who despises the position, than one who covets it."

I immediately think of my brother-in-law, Diogo Fuentes, Warlord of the Tucson Sanctuary. According to my sister Taran, the responsibility of the most prominent Sanctuary in what used to be America weighs heavily on him. There are times that he wishes he wasn't the leader, but knows his Sanctuary thrives because of him and because of my sister. They're both effective but reluctant leaders.

Uncomfortable with the direction of the conversation, I change the subject back to the doctor's group of underground women. "What do the other women do for work?"

She replaces the vial in my arm and fills another. "Anita is our resident engineer. She can look at an engine and know how to make it work, like magic. Dolly is our tech wizard. If you have any old technology, broken or otherwise, she'll make it work. Tabitha is an agriculturist. When we lived in New York she was responsible for creating vast gardens in our underground network. We shared with everyone in our group and those in need. Christine is Tabitha's wife. Obviously, they had to take their relationship underground so that neither was forced to marry someone else and produce his babies. Christine is a really fabulous cook, has a big heart and loves being around children. In New York, she worked as a teacher."

My heart aches as I listen to the doctor talk. She's talking about an impossible dream world. A place where there are fewer rules and restrictions. To even be able to survive in an underground capacity this group of women must've been fierce. I long to be part of them.

"Thank you for telling me all this," I murmur, my thoughts still filled with the images provided. Then another thought occurs to me. "But you're the doctor here in Santa Fe Sanctuary. You must practice out in the open, or you wouldn't be meeting with me. You're not underground anymore?"

Hannah answers for the doctor and I turn my attention to the other woman.

"In one word, Wolfe," Hannah says, watching my face carefully. "At first the women remained hidden, fearful that they would be separated and forced to marry members of the city security force, but Anita stepped in to show us her skill when the west wall fell after repeated attacks. She risked herself in order to save an entire city. She helped plan the new wall and actually helped build it with her own hands, alongside our men. When Wolfe found out about Anita and the others, he had them gathered up and brought to him. We expected him to marry them off to his eligible soldiers, but instead he demanded a full explanation and then allowed them to leave peacefully. He utilizes their skills when he needs them. Which is how you're having this conversation with Dr. Summers."

"He didn't force any of them to marry?" I ask incredulously. Even under Silas, a Warlord who ruled with unusual compassion, women were still forced to marry, whether they liked it or not.

Hannah shrugs. "We were all surprised. Since coming back to the city and taking over, he's made many improvements and worked diligently toward a harmonious city."

I nearly laugh out loud at the pairing of Wolfe's name with the word harmonious. Hannah's words don't jive with what I know of Wolfe. He's a soldier. A Warlord. No part of him is soft or understanding. But he is smart, and I have an inkling that he's decided these women can be far more useful in a professional capacity.

"I wish I had a skill that he coveted more than marriage," I say bitterly, thinking back to our conversation earlier.

The doctor squeezes my arm comfortingly and gently removes the needle. She presses a small piece of gauze against the pinprick of blood that wells up.

"You're set to marry the Warlord." It's not a question, which means both women must know already.

Hannah speaks up. "If it makes you feel better, I don't think it would matter what kind of profession you were skilled in, he would make you his wife anyway. It's about you, not what you bring to the table."

Hannah's words sound wistful and I frown at her. "If you want the job, please take it. I have no desire to marry him and the first opportunity I have to get out of here, I'm leaving."

"He doesn't want me, he wants you." Hannah turns away abruptly, mumbling, "The favourite... always the favourite."

Then she shakes her head as though to dispel the bitterness that takes everyone in the room by surprise. Hannah is usually a gentle and loving creature with no bad thing to say about anyone.

She continues, her moment of annoyance over, "That man has been obsessed with you from the moment he laid eyes on you when the Outsider Talon brought you in and presented you to Silas. Wolfe has waited years for this moment. There's no chance he's letting you go this time."

I stare back at Hannah, our eyes clashing. There's something different about her, less forgiving, harder. The past year has had a significant effect on her.

"It doesn't matter." I shake my head. "I won't marry him."

Hannah laughs. "As if that ever stopped a Warlord. As if it will stop Wolfe."

We fall silent. Hannah's words ring true in a way we've all experienced. Warlords rule over everything: land, resources and people, particularly women. The doctor finishes up and she and Hannah leave together. Once more I'm alone in the harem, contemplating a future that I want nothing to do with.

Exhaustion hits me as I make my way to the harem, to Skye. She's been in my city for four days now. Enough time to calm down. Enough time to contemplate her new reality and reconcile herself to the inevitable.

I run a hand over my face and beard, then slap a cheek, trying to wake myself up. Skye is a sharp woman, always coming at me with something, so I need to be alert to handle her. Which is hard to do when this fucking city is sucking everything out of me.

There's a reason I never wanted to be Warlord. I could've had my pick of cities. When I left Tucson, I toyed with the idea of going back to Tijuana, taking out the Warlord there and creating a viable Sanctuary out of my birthplace. Ultimately though, I dropped the idea. I didn't want the responsibility and I sure as fuck didn't give enough of a shit about people that I'd ever prioritize their health or the health of a city. There's a big difference between being able to do something and wanting to do the thing.

Then I ended up in Santa Fe, saw the destruction and people struggling to rebuild, and stepped in with the necessary expertise. Over the course of months, the citizens of Santa Fe Sanctuary began looking to me more and more for leadership, until it became official. Now I find myself in the exact position I'd been avoiding for years. Warlord.

The woman on the other side of the harem door is another matter. She was born to lead. Unfortunately, she was also born in the wrong time. Had she been born seventy years ago, she would've ruled the world. Now, her potential is crippled by a world descended into Primitive brutality. I've decided to change that. I'll start with this city and see where I can go from here. Give her a place to rule, to shine, to become the leader she's meant to be.

I stop next to the guards at the harem door. "Any problems?"

They both stand straighter, chins up, shoulders back. I don't have time to develop relationships with my people, so I rule through a combination of fear, fairness and sheer brute strength. I work alongside my people, proving my worth, but I also elevate myself above. There must be separation between the Warlord and his citizens, in order for him to make an effective leader. I am different, and I don't want them for one moment to forget. I would as soon kill these men as talk to them.

The one nearest to me, Denny Torrance, speaks first. "She tried to escape a few times. Once through a window and once by tricking us. Neither worked."

Of course, neither attempt would work. The harem is located on the second to top floor of the palace, thirty floors above the ground. Even if she manages to make it through a window, most of which are sealed shut, she has nowhere to go but down. As for tricking my security team, Skye is smart and determined, and given time she might be capable of such a feat. But for now, my men are alert to any tricks.

"Open the door." I give them enough room to unlock and open the portal to the harem. Not a regular door, but closer to the door one might find on the safe of an old bank. Steel, reinforced, blast proof. As I step through into the harem, I say, "Bring the food when it arrives."

Skye is standing by one of the windows, her legs spread, her arms crossed, her back to me. Her spine is so straight it looks like there might be a steel bar trapped in her back. Her ass, the finest ass I've ever seen, is encased in a pair of supple leather pants, so tight that they mold to her thighs and ass, showcasing every detail. She's wearing a loose beige shirt. A man's shirt. I wonder where she got it from. It'll be the first item of her wardrobe to go. I can't have my woman wearing another man's shirt.

She has a veritable artillery strapped to her thighs and waist. When she was brought into Sanctuary, I made an unspoken statement to her by allowing her to keep them, *I want you to feel safe within these walls.* Now she's making a statement to me by wearing them, *I will fuck you up at the first opportunity.*

She doesn't need weaponry in the harem. This room is the safest in the city. But the fact that she wears them makes me want her even more.

"How are you settling in?" I'm not a man of words, never have been. But I want her to talk, need to hear her voice, and the only way that'll happen is if I get her talking.

She turns her head to the side but doesn't turn around or look at me. Her long dark brown hair with its reddish tint spills down her back in soft waves, ending in an arrow just above her waist. It's grown several inches since I last saw her. It's ragged, wild and beautiful. Just like her.

"I'm trying not to settle in since I'll be leaving soon," she says scornfully.

I bite back a smile. She doesn't need to see my amusement or know that I think her resistance is both stimulating and cute. Something tells me if she knew of my sentiment, she would become murderous. As much as I would love a tussle with her, now is not the time. I need sleep before I engage in physical combat with this woman.

"The quicker you settle in, the more freedoms I can give you. Starting with a tour of the city." I can tell by the tilt of her head and the stiffening of her shoulders that she's interested. I knew she would be.

When she first arrived in Santa Fe seven years ago, she fought against her new role, fought against her new Warlord husband. She wanted nothing to do with him. But Silas had been nothing if not patient. He'd waited her out, wooed her, showed her how important she was becoming to him. I'd stood by and watched the entire romance unfold. After her first year in the city, she'd become involved in the inner workings. Involved in things like education, food supply, medicine, everything. She was the perfect companion to the Warlord. Graceful, intelligent and compassionate. Though she was impetuous and sometimes emotional, they were character traits that helped her rule at her husband's side efficiently and effectively.

That was the closest I'd ever come to murdering Warlord Silas and taking his place. Jealousy had eaten at me, but I'd decided to wait, to bide my time. The woman I had fallen in love with would never have accepted the man who killed her husband. Now, my time has arrived.

"I have no desire to settle or to see the city," she says tartly, turning to look at me, her beautiful grey eyes narrowed in anger. "You'll have to kill me or keep me locked up forever. I won't stay here."

I step toward her, incapable of resisting her lure. She's

so fucking beautiful in her warrior clothes with her weapons and bad attitude. I want to lay her out on the table and show her how much I worship her. But she can't know yet how much she has come to mean to me. That her attitude, who she is, is the only thing in this world that keeps me breathing, working, living. I don't know when the transition happened, but one day I was a dead man breathing, the next I was living for her.

I raise my hand and she flinches. I pause and then slowly brush my fingertips down the side of her silky cheek. I tell myself to go slow, not to frighten her, but I've ached for her for so long it's hard not to just reach out and take what's mine.

"Neither option works for me. Alive and with me is your only option." Before she can reply, there's a brief knock at the door.

"Come," I call.

The door opens and two men walk in with platters filled with food. Though the palace kitchen is run by women, I decided not to let them in the harem just yet. Skye is fully capable of taking down a grown man; a few women would be nothing to her. For now, the only people allowed in the harem besides Hannah and the doctor are my soldiers. And even then, I'll only send in the best. Skye is sneaky, aggressive and capable. I don't want her attacking my people just yet.

"Oh good, the food's here," Skye says, snark clearly evident in her tone. "You can leave now. I'm going to eat."

I can feel my lips tugging upward, despite my best intentions. This woman and her sass speak right to my dick.

"I'm staying."

"Then I'm leaving." She strides past me toward the door, as though I would actually allow her to leave.

I don't bother to stop her. She knows she's not getting out of the harem. My guys locked the door behind them, slamming the bolts home in an echo of her imprisonment. This isn't how I want to keep her, but she's proving as stubborn as I expected. She needs time, and the harem is the safest place for her to stay as she settles into her new life.

She whirls around and gives me a glare, looking at me as though I'm lower than a Primitive. "I'm not eating with you." She crosses her arms stubbornly over her chest.

I shrug. "Then you'll watch me eat."

I stride past her to the table, jerking a chair out and sitting down. The damn chairs in the harem are too delicate for a guy like me. I feel like I'm going to crush the fragile wood beneath my heavy body. I shift gingerly on the chair as I reach for the nearest platter, piling a plate full of meat, vegetables and bread.

I ignore her and begin eating. Eventually, she lets out a huff of annoyance and drops into the seat across from me. Her movements are jerky and loud as she throws food onto a plate and slams it down in front of her. I cringe as the tines of her fork scrape across the bottom of her plate while she eats forcefully. Occasionally, her temper can take a juvenile turn, something I'm sure will smooth out as she matures.

"If you promise not make an escape attempt, I might consider taking you on a tour." It's more than I had planned on doing. I'd wanted her in the harem for at least a week before taking her to the city, but I despise watching her be caged up like an animal. She's meant to be free.

"First of all, I won't be making an escape *attempt*, it will be a successful bid for freedom. Second of all, the moment you let me out of here, I'm leaving. I refuse to spend one minute more in this city with you than I have to." She shoves a piece of bread into her mouth and chews belligerently.

"Then you won't be leaving the harem." I watch her face fall as the words leave my mouth and almost regret them, though she's the one throwing down the gauntlet.

In an effort to change the subject, I ask her which Sanctuaries she's visited since leaving Tucson. At first, she doesn't answer, ignoring the question. Then, as if unable to help herself, she starts to speak, telling me the story of her journey.

"We left Tucson shortly after the creation of the vaccine. The doc figured the faster we stopped *Necrotitis Primeval* from spreading the better. We put a team together out of the best soldiers from Tucson and the refugee camp. Well, you met them."

At my nod, she continues, "It took a long time to get from Tucson to Sacramento. There were still hordes of Primitives moving west, almost in a tidal wave. We kept coming across them and we kept having to fight. We lost two men in our first week out." She falls silent for a moment, the weight of her responsibility toward her team still heavy on her shoulders. Then she straightens in her seat and hardens her voice. "A few weeks in we began acting like more of a team, hitting the Primitives in a tactical sweep. It reached the point where we could attack a group five times the size of our little team without any casualties."

Skye continues outlining attack strategies and defensive techniques she picked up along the way. She sounds proud of herself, and I can understand why. Primitives are vicious relentless killing machines. They are driven to feed their never-ending hunger for flesh. I'm impressed, but not surprised by Skye's ingenuity in fighting them. She's always had it in her to inspire loyalty in others.

"Sacramento was tough. It was our first Sanctuary out of Tucson. We didn't have a strategy, just went in blind with the vaccine and the idea that they would just take it and let us leave." She shakes her head and rolls her eyes at her own naivety. "At first they didn't believe that we had a vaccine. When we explained how it worked, described the effects on Tucson Sanctuary, they became interested. Very interested. Then I made a big mistake."

So far I've remained silent throughout her story, but I know exactly what mistake she made. "You told them about your blood."

She nods. "It was a stupid mistake, one that nearly cost my team their lives and me my freedom. The idiots in Sacramento didn't have a proper doctor, someone that could explain to them how vaccinations work. The Warlord couldn't get it through his thick head that they didn't actually need me there in order to re-create it. Luckily, Deacon figured out what was going on when I failed to meet the team at our scheduled departure time. He was able to bust me out. We left a box of vaccinations and the formula behind, but who knows if they were able to re-create it. I hope so. Despite the assholes running that place, there's plenty of innocent people living inside the walls."

That's the difference between Skye and me. She gives a shit about the people living in Sanctuary. I don't.

"Where did you go next?" I'm only vaguely interested, don't care much about the vaccine. But I want to hear her voice, want her to talk to me.

Skye opens up and tells me all about her journey with her team. My respect for Deacon grows as she speaks, and I feel slightly disappointed that I evicted him from the city without plumbing his full potential. The more she speaks the more I realize that there was nothing to be jealous about in their relationship. The two simply worked well together.

Finally, after over an hour and well past when our meal

finished, she stops speaking. She falls abruptly silent as though she realizes she's been dominating the conversation for over an hour. She blushes and turns her head away, masking her discomfort with her hair.

"What did you mean... when you said you wanted me for a wife?"

I stay silent and look at her. She knows exactly what I mean, and she wants me to give her a different answer. I won't. I can't. Maybe it isn't fair, but we don't live in a fair world.

"Fine, fall back on your usual thing. Nothing can induce me to marry you so you may as well forget about it."

Our evening has turned out better than I expected, so I'm disappointed that she's giving me attitude again. I sit back in my chair and cross my arms over my chest.

"You'll marry me. You won't have a choice."

She lets out a frustrated growl and swipes her hand at the table, catching the edge of one of the trays and sending it flying. I raise my eyebrow at her temper. She's not as controlled as I'd like her to be, as much as she's learned over the past year.

"I want you to leave." She points at the door.

This particular phrase of hers is beginning to grate, but I'll give it to her one more time. Soon she'll learn that I don't do a damn thing I don't want to. If I'm not ready to leave, then I won't be leaving. I stand and turn away. I'm fine with giving her small doses of my presence as she acclimates herself to me. Silence follows me through the harem door as I leave and the guards close and lock it.

As I stride down the hall, I hear a loud crash and the sound of breaking dishes. She threw a tray at the door. My lip tugs upward as I think of my hellion bride. She's going to be a handful, exactly the way I want her.

SIXTEEN

SKYE

I've had enough. Enough pacing. Enough staring at walls. Enough biding my time. I'm done waiting for fate to come find me.

It's been three weeks since I've arrived in the Santa Fe Sanctuary. Three weeks of being locked up in the harem with nothing to do but contemplate a shadowy and uncertain future. I've been mostly alone. Dr. Summers hasn't come back, though I've requested her presence more than once from the guards on the other side of the door. Likewise, when I ask for Hannah I'm ignored.

Even Wolfe has stayed away, but I don't demand his presence. I wouldn't give him the satisfaction. Except... I'm frustrated by his absence. What kind of future bridegroom who's forcing his bride to marry him completely ignores her? I don't understand him at all.

I bang angrily on the door and then step back, waiting for it to open.

The guards have learned since my last attack to treat me carefully. The door opens and two armed men stand facing me, prepared for anything. I smirk at them, glad that they learned a lesson at my hands. Too often, these big tough Sanctuary guards think they're undefeatable. They would never consider that a woman could take them down.

A week ago, when they brought my dinner meal in, I'd shown them otherwise. I'd shoved the trays at one, distracting him while sweeping the legs out from underneath the other and dropping onto his chest with my knees. I hadn't paused. I'd hurtled towards the open door and out into the corridor. Unfortunately, three more guards were waiting. I hadn't counted on Wolfe placing this much security on me. If I'm being honest, a small part of me is pleased that he doesn't underestimate me. Even if he won't visit.

Not that I want him to.

"How can we help you, Miss Skye?" The guard's tone is friendly and professional. Once, he'd made a sneering comment, shortly after I tried to escape. It was one of the few times Wolfe had been in attendance. Wolfe had turned on the man, slamming him against the wall and shoving an elbow in his throat. He told the man that if he couldn't keep a civil tongue, he wouldn't be having a tongue in the future.

"I want to see Wolfe." My voice is cold and steady as I glare at them. "Bring me the Warlord."

The first one, Denny Torrance, shakes his head. "Sorry, Miss Skye, he's unavailable at this time."

I grit my teeth and stomp away from them, glaring out the window. "And when exactly will he be available?"

"When he's ready to see you." Torrance again. He's lucky there wasn't a single smug syllable in that sentence or I would be assisting his balls up into his throat.

I glance over my shoulder and raise a brow at him. He shrugs. "Warlord's orders."

So, Wolfe is determined to put me in my place, to show me that my leisure is not his leisure. We'll see about that. If he refuses to notice me when I want him to, then I'll force his attention when he doesn't.

"You can go," I say dismissively, turning my back on them.

The second the door closes I bend down next to a shelf holding a variety of crafts that the women of the harem used to work on. I drag a metal container off the shelf and open the lid, examining my own personal stash. I started it years ago, when I first came to the harem. It contains a knife, matches, some bandages, painkiller medications and several books.

I pull the matches out, replace the lid and shove the bin back onto the shelf. I set about going through the rooms, systematically gathering up anything that I can light on fire that won't be important. For some reason I can't bring myself to burn anything I know has personal value to the women who lived here. Some of them didn't survive the fall of the city, some stayed behind after the dust settled and a few had gone with us when we'd escaped. The only ones I know for sure are still alive are me, Hannah and Scarlett.

I feel a pang as I think of Scarlett. Young, idealistic, annoying as hell, but loyal and a much-needed bit of fun whenever I needed a silly chat. When Wolfe had given my team his ultimatum to leave the city, he'd singled her out with an invitation to stay in Sanctuary since she had belonged to the original harem. Scarlett had decided to leave the city with Deacon and the rest of the team, saying she was now invested in distributing the vaccine. I'd been both proud and jealous of her dedication.

I throw pieces of cloth and paper into the middle of the floor, using an old roasting pot as a makeshift fire pit. Once I have enough flammable items inside, I strike a match and drop it into the pot. It takes a moment to catch, but when it does the paper goes up quickly.

I take a step back as the burning paper starts to light the bits of cloth. Satisfied that my fire is about to become a raging inferno I run to the window, lift a sewing machine and smash out the windowpane, which was bolted shut. I keep hitting it until all the shards of glass have fallen. We are high above the ground, about thirty floors. I hope no one is on the street below.

I drop the sewing machine and shove a chair up against the window, then knock it over onto its side. As smoke fills the room, I run to the pantry closet and hide just inside the door.

Moments later, having been alerted to the fire by the smoke streaming under the door, the harem guards fill the room. I can hear them shouting as they search for me and shout for water to put out the fire.

"Dammit, I think she went out the window," one of them shouts. "She's just crazy enough to do it!"

I smirk. It's about time they stop underestimating exactly what I'm willing to do to escape. Crazy? No. Determined, stubborn, hardheaded, argumentative? Absolutely.

I peek around the door in time to see men rushing to the window, one of them climbing onto the sill to lean out and check for me on the ledge. I waste a couple of seconds worrying that the idiot might fall because he actually believes I'd be foolish enough to go out a thirty-story window. Actually, maybe not so foolish. My sister is an excellent climber and she would absolutely have gone out the window long before now. Unfortunately, I didn't inherit her climbing talent.

While the guards are distracted, I race through the smoke and out the door. When I reach the other side, I bend over and grip my knees, coughing and pointing over my shoulder back into the harem.

"There's a fire!" I say to the guards running toward me. "Quick, I think someone might be going out the window to escape the flames. You have to help!"

They hurtle past me with buckets of water. The second they're gone I race through the corridor and head toward the nearest exit. I know I won't be able to make it to the ground before the guards figure out my ruse and alert the guards on the main floors of the building, but maybe I can hide long enough for them to stop searching and then eventually slip out. The building is massive, there are so many places to get lost. In fact, when I'd lived here with Silas, I'd gotten lost many times without even trying.

I decide to head to the Warlord's chambers, confident that they'll be empty. Wolfe is a solitary man. He won't want guards lingering in his personal space. And I'm relatively certain that he's out in the city working and not inside the palace. It's a gamble, but one I'll take. If I do happen to find him, I'll just have to find a way to take him down so I can leave.

Luckily, as predicted, the hallway leading to the Warlord's private chambers is completely deserted. In fact, the area is so empty that I start to wonder if Wolfe has inhabited the chambers at all or if he decided to make a space for himself elsewhere. As Warlord, it's his right to take over the Warlord's private floor. Silas enjoyed being surrounded by beautiful things, such as his harem women. He wanted the best, most unique of everything. He worked hard for it too. Thus, his chambers are filled with beautiful furniture, paintings, expensive rugs and priceless ornaments.

The doors are locked, but I have a key. A key given to

me long ago by Silas. I'd left it in the drawer next to my bed in the harem. I'd never thought to use it. I'd always been escorted in and out by guards, but his giving it to me had been symbolic and I treasured it at the time. It was an all access pass to see the Warlord whenever I wanted. Now, it will help me evade pursuit.

I unlock the door and slip inside, locking it behind me. The rooms are dark and cool. I run my fingers over a shelf and then hold them up in the dim light filtering through one of the windows, squinting. No dust. Which means that Wolfe is either living here or the palace cleaners come in on a regular basis.

Nostalgia hits me hard as I wander the rooms, touching things that belonged to Silas. I'm a little surprised that Wolfe hasn't had them removed, considering they're not even close to his taste. Actually, I don't know what his tastes are. From what I can tell that man only loves two things. War and death.

I continue through the chambers, heading toward the solarium. Silas's favourite room. The last place I'd set eyes on him.

I hold my breath as I step inside. I don't know what I was expecting, but the room is still and quiet. I'm amazed to find that much of the greenery has survived. Someone must be watering the beds. In fact, weeds seem to be taking over. I yank on one, pulling it out of the soil where it's choking another plant. It resists and then finally the roots give. I toss it aside with a sigh.

I did this so many times, with Silas. He told me that his garden would help me become more serene, more accepting of the life that he wanted me to live. He'd been partially right. Tending the garden had taught me about the value of life after a lifetime of living only death, but serenity is not an emotion I've ever learned to value.

"Thought I'd find you here."

I whirl around, bringing my fists up. Wolfe is standing just inside the solarium doorway, watching me carefully with that one single piercing eye.

"Then it would seem you're the only one. Are your people still battling the fire?" I give him a smug look.

He steps farther into the room, circling around behind me without coming too close. Almost as though he's stalking a wild animal. An apt comparison considering I'll scratch his face off if he touches me.

"It was hardly an out-of-control blaze. A few buckets of water and it was extinguished. You could've done better, gone bigger."

Unable to help myself, I laugh out loud. It's just like Wolfe to criticize my fire making abilities. The man is all about destruction. He doesn't care that I tried to burn down the palace, he only cares about how big the fire was.

"You're right, I could've done better," I admit, reaching back into the garden and plucking a few more weeds. Now that he's caught me, I may as well relax and do something I enjoy. Wolfe won't let me out of the room anyway until he's ready. "I couldn't bring myself to burn down the harem. Too many memories."

"Good or bad?"

I'm surprised he cares. Then, Wolfe has been doing that a lot lately. Surprising me. I'm starting to think I never really knew him well at all.

"Just... memories. Not good, not bad, but mine. I don't want to lose them."

Wolfe steps closer to the plant box that I'm working on. His gaze meets mine through the shrubbery. "Tell me."

I frown. "Tell you what?"

"A memory." As usual, he doesn't expound so I'm left trying to decipher what he wants.

Though I'm not particularly inclined to give Wolfe anything he wants as long as I'm his captive, maybe if I act more compliant he'll be willing to give me more freedom. Especially now that I'm on the outside of the harem instead of the inside.

I search for a memory that he might find pleasing but I'm left floundering. I have no idea what pleases Wolfe. Death and violence? Those things definitely didn't occur in the tranquil harem. Not before the city fell.

I might have something that'll work though. "You remember when I was first brought to the city and placed in the harem?" At his nod, I continue, "I resisted everything. I didn't want to settle down, no matter how hard everyone tried to make me feel welcome."

He continues to look serious, but there's a humorous glint in his eye. "You wouldn't stop. You were either shouting, throwing things or threatening anyone who would listen."

I smile at the memory. "I wasn't well behaved it all, but the memory is a happy one. Mostly because of the love and patience everyone around me showed. No one blamed me for my attitude or my terrible temper. They just continued to accommodate me until I was ready to settle down."

He nods. "It took damn near a year before I figured you stopped wanting to kill us all."

"I kept a knife under my mattress and carried in around everywhere with me, tucked inside my waistband, even once I accepted my position." I meet his gaze, pausing my weeding. "It was the only way I could feel safe."

"I know."

"You knew about the knife?" I ask incredulously.

"Yes, I knew about the knife."

"Why didn't you take it away?"

"Because you needed it." He says it so simply, but his words mean everything.

He allowed me to keep a knife because he knew what it meant to me. I didn't need it for safety, or because my life was being threatened or because I'd intended to hurt anyone, but because I needed the security of knowing I could defend myself if I had to.

"Why would you do that for me?" There's a catch in my voice and it's hard to get the words out as memories wash over me. Those first months of fear and hatred, then warmth, and finally acceptance. Of spending time with my husband and gradually falling in love.

Yet, the shadow of Wolfe had always been there. I just hadn't realized. Or I wasn't ready to see it.

"Because we're the same."

"We're not the same, not at all!" I step from the table and shake my head in denial, brushing the dirt from my hands onto my pants. "You love death. You thrive off of blood and the war. I hate it, hate everything about it. I just want peace."

He stares at me but doesn't say anything. I'm frustrated. This is the way he is. Enigmatic. Difficult. Impossible to predict.

"I suppose you're going to take me back to the harem now?" I demand, breaking our moment with my anger. I'm not ready to have the kind of honest conversation he seems to want. I don't know if I'll ever be ready.

"Not yet."

"What's that supposed to mean?"

He looks at me as though searching for words and

finally says, "You proved that you can't be kept locked in the harem. So, you'll only spend nights there for now."

I shake my head trying to understand. He sounds almost proud that I managed to escape the harem. "You wanted me to prove something to you? Is that it? You kept me locked up in there for three weeks, waiting to see if I could escape?"

He just stares back, his one amber eye bottomless and unfathomable.

I throw my hands up in annoyance. "If I'm going to spend nights there, then what about my days?"

This time he does speak, his words thoughtful and measured. "You're standing in a dying city. There's more for you to do than you could possibly know."

SEVENTEEN

True to his word, Wolfe has me taken back to the harem for the night. I'm excited for what tomorrow will bring. Though I don't trust him completely, I know that Wolfe is a man of his word. If he says he's going to let me out, then he will.

I don't bother to speak to the guards as they bring my food in, though I'm surprised when one of them asks if I need anything else. I turn a frown on him.

"You've never asked me that before." It's a statement with an implied question. I want to know what his game is.

He doesn't look at me but fixes his eyes on the wall behind me. "The Warlord has asked that we treat you with respect."

"So... you weren't treating me with respect before?"

He shuffles his feet and searches for an answer. "The Warlord has instructed us to treat you as we would treat him. We are at your disposal."

A slow grin spreads across my face as I think of all the possibilities. There's no chance that Wolfe will give me complete freedom, but I can have fun with this, or at least fun with the guards. They've kept me cooped up in the harem for three long weeks and though I know that it's on Wolfe's orders, I'm not feeling particularly kind toward my guards.

I turn in my seat to face the guard more fully. "I require my freedom. You will let me leave immediately."

I'm impressed with how straight he keeps his face as he answers back, "You may ask for anything you wish, but there are several things we have been instructed not to give you. Your immediate freedom is one of them."

"Then I guess I'm not being treated exactly the way Wolfe would be treated." My words are smug. "I don't see him locked up in the harem."

Finally, his eyes slide down to meet mine. A frown of disapproval draws his brows together. "You think that Warlord Wolfe is a free man? Then you know nothing about running a Sanctuary. It is as much a prison as this harem."

Well that got serious fast.

"What's your name?" I demand.

"Kingston."

"Last name?"

He continues to stare at nothing, but I can see the tension in him. He doesn't like answering my questions. I wonder if it's because I'm a woman or a prisoner.

"Kingston Carr."

I happen to agree with the man about what Wolfe's job entails, knowing exactly what it takes to run a Sanctuary, but I'm not going to get into an argument with him. Until I have my complete freedom, I refuse to be compliant.

I turn my back on him and reach for my fork. "You may leave, Kingston Carr."

I hear the door close and lock behind him. I've been left alone in the harem once more, but today the idea is a little less depressing since I know I'll be leaving tomorrow. Perhaps for good, if I can find a way out of the city.

Wolfe will have me watched closely, will expect me to act. I'd love to disappoint him, but I need to catch up with my team and they have a two-week head start on me.

I dig into my food, savouring it, knowing what it takes to put this kind of meal on the table. The succulent meat took manpower to hunt, the vegetables took time, effort and skill to grow. But the bread, oh my god, the bread! It's my favourite part. It's like heaven in my mouth and I know that it was baked recently. I eat three pieces, all smothered in butter that was cultivated in the palace. Again, the collective effort that goes into this kind of elaborate meal is not to be taken lightly. I wonder if Wolfe eats the same things as me; if everyone in the palace eats this well.

I frown at my plate. It almost seems wrong to eat food this delicious and plentiful bounty when I know that there are people in the city who are not as lucky.

Still, I eat everything on my plate. There's no point in waste. I vow to find out in the morning how food is being distributed throughout the city. Maybe Wolfe can use some tips. Food distribution was one of the things I oversaw when I lived here before.

I prepare myself for bed, taking a shower and changing into a long warm nightgown. I like to sleep with the windows open, I've always felt this way. Something about the fresh breeze floating over me as I sleep is as comforting as a blanket. Someone must know this about me because my bedroom window is the only one in the harem with the ability to open. It can only open a crack, but it's enough to let the breeze in.

What's less comforting is the way I'm woken up the next morning. Being locked up in the harem for weeks on end

I've grown lazy, sleeping in because there's nothing else for me to do. This particular morning, I find myself being rudely awakened just as the sun is beginning to peek through the window.

I roll over to look at my attacker and find myself blinking up at a scowling, scarred man. Wolfe. I'm not worried about the scowl since it's his go-to expression. I smooth the hair off my face and sit up, yawning.

"What's going on? Is the palace on fire... again?" I snicker.

"You wanted to get out of here," he says matter-of-factly. "Get up, get dressed, meet me outside."

He turns to leave before I can ask questions. Like, where are we going, why are we doing it so early, and should I wear anything special? The man of few words strikes again.

I mumble my annoyance as I start digging through clothes. Besides the outfit that I showed up in I have a few leather items that I'd packed from Tucson and several harem outfits. Filmy dresses mostly. I decide to wear the same leather pants and shirt that I'd worn the day we came to Santa Fe. Leather clothing is a particularly sought-after commodity in a world filled with Primitives sporting sharp teeth. Leather is a difficult material to penetrate.

I head out of my room toward the entrance of the harem. As I walk past the table, I notice a plate laden with food and a steaming cup of tea. I shove a forkful of fried potatoes in my mouth, a couple grapes and a piece of buttered bread. I grab the cup of tea and head out the door.

Wolfe meets me at the entrance. He glances at my tea and then turns and starts to walk. I assume he wants me to follow so I hurry to catch up.

"For someone who kept me locked up for three weeks,

you're in a hurry to get me out of here now." Not that I mind. I hated being locked up. "Where are we going?"

Wolfe continues walking until he reaches the main stairway leading down in the building. He shoves the door open and we start to descend together. It takes him a minute to answer.

"I kept you in the harem because you needed time to calm down and accept your situation. Your anger had to dissipate so that you wouldn't do anything stupid."

"Like set a fire?" I ask sarcastically.

He glances at me. "You did that deliberately, with careful precision. You didn't set anything more than that part of the harem on fire and you used the distraction to escape. It was a decent plan. Would you have come up with such a strategy during your first few days here?"

The fact that I hadn't come up with a plan proves his point. I'd been far too angry and emotional to think straight. I'd wanted to burn the harem down, but had I acted then I might've hurt myself and others. Dammit, I hate when this man is right.

When I don't answer his question he continues, "As for where we're going. We're heading out to survey the city and supply sheds. I want your opinion on some priority projects."

I raise a brow, but he doesn't see my expression. We're both going down the stairs at a rapid pace. "Why do you need my opinion? You're the Warlord, it's your job to figure that shit out."

I almost regret my words. I don't want him to change his mind and take me back to the harem. But I am curious. Why would he want my opinion about anything? Wolfe does what Wolfe wants, regardless of what anyone else thinks. Even when he had to answer to Silas, he was always doing his own thing.

I finish my tea before we hit the bottom level and pass my cup off to one of the waiting guards who takes it with a slight bow of his head. This respect thing the guards have to show me is pretty sweet. I step outside into the warm sun and tilt my face upward. It's been a long three weeks of captivity. After spending months on the road prior to coming to Santa Fe, I'd gotten used to outdoor living.

Wolfe strides around the idling vehicle and gets in the driver side. I assume he wants me to follow and I reach for the passenger door. One of the guards steps forward and opens it for me. I give him a tight smile and slide in.

"Seatbelts."

Ugh, the seatbelt thing again! This guy is obsessed with safety.

"You know I don't like them."

"Too bad." He reaches over to fasten my seatbelt for me, then grabs his from across his own shoulder and buckles himself in. "Unless you want to stay cooped up in the palace, you'll wear your seatbelt."

His tone of voice is oddly familiar. Stern, but caring about my safety. Like my parents, and my grandparents. Even my sister is motherly, always worrying over the well-being of others.

I can't think of Wolfe that way though. He's too dangerous, too bloodthirsty. He's nothing like my family.

Wolfe takes me on a tour of the city and I get to see firsthand the damage caused by the Primitive hordes when the city fell. It's not as extensive as I had originally thought, but it's still heartbreaking. Many buildings and homes that had been standing just over a year ago are now razed to the ground. Burnt out shells of what they used to be. I wonder if the families that once lived inside managed to escape or if they perished. Maybe they still live in the city.

As always, Wolfe is able to see my thoughts. "Most were killed. Some stayed to rebuild, others showed up from Sanctuaries that are now unlivable."

"Like the doctor," I murmur.

He nods. "Yes. Her and others."

I turn and look at him curiously. "You allow a female doctor to work within the walls of Sanctuary."

He glances at me. "I don't hear a question."

I sigh deeply. This man can be so aggravatingly difficult sometimes. He knows exactly what I want, but he's going to make me dig for the information.

"I want to know why you allow a woman to work as a doctor in a Sanctuary. The practice is pretty much unheard of. She's young and she's pretty, and she'd make a good wife for someone. She could have strong, intelligent babies. Why hasn't she been married off to one of your soldiers?" My words come out in an angry rush. I'm not exactly angry at Wolfe, but I am angry at the situation. I hate that this is what women have become.

He doesn't look at me but continues to drive. "She's a good doctor. We have need of a doctor more than we have need of more mouths to feed."

It's not exactly what I want to hear. I want him to tell me that women are capable of doing whatever men are. That he appreciates the doctor's tenacity in learning her profession and practicing it in a world that doesn't accept female doctors. I want to hear these things, because then I'll know for sure he appreciates me for who I am; a female warrior determined to make a better world.

Instead, he's told me the truth as he sees it. Where there's a need he'll fill it. If they did need more babies in the

Santa Fe Sanctuary, Dr. Summers probably would've been married off. A depressing thought. All that talent going to waste.

I fall silent as we continue our tour of the city. Most of the industrial section has remained untouched and is now a busy hive of activity. Wolfe tells me this is where they're keeping the city supplies, including food, building materials, clothes and seeds.

I watch in fascination as someone leaves with several bars of twisted metal under his arm. He throws them into an old rusty truck, climbs in the back and is driven away. Another person leaves a warehouse with a couple of sacks under his arms, likely food supplies.

Next, Wolfe takes me to the big gates of the city and waves for them to be opened. I'm growing more curious by the minute. It's rare to leave a Sanctuary city, unless a person is going on a hunting trip. Wolfe is acting as though this is an everyday occurrence. Maybe it is for him. He doesn't even speak to his men as they open the gate.

Instead of taking me for another tour, he drives straight to the water refinery plant. I see immediately why he's brought me here. Half of the plant has collapsed into a heap of rubble, probably taken out during the zombie attacks, since it was mostly intact a year ago when we fled the city. When we arrive, he parks as close to the gates as he can get and we walk the rest of the way toward the ruins. He cocks his rifle, which he pulled from the back of the vehicle.

Taking his lead, I pull my gun with one hand and my knife in the other. Wolfe taught me this strategy. Shoot the zombie, take it down to the ground, cut its head off.

He doesn't say a word as we walk. He doesn't need to. There could easily still be zombies in the area, hiding out in these buildings. Not all of them would've been able to keep up with their horde. Newer zombies would've taken a few days to finish their Turn and figure out their new state of being. They might've gotten left behind when the hordes moved on.

We move safely through the building until we reach the control center. I gasp in dismay as I see the disaster left behind. All of the computer equipment has been taken out. I'm not sure exactly how it worked to begin with, but I remember Silas telling me that we were lucky to have this plant. It was the sole reason why our Sanctuary was as successful as it was. Our ability to maintain a steady supply of clean water for the city.

"We don't have any water, do we?" I ask, fear creeping into my voice.

A society can't survive without water. The entire city will have to migrate to another. What kind of Sanctuary will accept that many thousands of people? Some of them elderly.

"We have what's being pulled up from the river. A tedious, tiring task that some citizens are unable to complete without help. I have soldiers pumping water when they should be protecting the city. For many weeks, our main focus has been on keeping enough water in the city. We have to boil it, which means we need fuel for the heat. As you know, it's not easy to come by."

He runs a hand over his hair and for the first time I can see his frustration. This is a problem he doesn't know how to deal with. Probably doesn't want to deal with it either.

"What are you going to do about it?" I ask softly.

I don't like that look of frustration on his face. Wolfe is always so controlled, so confident, that any other expression feels like a punch to my gut. It means that things must be dire.

"Not me." He looks at me. "You. What are *you* going to do about it?"

"What am I going to do about it?" I ask incredulously. "What can I do about it?"

He turns to give me his full attention, his arms crossed over his chest. "When Silas's health began to decline, you were there. You picked up the slack and you ran the city. Every part of it, including the water. You tell me what we should do."

I want to argue with him, tell him that this isn't my problem. My mission was to spread the vaccine as far and wide as I could get it. He interrupted that mission and now he's demanding that I solve his problems? I open my mouth to tell him all this, but then the truth hits me. This was my Sanctuary... is my Sanctuary. I care about the people here. If I can do something to help, then I should.

I bite my lip and pace away from him, the gears of my brain turning as I try to figure out a solution. Most cities are able to get water in one of two ways; a well, or a river and treatment plant. Our treatment plant is now off-line, which leaves us with one other option until we're able to fix the damage, which could take years.

"Dig a well." I turn to look at him, to see if he's considering my words.

He nods slowly. "It's a solution we thought of, but it comes with its own set of problems. We've had one well collapse and another dry out almost as soon as it was dug up."

"That's because you don't know what you're doing."

He raises his eyebrow. "And you do?"

I shake my head. "No, but I know who does."

EIGHTEEN

"Where is the Warlord?" I demand, walking swiftly through the front doors of the palace and addressing the nearest guard.

It's been five days since Wolfe dumped a city full of problems in my lap. Five days and I've only caught snatches of him as we passed each other in the halls, as our vehicles passed in the city. I'm frustrated and I need to talk to the Warlord.

"In his chambers," the guard I addressed answers.

I nod my thanks and begin climbing the stairs up to the Warlord's chambers. About halfway there I decide it would be in everyone's best interests to move the Warlord's chambers to a lower floor. I'm in good shape, but I'm huffing and puffing by the time I reach the top of the building.

I push the heavy doors to the Warlord's chambers open and walk inside, allowing them to slam shut behind me. Once again, there are no guards. Wolfe really hadn't been kidding when he said that I had free run of the city now. I'm still guarded at all times outside of the palace and I'm not allowed to leave the city limits without a heavy escort, but aside from not being able to actually leave I'm not restricted in any way.

"Wolfe?" I call out.

The Warlord's chambers appear to be untouched from the last time I was here. I walk past the solarium, ignoring the urge to stop and tidy the overgrown plants. I feel guilty as I glance inside and realize that the effort I put into weeding the garden is now overrun again. It's becoming clear that no one actually comes in here, except maybe to occasionally water the garden. I will have to change that.

I continue past the solarium, glancing into each room. Finally, I arrive at the Warlord's bedchamber and hesitate outside the closed door. It feels strange being here. I'd only entered this chamber as the wife of another Warlord when he summoned me for intimacy. Now, everything has changed.

I start to regret my impulsive decision to come searching for Wolfe. I'm about to leave when his voice calls out commanding me to enter the Warlord's bedroom. He must have heard me calling for him.

I open the door and then freeze.

His back is to me – it's bare. He's wearing only a pair of leather pants sitting low on his hips as though he unlaced them at the front. Scars crisscross his back in a horrific display of shredded and badly repaired skin. I lift my hand to smother my sound of dismay and step forward into the room, drawn to get a closer look at the map of scars across his skin.

I've never seen anything like it. It's both beautiful and horrifying. This man has been through so much, survived brutal attacks. Seeing this, some of my antagonism toward him melts away.

In the back of my mind, since finding out he took the

position of Warlord, I've thought of him as a usurper. Maybe not a fair thing to call him, but it's how I feel. Silas had been my Warlord. I don't want any other Warlord, yet this man stands here, steady and strong, proving himself daily.

Something inside me loosens and releases. Though we are in Silas's old chamber, it no longer looks the same. All the plush wall hangings, pillows and ornaments have been removed. There's only a bed, not even Silas's old bed, but a different one. The windows have all been pushed open, a light breeze caressing the interior of the room.

"You came here for a reason?" He doesn't turn around as he speaks. "You wish to scrub my back?"

I realize he's in the middle of bathing himself, a sponge in one hand and a bowl of hot soapy water in front of him. Unable to tear my eyes away, I approach slowly and cautiously, giving him a wide berth. I know how lightning fast Wolfe can strike and I don't want to be in the way if he decides to reach for me.

There's always been a certain kind of intensity between us. Several months ago, before he left the Tucson Sanctuary, I thought maybe... maybe... something was happening between us. But then he abruptly left.

I can't blame him. I'd been bitter and angry over the death of my husband and the loss of my Sanctuary, but it still hurt, losing the man who had become my anchor. I still don't understand why he left.

"Okay, I'll wash you." I decide to call his bluff, see what he'll do.

But of course, Wolfe never bluffs. Without turning to face me, he dips the sponge in the water and then hands it to me, water dripping down his strong, veined arm. I take it from him tentatively, already regretting my comment. I don't want to wash him, but I don't have a choice now. I need to learn when to keep my mouth shut.

I sidle up to him and place the sponge in the middle of his back, slowly dragging it down. It's not so bad, washing a semi-nude man. In fact, Wolfe is an interesting texture where my fingers brush against him. The scar tissue makes his flesh feel ridged, but not rough. He's still soft and smooth in places, like a patchwork quilt. His back should be ugly, disgusting even, but it's not. It's beautiful. A testament to his strength.

"You came looking for me?"

I'm so preoccupied with the sponge and buffet of male flesh in front of me that I almost miss the question. Then his words catch up to my foggy brain and I nod, even though he can't see it.

"The city needs to be more organized," I say to him, my voice husky. I clear my throat and try to speak with more conviction. "I can't be everywhere at once. I need someone to oversee the wells, someone else to oversee the treatment plant, and yet someone else to take care of food storage. And those are just the basic needs. We also need a better medical facility and someone to organize educational programs in the city. There's just too much work. Things are falling apart Wolfe. The city won't survive much longer without stronger leadership."

He turns on the spot and catches my wrist in a loose grip, holding the sponge aloft. Warm water trickles down my wrist and arm touching his thumb where he holds me. His golden eye blazes down at me and I can see his Adam's apple bob. The only indication that I'm making him as uncomfortable as he's making me.

"Then do it," he says, his voice hard. "Assign whoever you want. Get the city in order."

Frustration wells up and my hand involuntarily fists, causing more water to gush out of the sponge and run over our arms. He ignores it. I narrow my eyes at him.

"Isn't it the Warlord's job to assign city workers?" I say sharply. "I'm nothing more than a kidnap victim. I can't do everything for you."

He curls his lip in disgust and I'm surprised at the emotion. It's so rare for any kind of expression to cross his face. I get to him more than anyone else, perhaps force feelings from him that he's not used to feeling.

"If you're a victim then you belong in the harem. I can arrange for you to be sent back anytime you want." He plucks the sponge from my hand and tosses it back in the bowl.

"Of course I don't want to go back to the harem!" I snap, stepping back from him and putting space between us. I try to wipe the water from my arm onto my shirt. He catches my action and tosses a towel at me. "I'm just saying, it's not my job to put the city in order."

"Then what use are you?" His words are harsh, though his voice and face have gone neutral again.

"Excuse me?" I gasp, slamming my hands down onto my hips. "I had an extremely important job to do distributing the vaccine. You're the one who took me away from that."

"Your team is gone, get over it. Everyone in this city has a job to do, everyone must prove their usefulness, including you." He takes a step toward me. "If you refuse to help put the city in order, I'll have no choice but to find a use for you elsewhere."

"What's that supposed to mean?" I growl, frustration welling up and threatening to ignite into fury.

His gaze drops down my body. "Your womb."

I gasp and stumble back another step as he steps toward me. "You wouldn't do that to me."

He stares at me and refuses to speak. I'm starting to realize that this is how he navigates emotional situations. He places his words carefully and then stops speaking, allowing the other person to absorb what he said, to draw their own conclusions.

In this case, he's been extremely clear.

Either I do the job of a Warlord and get the city functioning again, or I become just another female baby maker.

What I want to know is, whose baby would I be expected to have? Wolfe told me he wanted me for his wife, but he hasn't made any moves since that declaration. I thought it was an empty threat. Now, I'm not so sure.

I hurry away from the Warlord's chambers, determined to show him how useful I can be as more than a walking womb for his seed.

NINETEEN

I look at the people assembled before me, looking back at me with expectation and skepticism. These are six of the most skilled people in our Sanctuary. Some of them are smart enough to figure out why I've gathered them here, which is why they look skeptical. I don't blame them; I'm skeptical too. This is never going to work.

But Wolfe directed me to put the city in order using whatever talent I see fit, and I need these people in order to do it.

I start the meeting. "Thank you for agreeing to join me today. I'm hoping this will be the first of many meetings, and the first step toward real change in the Santa Fe Sanctuary."

"I see what you're doing," a woman speaks up. She was introduced to me as Tabitha, our agriculturist. "I respect the thought, but it's never going to work."

"What's not going to work?" Dolly, the tech wiz, asks curiously. "Are y'all clairvoyant, because she's barely said a word? I have no idea what's going on. But the baking is damn good."

Dolly reaches out to take another cookie from the plate in the middle of the table. Christine, Tabitha's wife, murmurs her thanks. She brought in the tray of baking, which she made herself.

"Tabatha is correct, I do have an agenda. Maybe an impossible task but I'm going to ask your help nonetheless. We need change in the city and you are the right people to enact that change."

Tabitha bursts out laughing.

"Change," she says bitterly. "Change is what was supposed to happen in the New York Sanctuary. Instead, what we got was more oppression, more violence and a whole lot of death. The Primitives did us a favour by taking that Sanctuary down."

Christine reaches out to take Tabitha's hand, showing her support for her wife. There are murmurs of assent all around the table. No woman in modern times is exempt from the harsh realities of a male dominated world.

"Tabitha has a valid point," I agree. "I've travelled to many Sanctuaries and I can promise you, the harsh patriarchal system that we've all gotten to know and despise is everywhere. What I'm proposing is radical and different, but it's not new."

Again, murmurs rise up around the table. This time it's Dr. Sheela Summers who jumps in. "Hush please, I want to hear what she has to say. Bitching about an oppressive system and not doing anything about it isn't the right path and you know it. I love you Tabby, but shut up and listen."

The voices fall silent and all eyes turn to me. The weight of responsibility settles heavily over me. Not just my responsibility toward the city, but toward these women. If my plan to form a female dominated city council using the talents in this room fails, then these women will be crushed.

I force myself to continue, despite my trepidation over the scale of what I'm attempting to do. "Somehow, in a world meant to put us down and keep us down, you five women have managed to rise up and make careers for yourselves." My gaze travels to Hannah, an outsider in this group, but a valuable member just the same. "As far as I know, you are the most skilled in your professions in the city. We need you. What's between your legs doesn't make a difference when it comes to what's between your ears."

"An idealistic sentiment, but ultimately worthless in a world completely dominated by warmongering men." Again, Tabitha speaks, her bitterness shining through. "I get what you're saying, I just don't think it's gonna work. Who'll let a group of women run an entire city? Impossible. Unheard of. Not going to happen."

Anita, the engineer, speaks quietly, adding her voice to the mix. "Where is Warlord Wolfe in all this?" she asks, looking around the room as though he's about to pop out from the wall. "There's no way a powerful leader like him is going to let a group of ragtag women take over his city. I don't even know how you got us in the palace, let alone into the Warlord's planning room. We're all going to find ourselves arrested."

Tabitha nods her head while Dolly reaches for another cookie, a look of concern bright in her pretty brown eyes. I open my mouth to speak, but it's Hannah who jumps in to defend our Warlord.

"You don't know him." She pauses and then adds, "No one really knows him, except maybe Skye. She's spent time with him. He's not the kind of person you think he is. Yes, he's brutal, intense, a killer. He's all those things. But he doesn't look at people and see things like gender, race, age or anything else."

Tabitha snorts. "Yeah, he sees targets."

Everyone laughs, including me, which eases some of the tension in the room. Tabitha isn't wrong.

"Hannah's right though," I interrupt the laughter. "What Wolfe wants is a city that runs smoothly. He doesn't care who does it, who makes the changes, who runs the city. He may be the Warlord, but he's leaving the task of putting the city in order in my hands."

Now everyone's looking at me with a new kind of curiosity and I stand a little straighter under their collective perusal. I didn't ask for this monumental task, but if I'm going to do it, then I'll do it the way I want, which means pulling these talented women into my inner circle.

"Who are you exactly?" This is from the outspoken Tabitha. Her straight black hair falls in a shiny waterfall down her back. She's beautiful and delicate, but her spine is made of steel. "Why should anyone listen to you?"

Her question drives home a thought that I've had over and over again, especially since the death of my husband. Who am I? I'm nothing really. I don't have any extraordinary skills. It took a lot of hard work and practice to learn how to protect myself, to defend myself and my team from the zombies. Other than that, I don't have much to offer. Unlike the women in this room, I'm not a doctor, a teacher, an engineer, a tech wizard, or an agriculturist. I hate cooking and cleaning, children make me shudder, and the thought of trying to organize an entire city when I can barely manage my own damn self makes me feel so far out of my depth I may as well be swimming in the middle of an ocean.

Instead of saying all this, I simply say, "I'm the person who Warlord Wolfe chose for this project."

Despite the tension between us, I believe Tabitha and I

will make a good team. She's willing to challenge me, and probably anyone else who gets in her way. That sort of thinking leads to better decision-making.

"Look, I know that it won't be easy. We're challenging a system that's been in place for over 50 years. When civilization fell, after the initial Primitive attacks, humanity had to find a way to survive and they had to do it quickly. This patriarchal, brutal, unfair system is what they found. That doesn't mean that we have to live this way forever. We can question things. That is our right."

"That has never been our right." Anita's quiet voice interrupts. "We've been oppressed from birth. We've spent a lifetime being treated like cattle. How do we challenge a system like that? What if we fail?"

I nod thoughtfully. "Maybe we do fail. Maybe the Sanctuary falls, like so many Sanctuaries before it. Maybe we get carted off by Warlords and soldiers and forced to live in harems, under the thumbs of our oppressors. It's happened before; we've all had terrible experiences. But that doesn't mean we don't try, that we don't face injustice and try to change it. I know we're tired, that we've spent a lifetime challenging a system designed to keep us down. But it's time to stop hiding, time to fight for both our survival and our human rights."

I sit down, let my words sink in. Everyone looks serious as they think over what I'm promising.

"All right," Tabitha says, leaning back in her chair, her arms crossed over her chest. "Tell us what you have in mind. I'm not saying I'll agree to any of it, but I'm willing to hear you out."

I outline my plan for the city's future, both immediate and long-term. As I speak, I can see their expressions gradually change from skepticism to excitement. "Dolly, I'll need you working on the water treatment plant. We need to get everything back online. We need to get clean water running through the city again. Anita can help you with that. With you two working as a team, I'm hoping you'll be able to systematically start solving some of our more pressing engineering and technology problem." Dolly and Anita look at each other and nod. I get the feeling that they've already made a pretty good solid partnership.

I look at Hannah, who's looking back at me, her gaze dull. She doesn't have to say it, I can read her mind. Hannah is a sweet, gentle soul. Her entire job before the fall of Santa Fe had been to keep the harem in order. To keep the women fed, entertained, educated and happy. She'd done a fantastic job. I fell in love with Hannah long before I fell in love with our husband.

"Hannah, I want you to work with Christine on creating some kind of school system. She knows the job, but you know the people of this Sanctuary. You can talk to them about what they want for their children, and together you and Christine can design and implement educational programs. Basic to start and then more comprehensive as the city rebuilds itself. We need to get kids in classrooms. We need to teach the next generation our skills, history, geography, everything – before the older generations die and take their knowledge with them."

Hannah's face lights up with pleasure, and she turns to murmur excitedly with Christine, ideas already pouring out from both of them. This kind of project is right up Hannah's alley and I knew that she would love the idea. I give her a quick smile and then turn my gaze to Tabitha, the toughest nut in the room to crack.

"You'll be working with Floyd, our food production manager. I think he can learn a lot from you." She narrows her eyes at me and I can tell that she's met Floyd before. "I know he's not an easy man. He's older and set in his ways. I don't think I've ever seen him work with a woman. But the for the sake of our Sanctuary, you need to be on the same page with him. I know nothing about food production, so I would be useless to you. You think you'll be able to work with him?"

She thinks about it and then tilts her head to the side and shrugs. "I like to eat. I'm assuming he likes eating. I think we'll be able to find some common ground."

"All I ask is that you try." I look around the room at the faces, still hopeful, still skeptical. These are the people that are going to help save our Sanctuary. I hope to god I know what I'm doing. "You all can go now. I'll check in with each of you tomorrow. Set up meeting schedules, offices, job sites. Take the night to rest, spend some time with your loved ones, as we have a big job ahead of us and you're all going to be very busy." My gaze moves to Dr. Summers. "Doctor, our conversation needs to be a little longer, if you can stay behind for a few minutes, that would be great."

"Of course," she murmurs.

Everyone else gets up and leaves and I take the chair next to Dr. Summers.

"It looks like you're settling into your situation pretty well," Dr. Summers points out. The last time she saw me I was raging against the Warlord and his soldiers, demanding to be let out of the harem and insisting that I would leave the city the first moment I could.

I look at her and sigh heavily. "I have no idea what I'm doing. Wolfe has implied that if I do this, if I try my hand at putting the city in order, he'll..." I don't actually know how to finish that sentence. What will he do? He hasn't said he'll let me go. He essentially told me that he wouldn't force me to have babies if I did this. I close my eyes for a second. Having a baby might be easier than rebuilding an entire city, with limited technology, a few supplies and only a handful of ragtag women who are completely skeptical that this can happen. What am I doing?

Dr. Summers seems to understand my hesitation. "So far as I can tell, you're doing a great job. You've chosen some of the smartest people you have available to help you with the rebuild. It's going to be an uphill battle, but you're on the right track."

I nod and thank her. "I needed to hear that."

She smiles back at me. "What did you want to talk to me about? I already act as the city's doctor. There's another one here, a younger man, who handles the people that don't want to see me. But Wolfe has placed me in a position where I get final say over healthcare in the city."

"I have a special job for you, if you're willing to hear me out." The doctor indicates that she wants to hear more so I continue. "Back in my sister's Sanctuary, in Tucson, an accident led us to injecting a freshly turned Primitive with the blood that the vaccine is made of. She turned back into a human, but the toll the Turn took on her body eventually killed her."

The intelligent Dr. Summers realizes where I'm going almost immediately. "You want me to work on a treatment, don't you?"

"I know it's a long shot, but we already have the vaccine and soon, hopefully, it'll be well on its way to being distributed throughout the world. What we need next..." I trail off as I think of my encounters with Primitives. They've destroyed our world, my family, everything. I have trouble separating the actual victims of the virus from the virus itself. To me, they are one and the same, though I know otherwise. I'm angry at all that they took from me, but also sympathetic. They didn't choose the awful existence they're now forced to endure.

Dr. Summers seems to understand. "If we can find a treatment, we owe it to the poor people who were infected. No matter what they've done, they were human once. They were our family and friends."

"Exactly." I'm relieved that she understands.

"The only problem is, I'm not a virologist. Though I would've loved to specialize, my area of medicine is general. I figured that more people would benefit from that, living in the world we do."

"I anticipated that, so I propose that we contact my sister's Sanctuary and speak with the doctor there. I got the chance to get to know him over the course of a few months while he was coming up with the vaccine and he's a brilliant man. I don't know if he's a virologist either, but he definitely knows a lot about the virus. Especially this one. I think he made it his personal mission to study it."

She nods thoughtfully. "It can't hurt to ask. I'll start compiling a list of questions tonight. I suspect my conversation with Tucson's doctor will need to be long and detailed."

I smile my relief at her. This meeting has gone better than I could have possibly anticipated. I'm a warrior, not a diplomat. When Tabitha argued, I wanted to argue back. When Dolly ate the cookies, I wanted to take a handful too. I honestly have no idea what I'm doing and I think Wolfe is half insane for putting me in charge of this. But so far, so good.

We stand together and I promise the doctor that I will get in touch with her when I'm ready to attempt radio contact with the Tucson Sanctuary. I leave the meeting room and glance around for my guards. They're never far away.

I spot Kingston and wave him over. "Where's the Warlord?"

"He's working on the wall."

I nod and head toward the door. "Then take me to the wall."

TWENTY

"What are you doing?" I ask, approaching Wolfe from behind.

He turns around, his golden eye roving over me from head to toe. He always does that, like a private inventory. I want to tell him that yes, all of my limbs, fingers, toes, ears and nose are still intact.

"We're strengthening this section of the wall so the rebuild in the sections that fell will be stronger, sturdier. We don't want this to happen again. The Primitives shouldn't have been able to overrun the city. Silas did a poor job of wall maintenance."

At the mention of my husband's name, I'm instantly annoyed. "Silas was a strong leader. You have no right to say otherwise."

Wolfe says nothing and I'm forced to stew on my anger alone. I hate that he's right. In some ways, Silas was a strong leader. He was patient and fair. He loved his people. But Wolfe is right, he didn't put enough resources into security. He assumed his second-in-command, Wolfe, would take care of everything, but Wolfe could only do so much with the resources he had.

I move to stand next to him and look out across the construction zone. We're on the western section of the wall, facing the destruction caused by the Primitives as they forced their way into the Santa Fe Sanctuary. The men working construction are scattered across the wall. They look like tiny ants as they reinforce and reconstruct the wall using metal beams, the shells of old cars and concrete from fallen buildings.

"I want to know why you're putting me in charge of fixing this city. I'm a terrible choice. I don't know anything about anything."

I can feel the heat of his gaze he looks down. Goosebumps of awareness rush up my arms and I try to rub them away. I rarely think of Wolfe as overly tall or big, maybe because I've gotten used to him. But when I'm standing next to him, his size suddenly seems to matter. He is a huge, broad and tall man. He has long limbs, hard slabs of muscle, and no fat on him. Veins rope his arms and hands, showing that he's had a hard-working life. I know he has, because I've often seen him working in the city. When I lived in the harem, Wolfe was a very hands-on second-in-command. He was always doing something. He was not one to give orders and then step back while others did as he demanded.

"You had a meeting today. Did it go badly?"

I'm not surprised that he knows about the meeting, though I didn't clear it with him first. Knowing Wolfe, the kind of man that he is, he would just assume I was doing the task he assigned, putting the city in order. He wouldn't care how it got done. He's the type of person who likes to see action instead of words.

Suddenly, his last words to me before he left the Tucson

Sanctuary leap into my head. "Come find me when you're ready."

He likes to see action. Maybe I wasn't giving him the right actions back then? I thought that by learning to be a warrior, by working by his side, I could give him everything he needed. But, at the time, I didn't know what I wanted from him. Not until he left. Then I realized I'd been looking at him as my protection. Maybe that was wrong. Maybe he wanted something more. Or maybe, yet again, I'm over-thinking.

"No, actually, the meeting went very well."

"Then I fail to see the problem." His words are simple and dismissive.

I stand rigidly next to him, fighting with myself. "Well done, soldier. You just backed me into a corner, didn't you? If I continue to complain about the burden you've dumped on my lap, I'll look petulant and difficult. Yet, if I lie and say that the meeting went badly, you'll think I'm incompetent."

I tip my head back to look at him and find him staring down at me, an inscrutable expression on his face. Again, he doesn't say anything, but moves his gaze back to the work progress.

"What if I don't want this responsibility?"

"Anyone who wants this kind of responsibility shouldn't have it."

I frown. "Silas loved being Warlord. He loved running the city. Are you saying he shouldn't have had the position?"

He doesn't speak and once more I find my frustration growing. Yet, often Wolfe's silence speaks louder than words. I know that he's saying Silas shouldn't have been Warlord. And the more I see of the city, how easily it toppled, how badly protected it was when the Primitives arrived, I begin to agree. But it's hard for me to separate the love I felt for my husband from the disrespect I'm suddenly feeling for our former Warlord.

"Why are you doing this to me?" I ask in frustration. "I never asked for anything. I don't want any of this."

I'm surprised when he takes my arm and jerks me around to look at him, a thunderous expression on his face. My mouth falls open. I've never seen him look at me that way before. Not even when I tried beating him up in the harem. He's always so steady, so serious, I didn't think anything could anger him. Not really.

"Your choice doesn't matter. None of ours matter. Survival is the only thing we have. I gave you a choice: stay in the harem as the Warlord's slave, or come out of the harem and manage the city. You made your choice; you will stand by it."

I narrow my eyes at him. "And if I don't?"

He grips me by the back of the neck and drags me up onto my toes. I reach up to take hold of his wrists as his mouth touches mine. His kiss isn't angry, nor is it passionate. It's matter of fact, meant as a threat without actually being a threat. He's telling me without words what will happen if I back out of our agreement.

The only problem is, I love his kisses. I think I've been wanting them for years, I just never realized. Or wouldn't allow myself to want them. I was a married woman. Then I was a widow. Wolfe was a good punching bag when I needed one. But now... now, everything is different.

He breaks the kiss and I step quickly away from him. The look he's giving me, I expect him to reach for me again, but he doesn't. Instead, he turns his back dismissively.

TWENTY-ONE

"Skye!"

I turn from where I'm standing and look behind me to where my name's being called. I spot Dr. Summers weaving through people as she makes her way over.

I speak to Kingston, one of my bodyguards. "After my meeting with Dr. Summers I'd like to inspect the water treatment plant. Please get permission from the Warlord for me to leave the city with an escort."

I don't bother to see if he responds, instead turning my attention to Dr. Summers as she stops next to me, hand on her chest as she tries to catch her breath. She hands me a notebook and I glance down, reading the items on the page.

Her notes are messy, but I can make out enough to understand that it's a list of the things she wishes to discuss with Dr. Bishop when we connect with the Tucson Sanctuary.

"Looks good," I say, handing it back to her.

She flips the page on the notebook and shows it to me again. I look down and see another list, this one of supplies.

"So far, this is what I know I'll need to set up a lab in the city. I've no doubt that once we've spoken to Dr. Bishop I'll be adding more."

I narrow my eyes and scan the list. A generator, blood collection equipment, vials, a centrifuge, microscope, hematology analyzer, autoclaves, hotplate, cleaning supplies, and an assistant. Some of the items will be relatively easy to come by, others will need to be brought in from other Sanctuaries, and some will have to be made here in the city.

"Got anyone in mind for your assistant?"

She nods, but frowns down at the paper before saying pensively, "Dr. Kenny Starr is another general medicine practicing doctor in the city. He really knows his stuff, but he's hesitant to work with a woman. He's barely said two words to me since I arrived. He takes on the people who don't want to see me."

"Do you want me to talk to him?" I say to her. "Convince him it would be in his best interests to stop being a sexist asshole and get on board with Team Cure?"

She laughs and shakes her head. "I think it'll be better if I talk to him on a professional level. I can stroke his ego, which will hopefully convince him to help out. If he won't do it, we'll have to find someone else. They won't be as skilled, but I'll manage."

I don't like the idea of stroking any man's ego in order to get him to comply with something that should just happen, but I remind myself I'm a diplomat now. I can't stab people repeatedly with my dagger until they stop being stupid.

We make our way to the lift on the west wall and step inside. As we ascend toward the radio tower, I gaze out across the city – a city I've been tasked with saving. It looks like a concrete jungle with slabs of steel and metal twisted together and overrun by shrubbery. To my eyes, it's a beautiful sight. I've always loved the dichotomy of human ingenuity and nature. If I were to plan my ideal city, it would be overrun by greenery and human invention intermixed.

Dr. Summers either reads my thoughts or is a kindred spirit, because she murmurs from next to me, "Even though the human species has had some pretty hard knocks this century, I can see the beauty in Mother Earth reclaiming what was once hers."

I nod, my gaze tracing the vines winding their way up the western wall. It held steady during the Primitive attacks and is currently being used as a base of operations for the city's security forces. It also houses the radio tower.

Once we arrive at the top of the wall, the lift bumps to a stop and a soldier steps forward to open the door for us. I thank him and step out alongside Dr. Summers. We're escorted to the room beneath the radio tower, where they were told to expect us.

As we step into the shadowy room, I blink until my eyes adjust, then stop in surprise as I see Wolfe. I hadn't expected his presence here, though I know most of my activities are being reported back to him.

"Warlord," Dr. Summers says respectfully. "Will you be joining us for our meeting with the Tucson Sanctuary?"

I remain silent as Wolfe speaks with Dr. Summers, confirming that he will stand in on our radio conversation. It becomes clear that Wolfe and the Doctor have spoken often. They're relaxed and easy in their interaction. I'm surprised and a little jealous. I've never seen Wolfe interact with another human this easily, especially not me.

I turn to the radio operator. "Let's make the call."

Dr. Summers and Wolfe fall silent as the Santa Fe Sanctuary reaches out to the Tucson Sanctuary. Over the past fifty years, Sanctuaries have become increasingly more isolated from each other as they learned to protect themselves from attack. Supplies can be scarce and when a Sanctuary experiences shortages, it can be easier to attack another than it is to gain supplies through diplomacy. By connecting with the Tucson Sanctuary, we're setting a new precedent of cooperation.

Tucson is expecting us and picks up the radio communication right away. They were radioed ahead of time and given our message so they could make sure to have the correct people in the room for this call.

"Greetings to the New Santa Fe Sanctuary, you are speaking to Warlord Fuentes."

My brother-in-law is the first to speak and uses a formal greeting. My heart speeds up in anticipation as I know that my sister, wife to Diogo Fuentes, must be in the same room. I'm eager to speak to her, though our conversation isn't as important. We'll have to wait until the others finish.

Wolfe steps up to the microphone and talks to Diogo. The two men discuss security and wall rebuilds. The conversation is stiff and there's some clear hesitation on both sides before they each give away information about security. I'm gratified that they're able to unbend enough to see the potential for a future alliance between our Sanctuaries. If we can maintain peace, then we can only benefit from the sharing of information. I can't imagine ever going to war with a Sanctuary my sister resides in.

After the two men finish, Dr. Summers speaks with Dr. Bishop from the Tucson Sanctuary. Dr. Bishop doesn't hesitate over speaking with a female doctor, but quickly and simply outlines what she'll need as far as supplies and expertise for creating a zombie treatment. The two doctors rapidly go into territory that I can't follow so I step back and gaze out the open wall, toward the Santa Fe mountain range.

Wolfe approaches me from behind and stands too close for comfort, but I'm too close to the window to move away from him. I stiffen and continue to keep my back to him. He bends so that his lips brush my ear as he speaks. I shiver and tilt my head away from him.

"Tonight, you'll come to my chambers for the evening meal."

I don't like the he's making a dinner date sound like an order. "I won't be able to make it. I'm inspecting the progress at the water treatment plant. I won't be back in the city until after dark."

I can feel Wolfe stiffen behind me. "Unacceptable. You will not be allowed outside the city after dark without me."

I shrug. "Then come along."

His hand lifts and hovers over my shoulder as though he's debating whether or not to touch me. Finally, he drops his hand heavily onto my shoulder and squeezes. His grip is slightly too painful, an emphasis to what he's about to say.

"I've asked you to help fix the city," he says quietly so only I can hear. "But that does not give you the right to disobey your Warlord. Go to the water treatment plant tomorrow. Come to my chambers this evening."

I tip my head back to glare at him. "Thank you for so firmly putting me in my place."

He looks at me enigmatically, the patch over his damaged eye a vivid black spot on his badly scarred face. My eyes drift down his cheek, deeply marked from a knife to the face, to his lips, forever twisted in a permanent sneer where the knife crossed over his flesh. Though he has a beard, the scar is still prominent. He should be an ugly man, but he's not. I itch to trace my fingers over that wound, despite the anger I feel toward him.

"You don't know your place yet. That will come in time,

once I can see that you're able to manage your responsibilities."

My anger flares all over again. "How dare you do this to me? Give me responsibility I didn't ask for, place me in a position where I'm forced to either sink or swim, then decide how I'll do the job. I didn't ask for this, I didn't want this. Why are you doing this to me?"

His thick brows crash down and I see a flicker of anger in his eye. An emotion from an emotionless man. I turn more fully toward him, drinking in the emotion that I caused. I don't even care if it's anger or hate or whatever he feels toward me. I just want something. Something different from what he gives everyone else. I want to be special to him.

His hand tightens on my shoulder to an almost unbearable degree and I wince under the pressure. He leans toward me, his lips against my ear as he speaks, his voice a furious growl that only I can hear. "It's time for you to stop questioning your place, to stop questioning my orders. Yes, it's sink or swim. Do or die."

I jerk back, trying to pull my shoulder out of his grip, but he refuses to let go. "You don't get to decide that for me," I hiss at him.

"I do get to decide. As Warlord here I am owner of everything within this Sanctuary. I came, I took, I am now in possession of this city. It's time for you to stop acting like a petulant child and to step up to your position."

"And what position is that?" I snap, my voice raising enough that some of the others in the room turn to look at us. I don't care, I don't take my eyes off him. "Wife to the Warlord? Slave? That's what I'm starting to feel like. You've placed an enormous responsibility on me and you never asked if I wanted it."

Fury sizzles through the room like a lightning bolt, startling everyone inside, and possibly the people in the Tucson Sanctuary radio room, because the radio falls silent for a few seconds as Wolfe and I stare at each other. Have I gone too far? It doesn't make sense though. I have physically fought this man and he never acted like I'd gone too far. Yet when I question my role in his life, in the Sanctuary, he gets angry.

"I don't care if you want it or not." His voice has an icy chill to it, though fury still vibrates through him. "The right of the conqueror allows me to make you whatever I want. It's your choice whether that be wife or slave."

My heart is pounding and I'm praying that my sister and Diogo can't hear our low-voiced conversation. Humiliation colours my face. He's giving me the only choices that women in our world are allowed. I'm devastated that he's treating me this way, yet I almost asked for it by pushing him into this corner.

"I choose neither," I say, glaring coldly at him. "If you force me to choose, I will fight you, and one of us will die in the process."

The tension drains from him and his lip curls up in a half grimace. If his face wasn't so scarred and twisted, I would think he was attempting a smile. "Good." He sounds almost absent-minded as he says, "Make sure you're in my chambers by seven."

Wolfe leaves the room and with him goes most of the tension. I feel like I can breathe as soon as he disappears and I reach for the nearest chair, sitting because my legs won't hold me. It was a brief but powerful exchange.

Dr. Summers reaches out to squeeze my hand, clinging to me for a few seconds in solidarity. I give her a brittle smile and squeeze back.

"I think we've said everything that needs to be said," she tells me. "If you don't mind, I'd like to get to work on some of this stuff right away." She holds aloft her notes and I nod in agreement.

Dr. Summers leaves the room and I'm now alone with the radio tower operator. He waves me toward the control panel and I settle into the chair, leaning into the microphone.

"Taran?" My voice isn't quite as strong as I would hope. My exchange with Wolfe has rattled me.

"I'm here," she says excitedly. "So much has happened since you've been gone. I wish you were here so that we could talk in person, but this will have to do for now. Diogo says it'll probably be a long time before the Primitive situation is stable enough for visiting between Sanctuaries."

I smile at her excited chatter and let her keep going without interruption. Discovering that my sister was alive was one of the best moments of my life. It'd been devastating to find out that our grandparents hadn't made it into Sanctuary, but being able to hold my sister close, to see her happily settled with her Warlord husband and her baby, is enough for now.

"There are rumours of another wave of flu coming out of the North. Have you heard?" she asks.

I tune back in to what Taran is saying and frown. Flu took out our parents and half of North America's population. It devastated an already ravaged world. Now when I hear the word flu, my heart freezes with trepidation far more than it does when I hear the zombies are coming. We can fight zombies: cut off their heads, stab them in the heart, shoot out their legs. There's nothing we can do about an invisible killer. It comes, it takes some of us away, and then it leaves, the promise of its return still hovering in the air as survivors attempt to rebuild. Another major problem with flu epidemics is how much sickness can weaken a Sanctuary. If there are no people to guard the walls or bring in supplies, it makes us prime targets for Primitive attacks.

"Please, stay safe, Taran. Keep Blaze safe and all the people of your Sanctuary. We know what the flu can do, we've seen it with our own eyes." I plead with her, knowing that my softhearted sister would be the first person to line up to care for a flu patient, regardless of what it might do to her own health. So, I do the next best thing; I speak directly to the Warlord of the Tucson sanctuary. "Diogo, do yourself a favour, close the city gates. Don't accept refugees, keep out the Outsiders. Don't allow your people to hunt. Whatever you do, protect yourselves from this."

Diogo is a reasonable man, so I'm confident he'll at least consider my advice. He and I spent many weeks discussing the security of Sanctuary, in both a practical and theoretical sense. He's an intelligent man who knows not to underestimate the enemy, be it Primitive, human, or flu. He's similar to Wolfe that way. He looks at everything as equal; as in, everything is equally an enemy to him.

He takes my words seriously and doesn't treat me like I'm a hysterical woman, which I appreciate. "We will consider your suggestion. You should consider doing the same. As a Sanctuary in the process of rebuilding, you're far more vulnerable than we are."

I nod though he can't see it. "I'll speak with Wolfe about it, but I'm certain he'll agree." I'm not certain he'll agree, actually. I can almost never tell what Wolfe is thinking and he often chooses the opposite path of what I believe he'll choose. But I'll make him see how serious this is, if it kills me. I'll do whatever it takes to keep the flu out of our Sanctuary.

"Skye," Taran's voice comes over the radio again. "I worry about you, big sister. Your journey with distributing the vaccine ended so abruptly. I know you didn't choose to stay behind, that you were forced to remain in Santa Fe. Please take care of yourself and let me know if you need anything. I'll make it happen."

I smile, a genuine smile that I hope my sister can feel even though she can't see it. Reading between the lines, I understand that she's telling me she'll come straight to my side to help if I ask her, regardless of what her fierce husband says. She worries about me. Worries that I carry weapons, worries about my hot temper, worries when I go toe to toe with male warriors.

"I will, baby sister. I plan to be around for a long time to watch all of my future nieces and nephews grow into strong adults. You keep yourself safe too, and eventually we will reunite."

"I can't wait for that day," Taran says softly.

I blink back tears and push myself away from the radio, standing. I look over at the tower operator and nod, indicating our conversation is now finished.

He settles into the seat and speaks into the microphone. "New Santa Fe Sanctuary, out."

TWENTY-TWO

I walk swiftly toward the Warlord's chambers, trailed by my two guards, Kingston and Denny. When we stop outside of the massive door, I glance over my shoulder at the men. They stop and take up sentry positions on either side of the door. I find it curious that Wolfe doesn't post guards outside of his own door, yet he insists I take mine everywhere. I wonder if they're for my own safety or everyone else's.

Regardless, I find myself growing closer to my two guards by the day, relying more and more on their presence. Though my brand-new city council is all female, these two men play an important role by shadowing my every step, taking note of my needs and providing whatever I desire. Everything except my freedom.

I don't bother knocking on the door before pushing it open. The doors lead directly into a vestibule type room. There used to be plush couches, luxurious pillows, wall hangings and artwork in this room. Now it's stripped bare, with nothing inviting for guests. I walk through the room, toward the solarium.

Since he didn't greet me, I assume that Wolfe is in his

private rooms, so I decide to wait for him while tending to the plants. I immediately dig my hands into the dirt and go to work pulling up weeds. I'm pleased to note the soil is now moist, not nearly as dry as it was a few weeks ago when I'd been in here. The weeds are much fewer, too. Someone has begun taking care of the solarium plants.

"You look beautiful."

I look up sharply at the sound of Wolfe's voice. I frown at him and let out a skeptical laugh. "Beautiful?" I've never heard him say anything like that to me or anyone. Hell, I've never even heard him say a mountain or a tree or a flower was beautiful. The very idea that this man sees things in terms of aesthetics is ludicrous. He only sees blood, death and war. Not growth and beauty.

"You are uncomfortable with the idea that I think you're beautiful?" He circles around the table to the other side, as he did the last time we were in this room together. He gazes at me through the foliage as I work.

I can feel myself blushing and want to curse at my damn skin for betraying my discomfort. I don't look any different than usual. In fact, I haven't even changed that much. I continue to wear leather, though instead of pants I'm now wearing a floor-length leather skirt split up the front for easy movement in case I'm attacked. My top is a light, sleeveless shirt with a corset over top that Hannah helped lace me into. It looks good with the skirt. I'm devoid of jewelry, but that's a personal preference. Though I can appreciate a nice piece of jewelry, I've never liked having it on me. It's a hindrance when I need to move freely.

"I didn't know you could see beauty," I say sarcastically.

"Before you, I didn't know what beauty was." His words are simple, but they cause my heart to speed up in anticipation. Again, I want to curse at my physiology. Why am I so excited by a basic compliment? A compliment from a blood-thirsty Warlord. It should mean nothing to me.

"I never expected romance from you."

His gaze burns into me as he pauses before he speaks. I feel uncomfortable, so I drop my gaze to the soil where my fingers are working diligently. "Truth is not romance."

I'm becoming uncomfortable at the way my heart is pounding too hard. I want to grab my chest and force my heart to calm down before I have to loosen my corset, but my hands are now covered in dirt. I lift them up and look at them.

"Come with me, we'll get your hands washed and then we can eat." Wolfe circles the table and reaches for me.

I step quickly away, not wanting to feel his touch. Not right now. Not while we're speaking so honestly and intimately. It feels too real, too much.

Instead of grabbing me as I thought he might, he simply waves his hand toward the Warlord's bedchamber. I walk through the door ahead of him, moving toward a bowl on the table next to the window.

I use the pitcher next to the bowl to fill it with water, then dip my hands in and rub them together, scrubbing the dirt from beneath my fingernails. I smile down at the water as I realize the irony in dressing up for a fancy meal with the Warlord and then immediately sticking my hands in dirt. It's as though I think they belong there. In the dirt, in the trenches with the common people. I'm uncomfortable with the idea of being elevated. I always have been. Even when I lived in the palace harem with the other women, I longed to be part of the bustling city below. To live in a house, maybe with a family, to work a real job.

I jump as Wolfe steps up to my back, the barest hint of his chest touching me. He reaches around either side of me and dips his hands in the water with mine. I freeze, unable to move. I don't push him away, don't ask him to stop. Instead, I just feel.

Feel as his long, strong fingers slide down my wrists and wrap around my hands in the water. His hands are so much bigger that they cover mine completely. I watch, mesmerized, as one at a time he scrubs each of my fingers. He takes his time, going at a leisurely pace as he touches me.

My body grows warm as heat trickles through me, starting in my hands where he's touching me, in my back where his chest is touching, rushing through my body's nerve endings, sparking sensations throughout. This is a seduction. He's seducing me. It's the strangest seduction I've ever known, though. He makes almost no moves on me, but then invites me here for a meal and washes my hands for me. It shouldn't be so erotic, but I can feel my body flooding with desire. Feel the press of his cock against my lower back.

He lifts my hands from the bowl and turns me on the spot. Water drips from my hands onto my skirt and onto him, as he holds them aloft. He reaches behind me, his shoulder brushing first my face then my shoulder. He picks up a cloth and then proceeds to dry my hands, individually drying each finger as though prolonging the moment. By now I can barely breathe. Heat has taken hold of my entire body.

He drops the cloth, ignoring it where it lands on the floor. He lifts my hand to his lips and lingers over my flesh as he presses a kiss to my knuckles.

This is the most intimate, romantic moment of my life and I'm sharing it with a man who at times can be more enemy than friend. It's a strange moment fraught with tension... but it also feels right.

"Let's eat." His voice is unsteady as he takes my arm and

turns me, leading me from the room to the Warlord's dining chamber. I follow without complaint, still trying to sort myself out. We were both affected by that hand washing moment.

Wolfe holds a chair out and I sit. He pushes my chair to the table and then takes his place directly on my right. I look at him with a frown as I realize I'm sitting at the head of the table, in what would've been Silas's spot, while Wolfe is taking the right-hand position. Second-in-command to the Warlord. I don't correct him though. He knows the correct positioning. Either he doesn't care or he's making some kind of statement.

As if on cue, one of the kitchen staff starts bringing in plates. It's unfortunate that Wolfe has chosen this night to fuck with my equilibrium, because the food is an amazing display of what a Sanctuary can pull together with limited resources. Baked potatoes smothered in cheese curds, chives, cream and butter. The potatoes are accompanied by goat meat stew, made with onions, carrots and fresh herbs. A plate filled with mouthwatering fresh biscuits is also set in front of us.

Yet, despite the sumptuous meal, I barely taste a thing as I put bite after bite in my mouth, chew and swallow on reflex. My entire being is focused on the man next to me. It's like that moment when he washed my hands woke me up in a way I've never been before. I feel strange, uncertain, off-balance. The feeling makes me want to lash out at the person who's causing this.

"So, when's the wedding?" I demand, my voice as hard and brittle as I'm starting to feel on the inside.

Wolfe places his fork and knife down next to his plate and lifts his golden gaze to my face. I can feel the rebuke in that look even as he says, "What wedding?"

It's not like him to pretend he doesn't understand what a person is saying, so I'm led to believe that he wants me to spell out what I'm thinking. I follow suit and set my knife and fork down. I pin him with a glare.

"Our wedding, of course. You've informed me that I'll be your wife. I'd like to know when the nuptials will be so that I can prepare myself. It's not easy finding bridesmaids, dresses or a feast on short notice during an apocalypse." My words are sarcastic and biting and I can tell that they're having the desired effect of destroying the intimacy between us. I almost want to snatch them back, but it's too late.

"Skye." He says my name warningly, telling me in a single word not to go down the path I'm recklessly headed.

I choose not to take his warning. "You have everything planned, right? The big bad Warlord, bullying a woman into doing his job for him and threatening her with a marriage he knows she doesn't want. You treat women as equal to men in one breath, then talk about forcing me into subservience in the next. Tell me I'm wrong?"

His eye blazes at me and his lips become a jagged line of disgust. I can tell when I've crossed the line with him, when he's disappointed in me. I can feel a responding disappointment with myself. I miss the spark that flared to life between us just a few moments ago. Now, I'm destroying it in my mindless pursuit of fighting this man. But I can't seem to help myself. I'm also a truth seeker. I want people to be plain with me. I don't want Wolfe's ultimate plan to just unfold at his will. I want to know what the hell is going on and I want to be a part of it.

"I won't tell you you're wrong," Wolfe says, his voice a deep growl of displeasure. "But your truth may not be my truth."

"So... no wedding date then?" I ask sarcastically.

Of all the things I've said and done to Wolfe, for some reason that one sentence is the thing that pushes him over the edge. He shoves his chair back and stands to his full height, towering over me. He takes me by the arm and jerks me from my chair, forcing me to stand with him.

"Leave." That one simple word is spoken with a wealth of meaning.

Tears leap to my eyes and I feel crushed. Even though I goaded him into this response, I'm hurt that he wants me to leave. Then hurt quickly morphs into anger. I came here at his command. I even dressed up for him. I'm eating his damn food, conversing with him. Just because I'm not saying what he wants to hear doesn't mean he gets to throw me out early before I've even finished eating.

"What the hell is wrong with you?" I jerk my arm from his grip and step back. My ass hits the edge of the table, but I ignore it. "You act as though every move I make, every word I say is wrong. I don't know what you want from me!" Frustration wells up inside me and I shout in his face, my finger in his chest, "What the fuck do you want?"

He slaps my arm out of the way, grips me by the neck and shoves me back. I fall with a gasp, reaching up to grip his wrist so that my fall is controlled. He slams me down on the table and I gasp in pain as something hard digs into my back. I flail out, trying to grip the edge of the table so I can roll away from him, but he holds me pinned. Food flies everywhere as I scramble on the table. Wolfe covers my body with his, holding me in place, showing me how pathetic my struggles are.

"Fight me, woman," he snarls down at me. "You want a fight, you got it."

Fury sweeps through me and I give him exactly what

he demands, reaching for the slit in my skirt and dragging the dagger from the sheath between my legs. I'm not in a good position for stabbing so I slash at him, trying to force him off me. He knocks my hand aside as easily as though I'm a child with a child's strength. When I refuse to give up the dagger, he wraps his fingers around my wrist and squeezes so hard that my hand goes numb, then he slams my hand into the table until I'm forced to let the dagger go. As soon as my grip loosens, he reaches to shove the dagger out of my reach. I grab a plate and slam it into the side of his head.

The plate shatters against his skull in a satisfying crunch. I follow it up with a sharp knee to his hip. I can't gain enough momentum to do any real damage, but the flurry of my limbs must be bruising the shit out of him and that at least is somewhat satisfying. I know that Wolfe isn't trying to do any real damage to me, so I can do whatever I want to him – cause as much damage as I can without any real retribution.

It takes him a few minutes to fully subdue me, and when he does he's bleeding from the head from the broken plate, blood dripping down his cheek and chin onto my chest. There are bite marks on one of his hands and most likely bruising around his hips, waist and arms where I hit him with as many solid punches and kicks as I could get.

"You done?" Wolfe asks darkly, his hand tightening on my neck threateningly. He's telling me that he can break me if he wants to.

I shrug negligently on the table as though I'm not lying in a mess of food, my hair now a wild tangled halo around my head. "You started it. You tell me."

He lets out a growl of frustration and shoves me away from him. I fall sideways off the table and land on my hands and knees on the floor. I immediately scramble to my feet, picking food out of my hair and corset. I glare at him.

"Can I go?" I ask coldly.

He gives me a half nod, his own gaze just as cold as I step quickly back. I whirl around, my leather skirt snapping around my legs, and head straight for the door. My booted heels tap against the stone floor with angry intent as I try to get as far away from him as fast as I can. If I don't leave immediately, I will find a way to stab this man.

His voice stops me before I can leave the room. "You want to know what I want from you?" I glance back at him. He's tall, broad, muscular and still angry. "Everything. I want everything from you. And I won't stop until I get it."

His words reignite the spark between us and the room feels like an inferno of emotion. The intimacy, the fight, everything since the moment I stepped into the Warlord's chambers is raging between us.

I shake my head. "What if I don't want to give you everything?"

He stares at me for long seconds and I think he won't speak. I'm about to leave when finally his voice reaches out to me, quiet but ringing with authority.

"I live for the fight, Skye." His voice is a deep purr as it touches my name. "I will fight for you, I will fight with you and I will fight against you until I get what I want." His amber gaze holds me in place as he says the final word. "Everything."

TWENTY-THREE

"You need to take your head out of your ass and start thinking clearly, not with all this close-minded prejudice. If you can't figure it out, I'll figure it out for you!"

I'm startled at hearing Dr. Summers's angry voice as I walk into her new lab, located a couple of blocks away from the palace. I realize right away that she's speaking to her new assistant, Dr. Starr, the man she predicted she might have some trouble with. I stand back, watching the scene play out. Waiting to see which side things will fall on. If I need to step in, I will.

"I am convinced more than ever that you are the wrong person for this job. You think with your emotions, not the logic born to doctors." Dr. Starr's nose is stuck up in the air in a way that makes me want to punch it to see if I can straighten him out.

"You mean the logic born to male doctors," Dr. Summers says scathingly, her arms crossed tightly over her chest. "That's bullshit and we both know it. The fact is, you don't like that I'm the lead on this project. You don't like being put into the position where a female is superior to you."

"You're *no* one's superior," the soon to be dismissed doctor shouts back at her. "Your ideas are half-baked and based off poor science. The very idea of a cure, or even a treatment, is idiotic at best. It's impossible and we both know it. The best we can do is a better vaccine."

I feel my blood begin to boil. This man clearly doesn't realize that he's insulting me along with Dr. Summers, since this whole idea is my conception. It doesn't matter that he's echoing the same words Dr. Summers said to me when I asked her about a cure. At least she didn't call me an idiot.

"Then why are you here?" Dr. Summers demands. "You're an intelligent man. Your expertise is welcome in this lab, but your ego is getting in the way of your work ethic. If you can't contribute, then you shouldn't be here."

"I'm here because the project sounds exciting," he snaps back at her. "Unfortunately, your methods leave much to be desired. If you can't come up with better medicine, then I'm out."

"The door is that way." Dr. Summers throws her hand out and points directly to where I'm standing in front of the door. Both sets of eyes turn to me.

Dr. Summers smiles wanly and drops her arm, pulling her shoulders back in an attempt to look more professional. Dr. Starr doesn't bother, he turns his annoyed gaze on me and scowls. I walk straight toward him, my gaze travelling him as I move. He's a small man, shorter than my 5'8", slim and younger than I'd expected.

I keep my cold gaze on Dr. Starr as I speak. "You were showing yourself to the door?"

He looks startled for a moment and then shakes his head. "You're the one in charge of this mess, aren't you?"

I narrow my eyes at him. "I am in charge of the functioning of this entire city, including this lab. Any problems you can't solve with the head scientist will be addressed to me."

A slight smile curves Dr. Summers's lips as I acknowledge both her position and mine in one sentence. Dr. Starr is starting to look distinctly uncomfortable. He's standing in the same room with two powerful women while throwing out some very reckless comments.

"Of course, ma'am." His voice takes on a tone that is fractionally more respectful as he realizes he's talking to the woman who has the Warlord's ear.

"Do you mind telling me why you're describing this lab as a mess?" I ask him calmly.

The fury rises to snap in his eyes as he flings out a hand to point directly at Dr. Summers. "This woman is reckless and she lacks a basic understanding of the science behind medicine. A cure will not be possible, but with the proper leadership, we may be able to strengthen the current vaccine."

"Oh," I say, my voice reflecting fake surprise. "Please explain why a cure won't be possible. One of the best doctors on this continent has already sanctioned the idea and is giving his advice when we need it. Have you heard of Dr. Bishop from the Tucson Sanctuary?"

Dr. Starr looks startled and his gaze falls back on Dr. Summers, a look of accusation in his eyes.

She shrugs. "You didn't ask who was involved in the project, you just freaked out at my plan."

"What plan?" I demand looking at her.

"In order to even begin working on a cure, we need to have a better understanding of Primitive physiology."

I nod my understanding. "That makes sense."

She waits a beat before finishing, "Live physiology."

I raise an eyebrow at her as I realize what she means.

"You require a live specimen to study in order to begin work on the cure? Am I getting this correct?"

"Several live specimens preferably." Her voice is deadpan and her gaze flat as she essentially asks me to bring her several live zombies to work on.

I turn to Dr. Starr, sympathy in my gaze. "I begin to understand why you no longer want to take part in this project."

He looks relieved. "Now you understand. Our efforts are better directed toward the vaccine."

I shake my head. "The vaccine already exists. There's no point in reinventing the wheel." When it looks as though he'll speak, I hold up a hand to stop him. "There's no point in you trying to convince me that you can come up with a better vaccination. It doesn't matter. That is not our priority. Our priority is the cure, or whatever treatment we can get that's closest to a cure. If you can't get on board with this plan, then you'll be asked to leave the project."

"B-but... it's so reckless to bring live Primitives into the city." He looks truly frightened and I have to hold in my laughter as he clutches his throat and exclaims, "We'll all be killed!"

I glance at Dr. Summers who's watching me steadily. She doesn't know me well enough yet to understand that I am completely on her side. Even better, the more reckless the plan, the more on board I am. There's something about the idea of capturing live Primitives to bring into the city that gets my blood pumping. I can't wait to go hunting.

"I agree, it's very reckless. That's why I'm excusing you from this project. The last thing this city needs is to lose both of its doctors. You're far too precious for that." I can tell by the smile on his face that he doesn't hear the sarcasm in my words. "Please, excuse yourself. I would like to talk to the doctor about this so-called plan."

"Thank you so much, Miss Skye. Please give my warmest regards to the Warlord and let him know that I'm always available if he needs a personal physician."

I nod and agree to take the message, but as he walks away from me, I say, "Please present yourself at the palace tomorrow. We will go over your new position."

He turns slowly on the spot to look at me quizzically. "My new position?"

I smirk at him. "Obviously, since Dr. Summers will be occupied in the lab, you need to take on some of her patients." He looks horrified by the idea of taking on more work. "You have a problem with that? Warlord Wolfe has made it very clear that everyone in the city will have to pull their weight. You're very lucky that you work in a profession that's in high demand. You'll always have plenty of work."

He looks a little green as he nods and then leaves the room. I laugh out loud as the door slams shut behind him.

"I think my respect for you just went up." The expression on Dr. Summers's face softens to a wry a smile. She turns her gaze to me. "But what are we going to do about an assistant? I can't take on a project of this magnitude by myself; it's too much work. I needed his expertise."

I nod my head. "You definitely need someone, but I'm convinced he would've held you back by constantly questioning both your ability and your method. You need an assistant who can help and is willing to take direction from a woman. You might have to teach them on the job, but I think we can find someone with an aptitude for this kind of science in a city of thousands of people."

She brightens and nods her agreement. "Thank you, I hadn't thought about it that way. I'll start looking tomorrow.

I'll put the word out and see if Hannah has any ideas. She's brilliant with people."

"Yes, she is, and she knows a lot of the citizens personally," I agree. I switch subjects back to her desire to house live zombies in her laboratory. "I think my respect for you just went up as well. Live Primitives in a city full of people?"

Now it's Dr. Summers's turn to look a little green around the gills. "Yes, I tried to think of a way around it, but I need them. We can't do this unless I can get a better understanding of their physiology and behaviour."

"I understand," I say, moving toward the door. "I'll speak with the Warlord tonight."

"Do you think he'll agree?" she asks hesitantly.

I think about it for a minute and I honestly can't come up with an answer. For the most part, Wolfe has given me everything I want when it comes to putting the city back together. But live zombies inside the walls? Even Wolfe, the psycho warrior zombie killer, might have a problem with this.

"Leave it to me."

TWENTY-FOUR

Since our ill-fated dinner when we fought and half the meal ended up on the floor, Wolfe has sent me an invitation to dine with him every evening since. One week. Seven meals.

With each sit-down interaction I have with him, my level of comfort around him grows. I'm becoming used him in a strange sort of way. He's gradually becoming less larger-than-life and god-like and becoming more of a man in my eyes. There's still an invisible tension that constantly brews in the air between us, but I've become more used to the feeling. I don't yet know what it means, but I don't hate it anymore.

As usual, I put extra care into my outfit while berating myself that it doesn't matter. Not only doesn't Wolfe care about what I wear to dinner, but I shouldn't care what he thinks. Still, every evening I go back to the palace and prepare myself. After saying a quick mental thank you to the crew who built our new wells and restored running water to most of the city, I take a long leisurely bath, running a blade over my legs and in my armpits to remove any excess stubble. While many women allow their hair to grow, I've developed an appreciation for bare skin. It comes from my time in the harem when all the women were ordered to maintain a certain appearance. Though I resent the idea of having to be perfect in order to please a Warlord, I do love the smooth silky texture of my legs as I run my hands over them, as I rub lotion into my skin. It makes me feel more refined in a world forced to embrace the wild. I like the ritual of grooming myself, emphasizing my femininity, while maintaining a deadly quality underneath.

Tonight, I choose a pair of soft leather pants that cling to my thighs. A leather corset is cinched at my waist with a sleeveless white shirt underneath. I leave my shoulders and arms bare except for leather wrist cuffs which are a common symbol worn by warriors. Leather is difficult for zombie teeth to penetrate so warriors often wear leather strategically across their bodies to protect potential bite zones.

I also wear my holster low on my hips, just above the edge of the corset. Strapped to my thigh is my knife. No matter what I'm doing, my weapons go with me.

I make my way to the Warlord's chambers, nodding distractedly at my guards as they escort me and then take their sentry positions on either side of the door when I go in. As has become my usual, I make my way through the chambers to the solarium where I work on the plants that have begun to blossom under my care.

It has become a ritual that Wolfe comes and finds me here when he's ready to eat. Sometimes he shows up within a few minutes, other times it takes him an hour, depending on if he got held up in the city. Like me, Wolfe likes to shower and change before dinner.

"Skye."

His deep voice comes from behind me. I don't look, but

I pull my hands from the dirt and briskly shake them off then reach for the wet towel that I've set aside for myself. Since the night that Wolfe washed my hands for me, I've taken to keeping a wet cloth close by so we don't have a repeat of that moment. It was far too disturbing for me to explore again.

I turn to him with a smile on my lips. "I'm glad you didn't take long tonight, I'm hungry – " I gasp before I can finish the sentence as I get a good look at him. His face is a mess with a deep cut bisecting the scar over his eye and making its way across his nose. There are three stitches in the wound, holding the gash together. My heart speeds up in fear and I have to mentally stop myself from rushing at him. "What happened to you?"

"Unrest over the wall." As usual his lack of words leaves an unsatisfying answer.

"Not good enough," I chastise him with a shake of my head. "Give me details. Who attacked you? Why?"

His eye darkens as he gives me his laser focus, an expression that makes any subject of his scrutiny feel deeply uncomfortable. I shift on the spot and glance away. Perhaps I shouldn't be making demands of the Warlord, but we've been growing closer and he has made mention of me becoming his wife. Doesn't a future maybe-wife get a say in things like this?

"Some of the city's residents believe that we aren't doing enough to reconstruct the wall. They fear an imminent attack and are protesting our work progress."

"But you're making the wall stronger than ever!" I defend him, my voice rising in anger. "Did you explain that to them? There's no point in rebuilding the wall quickly if it's just going to come down again."

His gaze softens a fraction as it travels my length. The

edge of his lip quirks up in a semi-smile. "Your defense is appreciated, but not necessary. I did indeed explain it to them."

My eyes narrow in suspicion. "How did you explain it to them?"

His shoulders stiffen and I can tell by the slight shift in his eye that he's about to say something I won't like. "The main voice of dissent has been stopped; the others will fall in line."

"Did you kill someone?" I demand.

"Not yet." His voice is flat, as though telling me not to argue or interfere. "He has been imprisoned and there will be a trial."

"But that's so harsh!" I protest.

"It is the Warlord's job to stomp out any potential threats in a brutal and decisive manner. This man will not be allowed to convince others to go against the laws of the city. We will end up in all out civil war at a time when we can't afford it."

I wrap my arms around myself and shake my head. "I don't agree. You're following the example of the Tucson Warlord, and he ran into huge problems by dealing too harshly with his citizens. He striated the communities, caused them to fight against each other. You'll end up causing a civil war if you start executing citizens."

"The striation came when he began dealing less harshly with the voices of dissent. When your sister got into his head."

A protective fury wells up inside me. "My sister was correct. Murdering your people, the people you're supposed to be protecting, makes you the monster in their eyes. You have to do better."

He takes a step towards me. "How would you do it?"

"What?"

"How would you deal with this man who I have arrested?"

I'm taken aback by the question since I know Wolfe will do what he plans to do anyway. But I give it some real thought, since he also seems to pay attention to what I think and want as well. "Well... you're right that you can't have that voice of dissent stirring up anger in the city. But instead of killing him, I would talk to him. Find out where the dissent comes from. It probably comes from a place of fear. He and others want that wall up as fast as it'll go because they see it as their best chance at survival if we're attacked again. I would talk to him, explain calmly why he's wrong."

"You would go the diplomatic route," Wolfe says thoughtfully. "Noble, but how would you deal with his infraction? He took a knife to me, attempted to kill me so that I could be replaced by someone who might deal differently with the city's security. Attempted murder can't simply be shrugged off as a man afraid for his life."

"I completely agree with you," I assure him. In fact, I'm very angry that someone would take a knife to Wolfe. If I could end this man's life myself, I probably would. But calmer heads must prevail. We must think of the entire city – not one man. "He needs some kind of punishment that makes your position clear, along with the statement that it is never okay to harm other citizens of the city, Warlord or otherwise."

"How would you punish him?"

I think about it. "I would put him on wall duty; make him help with the rebuild since he wants it done faster. Give him what he wants but punish him at same time. It has the added benefit of giving you an extra labourer."

Wolfe remains silent for a minute and I can see the

gears turning in his brain as he considers my solution to his problem. Finally, he nods sharply. "Agreed."

I'm so surprised that I can't keep the look of shock from my face. "Just like that you'll pardon the man?"

"No, he won't be pardoned. He'll be put on the wall until I'm satisfied that he's not a threat to me or anyone else."

I'm surprised he's bowing to my plan, but I suppose I should have seen it coming. Wolfe doesn't speak unless he intends to say something important. By asking me what I would do with the man, he genuinely wanted my advice. A warm glow spreads throughout my body as I realize the extent of his regard for me. He trusts me enough to listen to what I have to say. To implement the changes I suggest if he thinks they're sound.

Before I can say anything else, he holds his arm out to me and says, "Let's eat."

I smile and reach for him, wrapping my hand around the thick muscle of his forearm, allowing my fingers to slide over the veins in his wrist and hand, marveling at the strength in just that one limb.

As we walk toward the dining chamber, I say to him, "Since you're in such an accommodating mood, I have a question."

He nods for me to continue.

"Can we go on a hunting party to capture some live zombies and then bring them into the city to play with?" I purposely word my request as irreverently as possible, eager for the shocked look on his face. Wolfe does not disappoint. He stops walking, stands rooted to the spot, a frown of consternation marring his brows.

He looks down at me, the eyebrow over his eyepatch rising in question. "You want me to let you have live zombies in the city?"

"Yes, that's what I want."

He thinks about it for a minute and then surprises me back by saying, "Sounds like fun."

TWENTY-FIVE

Two days later we finish preparations for the hunting party, set to leave the city the next morning. We're taking three cars with nine warriors, including Wolfe and me. The plan is for each car to transport a live Primitive to the city.

I finish my bedtime ritual, smoothing the homemade lotion that Hannah gave me over my skin after my bath. Since we need to leave early in the morning, Wolfe and I agreed that we should skip our usual dinner and I should have a tray brought to the harem. He also wants to take some extra time to instruct his soldiers on city security during his absence.

I pull on a nightshirt that I've been given to wear by the Warlord. He gave it to me one evening after our meal and suggested I might find it useful. It seemed strange, but I suspect he wants me to wear something that belongs to him.

I've worn it every night since. It falls midway between my thighs and my knees and is big enough to contain two of me. I leave the buttons undone to just below my breasts so I have lots of room to move in my sleep. I crawl into bed and assume my usual position, on my side with the blanket tucked between my legs. I curl an arm around my head and allow sleep to claim me.

It feels like I only get a few hours before I'm being gently shaken awake. I roll onto my back with a moan and glare up at the Warlord standing above me. He's the only person in this Sanctuary who would dare to wake me. Mostly because if I launch an attack, he's one of the few that might be able to fend me off.

How does he look so goddamn put together at this time of morning? He's wearing his beat-up leather pants, a long-sleeved shirt with a leather vest and a pair of heavy boots. He's a large man, but up close he looks impossibly huge, like a god. His dark hair falls to his shoulders in wet strands, dampening the fabric of his shirt. He must have bathed before coming to get me.

I squint toward the window and see the first rays of morning sunshine starting to light up the sky. It's maybe 5 AM?

"Too early," I groan and roll back over, covering my face with my arm.

At first he says nothing and he's so silent that I think he might have left the room but then I feel the heaviness of him dropping onto the bed beside me. I open my eyes, startled, and roll away from him.

I sit up and drag the blanket up my chest, covering myself where his shirt has gaped open. "There's no reason for us to leave so early," I grumble with annoyance. "I'm pretty sure the Primitives won't care what time of day we capture them."

Instead of getting angry back, he merely raises an eyebrow. "We have a lot of ground to cover. You knew we would be leaving early to get a head start."

I narrow my eyes at him. "Early is subjective."

We had agreed there would likely be hordes of zombies to the northeast of us, along the Rio Grande River. Our plan was to follow as close as we could on the nearest road that was still drivable. We would periodically check closer to the river valley for rogue Primitives. They hate water, but they have an understanding that humans require water sources to survive, so they aren't usually far away.

"Just give me a few more hours and we'll get going as soon as I'm awake," I assure him, snuggling back under the covers and closing my eyes.

He stands and I think this time he might actually leave, but he doesn't. Instead, he slides his arms underneath me and lifts me high up in the air, pulling me against his chest. He carries me, blanket and all, striding through the harem. I let out a squeal of surprise and grip his shoulders so I don't fall, but it's not likely that he'll let me go. I can feel the tensile strength rippling through his arms as he carries me like a child.

At the door of the harem he says to Kingston, "Her bag is in her room. Bring it down to the car."

We agreed to take one of my bodyguards with us, and since Kingston is somewhat more respectful toward me, I requested him. Now that I see him obeying the Warlord and heading into the harem to pick up my bag, I change my mind. I don't like him one bit.

"Please put me down. I'll get ready and we can go."

He shakes his head. "Too late; if we want to get out of the city on time will have to go now."

"What the hell, Wolfe! It'll take me two seconds to get dressed." I smash my fist into his shoulder for emphasis.

He looks down at me, his amber eye blazing with mischief, an expression I've never seen before. It takes my breath away, it's so sexy.

"I like you this way," he assures me, hefting me tighter in his arms.

He shoves the door to the stairwell open with his shoulder and starts descending through the shadowy stairwell to the underground parking lot.

"You like me with morning breath, tangled hair and a bad attitude?"

If I think to disconcert him, I need to think again, as gaining the upper hand with Wolfe is like tackling a horde of zombies single-handedly without a weapon. Difficult, fruitless and likely to end in death.

Wolfe pauses our downward descent and looks at me. There are very few windows in the stairwell so I can only just make out his expression in the shadows. I can feel the heat beneath his skin, the tightening of his hands on my limbs where he holds me. The softening of his jaw as he drops his head to mine.

My heart explodes and starts racing in my chest as I realize he's about to kiss me. My eyes drift shut as I anticipate the feel of his lips on mine, but he stops, hovering just above my mouth as he says, "Yes."

"Yes?" I say faintly, having completely lost track of the conversation.

"Yes," he confirms. "I love the hair, the breath and especially the attitude."

I laugh and a burst of happiness goes off inside me like fireworks. My heart is beating so fast, my skin is so flushed that I feel like I'm about to faint. How can such a big, tough, uncompromising warrior say the sweetest things imaginable?

His lips close on mine and a shower of sparks erupts between us. His kiss is perfect, his mouth slanting just enough that he can gain access with the barest push of his tongue. I melt beneath him, opening my mouth to his and tightening my arms around his neck.

He's been leading me to this moment, to this intimacy, with the dinners in his chambers, the position he's given me in the city, and the brief interactions he has with me. He's allowed me to get to know him, to get used to him. As much as a person can get used to a man like Wolfe. I'm not afraid of his kiss or his touch, though if you'd asked me several months ago, I would have denied ever allowing such a thing. Now I find myself eagerly returning kiss for kiss as he devours my mouth.

Heat ratchets up between us as the constantly smoldering embers explode into an inferno. He turns on the spot and leans against the wall, slowly sliding us down to the stairs until my back touches the concrete. It should be uncomfortable, but I don't feel a thing since his arm is wrapped around me, protecting me from the rough concrete steps.

I breathe in his scent when he lets me up for air, taking it in, absorbing it and feeling the sizzle of sheer desire as it floods through my veins. This man gets to me in every way. The way he smells, his size, his roughness, even his broken face.

His body is so big that it covers mine completely. Wolfe can kill a man twice his size as easily as I can sneeze, yet he checks his strength with me. Even when he's annoyed or angry.

I cling to him, surging against him as his hand roves over me. One arm is wrapped around my back, while his other hand tugs at the blanket, pulling it away from my skin. He pulls back just enough to watch as he brushes his knuckles against the dip in my throat and slowly draws them down over my skin until he reaches just below my breasts where the buttons start. Then, he deftly unbuttons the shirt. There is no fumbling despite his twisted and scarred fingers.

The breath catches in my throat as he pulls the shirt to the side and stares down at my naked breast. I try to see myself through his eyes, wantonly laid out across the steps on top of the blanket, his body covering mine, my skin a beacon in the shadowy hall.

His head descends and I watch with frozen expectation as his mouth slowly touches my naked breast. At first, he just sets his lips against the soft skin, but then he slowly moves to open his mouth and trace a scorching path of wet heat over my flesh. I arch my back and cling to his shoulders as he lovingly takes my nipple in his mouth. I moan so loudly the sound echoes through the stairway, igniting his passion.

He groans against me and clutches me so hard I feel as though my bones will crack, but I don't protest. I love his painful hold because it means that he's losing control. It means that I'm doing this to him, this man whose every word and every action is planned out. He didn't plan this interlude and the moment feels like a prize I want to hold tight against my heart.

I open my knees and lift them to clutch at his hips and draw him against me. I don't wear panties when I sleep, so his leather clad cock fits nicely against my bare pussy. The feel of him against me is enough to send a shower of sparks right through my body. A couple more rubs and I'll be able to orgasm. When he doesn't move to stop me, I wrap my legs more tightly around his waist and lift myself against him, undulating my hips and rubbing my clit against the leather of his pants. He lets out a low-throated growl that reverberates right through me.

My head drops back onto the stone step and he attacks

my neck with his teeth, his hand enveloping my bare breast, still wet with his saliva, while I slowly, luxuriously reach for my climax.

His cock is so hard that I wonder how he's not bursting from the laces of his pants. Instead, he holds his hips still and allows me to work myself against him, his hands holding me tight, his mouth a heated suction against my skin. He bites down hard on the tender flesh between my neck and my shoulder and I let out a scream as an orgasm rips through me. It's sharp but so sweet that I ride it right through to the end, my breath rushing from my lips and moving the hair on top of his head.

He lifts his head to look down at me, his eye glowing with satisfaction. As I return to earth, I realize with a pang of shame what I've done. I used him to reach my own orgasm. It's not fair and I know it. I can still feel him straining against me, his rock-hard cock nestled between my thighs. I reach down to stroke him through his leather pants.

"Your turn?" I ask uncertainly.

He shakes his head. "Not yet."

I feel ashamed of myself. That I came so easily, using his body to satisfy mine while he had no intention of losing his control completely and fucking me right on the stairs. I squirm underneath him and try to close my legs, but I can't because his hips are still pressed snugly against mine.

"I'm... I'm sorry, I shouldn't have..." I stammer, both ashamed and angry at myself.

He takes my chin in his hand and forces my face up until I'm looking directly at him. He gives me a little shake and says, "Never be sorry for expressing yourself sexually. You've never been more beautiful to me then you are right now."

Tears rush to my eyes and I look sideways to blink them

away. I don't know why I suddenly feel like crying. Maybe because his words mean so much? Or maybe because I suddenly feel so bloody awkward that I want the hell out of the situation.

I wiggle underneath him until he finally lets me up. I stand, brushing myself off and wrapping the blanket back around me for an added layer of protection. I keep my gaze on the floor. "We should go."

He nods but doesn't move.

He reaches out to tip my chin so he can look me in the eyes. "I will fuck you, Skye. It's a matter of when and where, not if." He glances around, his lip curling in distaste. "It was never going to happen in the palace stairway. I may not be a good man, but I'm better than that."

I let out an unexpected laugh and grin at him. I don't know what this man is doing to me, but I think I like it. He's leading me down a path toward an unknown goal and I'm helpless to stop it. Does he want me as a wife? Does he want me to fix his city? Does he want my soul? I don't know... and I'm starting to not care if he takes everything he wants and more.

TWENTY-SIX
WOLFE

"Stop."

Skye stops and looks over her shoulder at me, a frown marring her perfect features. She was about to get into one of the vehicles heading out of the city on the Primitive hunt that we've organized.

"You ride with me," I tell her as I stride past her, catching her arm and tugging her along with me to the lead vehicle.

I open the door and push her down onto the passenger seat. She opens her mouth to yell at me, probably for manhandling her, but it could be for any number of things. Maybe the orgasm I helped her achieve in the stairwell. I slam the door in her face before she can speak, but I hear her muffled shout of annoyance as I round the car.

I must admit, I enjoy pissing Skye off. I'd rather have her fight me every step of the way, her anger piquing her interest as I prod her. Her annoyance is far better than her clever mind picking out ways to escape the city and leave me. I won't allow that to happen, but I'd rather she not hurt herself in an attempt. Skye can be determined, but also reckless.

I point at Kingston and silently tell him to ride in one of the other vehicles. I want some alone time with my woman before the hunt. Besides, she's still wearing my nightshirt, gaping open over her perfect breasts. A sight for my eyes only.

I open the driver's door and drop into my seat. "Buckle up," I say to her without looking.

"Fuck off." Pause. I hear the click as she buckles her seatbelt.

I bare my teeth in some semblance of a grin as I turn the ignition and the car rumbles to life. I love cars. Everything about them. They represent the past, the endurance of human ingenuity. They represent strength, since only the strong have access to vehicles. And they represent the future. A way for us to remain connected. They are a surviving technology that will push us in the right direction rather than backsliding even further into the Apocalypse.

We head out of the city and hit the nearest highway east where we skirt the mountains. It'll be easier to pick off our victims on the open plains. Our plan is to follow the river as closely as possible until we're able to find a horde. Then we'll divide and conquer, hopefully keeping enough of them alive to deliver back to Dr. Summers for her experiments.

Though zombies avoid water, they seem to have figured out that humans require water to survive and have a tendency to either settle down near or visit water sources often. Our nearest water source is the Rio Grande River, so we follow the highway parallel to the river, occasionally taking back roads into the river valley to search for hordes.

After a few hours of driving, Skye sighs her annoyance.

"It's just like these assholes to play hide-and-seek with us. They're everywhere all the time unless you actually need one, and then good luck finding them."

I don't reply, instead scanning the area for a good place to stop. As I pull the vehicle into a copse of trees next to the river Skye asks, "Are we stopping?"

I put the car in park and turn the ignition off. Dust floats up around us as the rest of our hunting party arrives, parking their vehicles on either side of ours.

"We'll set up camp here, see if we can lure them to us," I answer.

I open the door and step out of the vehicle, searching the area with a narrowed gaze. Something moves in the bushes then leaps out into the clearing. I pull my gun from the holster at my hip and shoot the antelope mid-leap. It hits the ground, tries to get up and then collapses, a pool of blood spreading from its chest. A slight pang hits me as the beautiful animal with its long, curved horns hits the dirt and dies. I have more empathy for these creatures than I do most people. They are innocents in a world made dirty by humans.

"Nice shooting," Skye says sarcastically, slamming her door shut and rounding the vehicle to stand next to me, her arms crossed over her chest. "Too bad it's not what we're looking for."

"It'll feed a family for a few months," I say without looking at her. I turn to Kingston who comes to stand next to me. "Make sure it's prepared and packed up to go back to the city. Leave some meat for our evening meal."

"Yes, Warlord." He goes back to a vehicle for the supplies he'll need to butcher the animal.

Skye starts to wander away from me toward the river and I reach out to grab her arm pulling her back.

"Take your bag into the bushes and get dressed."

She swings around and glares up at me, her stormy grey eyes narrowed in annoyance. I've rarely seen another expression on her face, but there'll come a day when I will lay down everything, including my life, to see even the hint of a smile on those beautiful lips. For now, I will continue down the path that we've started together, the path that will lead to her emancipation. She doesn't know it, but she's too important to let wallow in her own grief.

Without answering, she reaches into the car, jerks her bag out, yanks a gun out of the bag and stomps toward the tree line. I follow her bare legs with my gaze as she walks away. They're long and strong. When she wrapped them around me earlier and rode me to orgasm, her legs had held on like a vice. It was incredible.

I shove the thought away as my pants grow tight once more. Business first, pleasure later.

She stomps back out from behind the bushes, walks to the car, throws her bag inside and moves to walk away again. I catch her arm to stop her and check her over, starting at her neck to make sure that she's wearing the proper equipment. I run my finger along the thick leather neck guard she has on, touching the smooth material as I run my hand down to her shoulder where it ends. Beneath it she's wearing a heavy shirt with a jacket. Her legs are encased in leather pants and her forearms are wrapped in leather shielding. She should be safe from zombie bite. Even if her blood protects her from the Turn, it won't protect her from having her throat ripped out.

I release her. "Don't go far."

She glares up at me. "You do know I ran my own team successfully for several months, right? I know what I'm doing, Wolfe. I know how to avoid zombie bites, how to fight them and how to kill them. I don't need you watching out for me."

"Have you ever captured one alive?" I ask her.

Tension vibrates through her body, excitement at the thought of capture instead of kill. She shakes her head. "Have you?"

"No," I answer honestly. "None of us have. We don't know what to expect, so we need to be extra vigilant."

She shrugs negligently and take several more steps away from me. "You sound like a worried old lady. Capturing them isn't that different from killing them; we just have to stop before the blade touches them. Or maybe not. We could play for a bit and still keep them alive."

"You've turned into a bloodthirsty little warrior," I say to her.

It's not meant as a compliment, but the image of her covered in blood and leather is too erotic for me to ignore. There is nothing more I love in this world than a woman who can fight. This woman specifically.

"Thanks to you!" she says cheekily.

She takes a mock bow, turns on her heel and heads to the river. I nod toward Kingston, silently sending him after her. Of all the palace guards, Kingston is the one that she seems to be developing a friendship with. A part of me feels jealousy. Not because I fear she'll fall for him, I won't allow that, but I dislike the easy banter between them. Meaningless conversation is not something I've ever been capable of. Words and sentences don't come easy to me. I lost my parents when I was very young and was raised on the road. No one cared enough to teach me the art of conversation. I had to learn on my own, most of my education coming from Silas's palace. One thing I can thank our old Warlord for.

We set up camp, including a fire pit, and one of my men

starts a fire. We brought dried soup along that we'd intended to reconstitute with the water, but our meal plans have now changed to include fresh antelope meat. The men quickly organize themselves into security details, taking turns patrolling the area and reporting back.

I allow Skye to take a rotation and agree to do a few myself. If I didn't think her capable, she would be forced to stay at my side, but I've seen her in action. Skye can take care of herself. Better than most of my men.

We settle into camp, making as much noise as possible in the hopes of drawing a horde to us. Hordes usually consist of between 5 and 20 Primitives, though I have seen far more. When we were attacked at the Tucson power plant there were at least 100. I've also seen single Primitives, though they're usually weak and dying, easy to pick off. Primitives don't do well without hordes. Which leaves an observer to conclude that they have some kind of social hierarchy in which they're able to care for each other to some extent.

I have studied Primitives for most of my life, usually taking mental notes of their behaviour directly before disposing of them. Though on the surface they appear to be unthinking killing machines, not capable of any kind of organized thought, in reality they do have some basic ability to reason. They group together for survival. They hunt in packs, exhibiting pack behaviour. They are fascinating creatures, and in a way, I can relate to them.

I'm a loner. I prefer to work alone, sleep alone, eat alone. But I can also understand the merit in being around other people. Groups are stronger than individuals. Primitives seem to have figured out this basic survival technique.

I have created a strong security presence in the Santa Fe Sanctuary, but I lack the ability and desire to organize people on any other level. Which is why I've forced Skye into helping. Maybe not fair, but it's for the betterment of our Sanctuary.

Skye isn't a loner and she's not an Outsider. Though she can physically survive the elements, the Primitives, and anything man or beast can throw her way, her heart is too soft to survive outside of Sanctuary. Skye needs people, she needs society. And I go where Skye is, so our only option is to put our Sanctuary in order and rule it together.

It's currently Skye's security rotation and she's been gone for about 20 minutes. Nothing to be alarmed about, but when she's out of my sight, whether inside of Sanctuary or out, I feel restless. I've always felt this way about her. As though I need to keep my gaze on her at all times lest she disappear.

In fact, this past year has been utter torture. Letting her go find her own path, deal with her grief over losing Silas and Sanctuary, then find her way back to me, was the most difficult thing I've done in my life. And that includes losing the sight in one eye. I would lose that eye all over again if it meant keeping Skye with me at all times. She doesn't know it, but she's my anchor, the single thing that keeps me tied to this world. If she didn't exist, I would be a different man. If anything happens to her, I will follow her into the grave and rest alongside her until death claims me too.

I walk to the river, sliding part way into the valley, rocks and dirt falling around me. Instinctually I know which way she'll go. Skye loves nature. She loves trees, she loves water, she loves sky. She would find the prettiest spot near the river and then attempt to attract Primitives to her position. Not exactly what she's supposed to be doing, but I know my woman. She's a hunter.

I hear a skirmish off to my left, in a copse of trees that

spills from the top of the valley down into the river. Grunts and growls alert me to the presence of Primitives. I pull the gun from my holster and unsheathe my knife, striding rapidly toward where I'm hearing the noises.

I round a boulder in time to see Skye launch a full-on attack against three zombies. They have her surrounded and are lunging at her, teeth snapping, limbs flailing. Every instinct in my body screams at me to run into the fight and take them out before they can touch her, but I hold myself back. Skye is a creature of intense beauty. The way she moves, fluid and graceful, her weapons slamming home with each strike. She doesn't miss once as she cuts each zombie down, killing them before they can hit the ground.

In a matter of seconds, she's surrounded by a twisted bloody heap of limbs, torsos and heads. Blood is splattered across her shirt and legs as she turns to face me, her weapons raised, her pistol pointed straight at my face.

My lips twist into a grin and I say to her, "That was a beautiful fail."

She cocks her head to the side and blinks at me. "Fail?"

I nod. "We want them alive, right?"

Her bloodthirsty gaze lands on the gruesome mass at her feet and her pretty face twists in a grimace. "Oops."

TWENTY-SEVEN

Despite the three zombies that Skye found, or that found her, the night passes uneventfully. We leave the fire raging in the hopes that it will attract our prey. Two men take guard duty while the rest of us sleep in the cars. We do guard rotation every few hours.

Though Skye attempts to take another rotation, I tell her to remain in the car. While I may trust her to fight, I want her fresh for the hunt, not exhausted with slow reflexes.

The next morning, we have a quick breakfast of fresh buns made for us by Hannah, paired with another round of antelope meat and soup.

We agree to drive further northwest, still skirting the mountains and remaining as close to the river as possible. It's starting to look like our zombie hunt is going to be a bust, but we push on anyway.

After several more hours of driving we find an old abandoned gas town.

Shortly after the Fall, before survivors began organizing themselves into Sanctuaries, small towns with resources like gas, crops and water were inhabited. Unfortunately for the inhabitants, the Primitives found easy prey in these small, isolated towns. As the years passed and Sanctuaries cropped up, survivors moved out of the smaller towns and into the heavily walled and guarded Sanctuaries, turning gas towns into ghost towns.

When we attempt to fill the vehicles with fuel, we discover empty tanks. This isn't a problem for us since we didn't anticipate a fuel stop and calculated our mileage accordingly.

"Zombies like these old gas town settlements," Skye says casually as we drive through the main street of the empty town.

I don't reply, my gaze on the cracked pavement as I carefully maneuver through the town.

"No recent activity," Skye murmurs, her sharp eyes scanning the area for movement.

"They might still come looking for survivors," I say to her, stopping the car outside of a group of buildings that look like they'll make good cover if we can lure a horde our way. "We'll spend the night here, use the buildings for cover."

I climb out of the car and she follows my lead, gazing around at the ramshackle buildings with a critical eye. Half of them are in such disrepair they'd be dangerous for us to explore. Everything is covered in weeds, vines and dirt.

"What if they don't come?" she asks.

"Then we head back to Sanctuary and prepare another party. Try our luck again in a few weeks, maybe head out in the opposite direction."

Skye turns to me, hands on her hips. "You know what I like about you? You're tenacious. You're willing to play the long game, give a good idea a chance to work."

I'm damn near stunned by her words. "Didn't know you liked anything about me."

She shrugs and sets off for the nearest building that looks semi-inhabitable. "Well, you can't be all bad all the time."

I would argue that I can be bad all the time, but I like her playful mood too much to contradict her.

She tries to open the door of a building that looks like it was once an old hotel, but the door doesn't budge. She puts her shoulder against it, braces her feet and shoves harder. Still, it doesn't move. I throw my shoulder into it next to her and it flies open with a poof of dust. I catch Skye's shoulder and steady her so she doesn't fall over from the momentum. We both cough as dust settles all around us.

We step into the shadowy building and Skye looks around critically. The entire room is a ramshackle mess. Roots have broken up most of the floorboards and vines have creeped through the windows to wrap themselves around old rotted furniture.

"Home sweet home," Skye says dropping her bag on the floor.

I assess the hotel with narrowed eyes, deciding that she's right, this will make a good base for luring zombies. I head outside and gather my men around. Skye follows behind and stands next to me as I speak, her arms crossed under her chest, her leather armbands gleaming in the sunlight.

"Kingston, take two of the men and check out the rest of the buildings on Main Street. Pair up in teams and choose buildings to stake out. Make sure you stay hidden. We'll lure them here to the hotel and you can ambush them from behind. If there's too many, kill the ones we don't need, but remember to grab at least three of them."

As the men scatter to search through the buildings, Skye

comments from next to me, "Good plan, bringing an entire horde down on top of us." She grins her approval. "I like it."

She stuns me with the heat of her smile. It's so unexpected, so rare that I can't help but stare at her. She's in her element, out in the wild, flexing her zombie hunting skills. I recognize the look, because I feel the same. I wish I could take that smile, or the feelings that smile engenders, wrap them up and hold them next to my heart forever.

"Let's check out the hotel," I say gruffly, turning to go back inside. "Stake out some attack points."

"You say the most romantic things," she says with a laugh, following behind me.

I wish I was smooth speaking enough to banter with her. When she's in a good mood like this I want to bask in the heat of her attention. But I've never been able to engage in meaningless conversation with people. Instead, I listen and learn, looking for weaknesses in the people around me before exploiting them.

Skye doesn't seem to care about my lack of conversation. She chatters to me as she wanders through the hotel, gingerly placing her feet so as not to fall through any of the rotted floorboards. I follow her closely, intent on keeping her safe if she does happen to find something harmful. We carefully make our way upstairs and check out each of the guestrooms. There are twelve in total, though four at the back of the building are missing the outside wall. The elements have rotted all the furniture and rusted all the metal.

We make our way back downstairs and attempt to find a way to the basement to see if there are any lurking Primitives who want to fall in with our 'catch the zombie' plan, but the stairs to the basement have long since fallen, leaving a gaping hole in the floor. One of us could drop down and search, but I decide against it.

Skye runs outside to grab a solar flashlight from the vehicle. She comes back in and we shine it through the hole, squinting into the darkness before determining that there's nothing down there except for possibly rats and cockroaches.

Skye sits back on her haunches and says to me, "I think we'll just have to wait. Hopefully they show up tonight."

I grunt a noncommittal response that seems to satisfy her. She heads back out to the vehicle to bring in our packs, including bedding and food and water. She tosses mine at my feet and sits down, her back against the wall, and starts digging through her pack for some of the food Hannah packed for us.

I leave her for a few minutes as I check on my men, making sure they're in place for a potential ambush. I determine that everything looks good and head back to the hotel.

I follow Skye's example and reach into my own pack, pulling out a flask filled with water, unscrewing the lid and drinking deeply.

We don't speak, just sit in companionable silence, eating and drinking. Eventually, Skye's eyes begin to drift shut and I think about waking her up enough to get her to lay down on her bedding, which is now spread out on the floor in front of her.

Without opening her eyes, she speaks, showing me that she hasn't fallen asleep, "Tell me, Wolfe, if you wanted to be Warlord so bad, why didn't you ever try to depose Silas? It wouldn't have been too difficult after he got sick."

It's possible her words are meant to incite annoyance or anger, but I feel neither. Skye likes to test me. She likes to push me to see if I'll lash out at her. I believe this attitude is a combination of a life filled with grief and hardship, and an inability to find her place in the world. If she goes on the attack first, then she won't be hurt when her assumptions are proved correct and the worst happens to her.

When I don't immediately say anything, she pipes up again, her piercing grey eyes opening to meet mine. "Were you afraid that you'd lose? That Silas would defeat you?"

My lip tugs upward in a twisted grimace and I shake my head. "There's no chance that Silas would've won in a battle against me. Not in full health, not even with an army at his back. His security force was loyal to me, not him."

"Then why did you choose to come back here..." she looks around the room, realizes that "here" is a broken-down hotel in a nonexistent town in the middle of nowhere. "The Santa Fe Sanctuary, I mean. Why did you take over as Warlord?"

"You've asked me that before." I don't like repeating myself.

"You didn't give me a good enough answer before," she says, her voice challenging.

I debate whether or not to indulge her. She's right, I have a very different motivation for taking the position of Warlord in Santa Fe.

Skye is a complicated and challenging woman, one who doesn't scare easily, but who also gets skittish when it comes to some things, like intimacy and responsibility. I was unwilling to give her my entire plan, knowing that it could drive her away. It's been enough of a struggle getting her to engage in Sanctuary, engage with me. I didn't need to give her one more reason to attempt an escape.

Perhaps it's time to tell her the whole truth. She's worked hard over the past several weeks to create a solid city council to help strengthen Sanctuary, to connect with the citizens. She's setting down roots and becoming more reconciled to staying. Perhaps she deserves to know what the ultimate plan is.

"I never wanted to be a Warlord," I tell her.

She nods and I believe that she understands. I'm a lone wolf. I don't like being around people. I don't solve other people's problems. I don't rebuild cities. Unless Skye is involved. I'll do anything for her, including taking on the burden of Warlord in order to create a city that will satisfy her every need, a wall that will protect her, and a position that is worthy of her.

"Then why did you take the position of Warlord?" Bewilderment infuses her tone.

"For you." I try to get her to see the truth in my expression, but she shakes her head, not understanding.

"That doesn't make any sense, you couldn't have known that I would come back to Santa Fe."

"I knew," I grunt.

She frowns at me. "Explain."

I lean back against the wall opposite from her and sling my arms over my knees. I tip my head back into the wall, the vines cushioning me as I think. Finally, I say, "I wanted to give you a place to call home."

I can feel her eyes on me though I don't look at her. Her voice reaches out to me from the shadows, sharp but beautiful with the husky tones that are uniquely hers. "Home can be anywhere. You didn't have to go through the process of taking over an entire city, kidnapping me away from my vaccination team and forcing me to fix a bunch of problems that shouldn't have been mine to fix. You could've just stayed in the Tucson Sanctuary with me. We could've... built a home there."

My heart aches at the longing in her voice. I understand. She misses her sister and she was sad when I left her behind. But she's still not getting it.

"I didn't want you to just have a home, I wanted you to have a Sanctuary. Your Sanctuary."

She growls her frustration and snaps, "Just say what you're trying to say, I don't understand."

I tilt my head back up and pin her with a look. "Warlord." When she continues to stare, I spell it out, "Your place is Warlord of the Santa Fe Sanctuary."

Her expression slowly melts into understanding. She finally gets it. As soon as the truth sinks in, she shakes her head, stiffening against the wall as she says, "You can't be saying what I think you're saying. Me become a Warlord?"

"Yes." I don't say more. I don't need to. She understands now.

"I can't be Warlord," she scoffs, laughing bitterly at the thought, though I can see her brain whirring at the possibilities. Her head continues to shake as she ponders the idea. "A woman can't be Warlord."

"You will be Warlord," I assure her quietly.

"I can't," she whispers, the agony of longing in her voice. She's realizing how badly she wants what I'm offering, but she's holding herself back from taking it with both hands, which means she's not ready for it yet.

The time will come when she is ready and the position will be hers. I will step down and she will step up.

I look her dead in the eye and say, "You will."

TWENTY-EIGHT

SKYE

Anger surges through me as I scramble to my feet, leap over my sleeping bag and plant myself in front of Wolfe, with legs spread and hands on hips.

"You can't force me to become Warlord!" I snap at him.

The whole idea is absurd. Me? Warlord? Ha! It's the stupidest thing I've ever heard. I don't know where Wolfe got such a terrible idea, but I'm going to set him straight if I have to bash the idea right out of his head.

When he just continues to sit on his ass, gazing steadily ahead, chewing on his piece of deer jerky I growl at him, "You think you can force me to stay and be Warlord? You're wrong, I will find a way to leave the Santa Fe Sanctuary."

His eyes travel slowly up my legs, linger on my hips, move up to my breasts and finally settle on my face.

"You won't be leaving. If you try, I'll find you and drag you back." His voice is steady and the authority that constantly surrounds him is still there, despite him sitting on the floor while I tower over him angrily. "You don't have a choice. Eventually, you will take your place as Warlord."

"You have no right to constantly dictate my life!" I shout,

storming away from him so I won't do something incredibly stupid like try to kick him in the head. I can only imagine how badly that would end. The man has the reflexes of his namesake. He'd have me pinned to the ground, my fragile neck under his fist in seconds. I whirl back around and glare at him accusingly. "I've put up with enough of this. It's time for you to stop forcing your agenda on me and to let me go my own way."

His thick brows draw together. "You've had enough?" he growls, his deep voice reverberating through the room. "We haven't even begun yet. You'll be unrecognizable by the time I'm done."

"Are you threatening me?" I reach for my knife, my hand settling on the hilt.

"I'm promising you." He stands slowly, reaching his full height and going for maximum intimidation as he towers over me, his shadow stretching across the floor in the bright light of the setting sun as it creeps through the broken windows. He steps toward me, his stance intimidating. "You will be Warlord."

"I will not." Unable to contain my anger anymore, I reach out and slap the deer jerky out of his fist, my hand making a red mark on his wrist. The jerky flies across the room.

Wolfe looks at the jerky unconcernedly, then raises his gaze to me. "You hit me."

I laugh out loud, my tone unamused. "You can't handle a light slap?" I taunt. "No wonder you want me to take over as Warlord. You probably can't hack it."

I know I'm being as asshole, but I can't help myself. When I'm faced with emotionally charged situations I fall to pieces. I've never been taught how to properly handle anything like this. My family was torn apart while I was still developing. All of my teenage angst was poured into mourning my parents and then, later, my grandparents and sister. I've never had the opportunity to understand how real relationships work. Even my relationship with Silas had been lopsided. He had many wives, and though I was favoured, I still had to share him. I'd bottled my emotions and played the dutiful wife. Yes, I loved my husband, but I can also recognize that he hadn't necessarily been good for me.

"You *hit* me," Wolfe says again, emphasizing the word hit as though he wants me to understand something.

"What's your problem?" I shout at him.

It finally occurs to me, a split second before Wolfe strikes. When I was first brought to Sanctuary, when I tried to fight him, he countered my physical attacks with kisses. Apparently, the rule still stands.

He shoves me back so hard, when I hit the wall it shudders under my weight and the entire hotel creaks ominously. I'm too stunned to immediately fight back as he falls on me. I open my mouth to tell Wolfe to take it easy before we do some serious damage to the building with us inside, but he uses the opportunity to slam his mouth over mine, thrusting his tongue into my mouth.

Before I can even think to bite him, he grips my jaw and holds my mouth open wide. I'm not sure if this is to protect himself from my bites, or if he's trying to gain better access, but either way, he sweeps my mouth in a kiss so all-encompassing it can barely be called a kiss. It's painful, it's exhilarating, it's everything I've come to expect from Wolfe. Wild, untamed, completely feral. His teeth cut me until I taste blood. The blood doesn't bother me though. If anything, it turns me on.

I slam my hands against his chest, wrap my leg around

his knee and shove him. He starts to fall, then catches himself and stumbles back a step. Somehow, he retains his hold on me. Our kiss breaks for only a few seconds, long enough for my grey eyes to clash with his single golden one. Then he bends his head and slashes his mouth over mine again. Once more I'm forced to accept his brutal kiss. His fingers bruise my flesh as he grips my biceps.

I try to fight him, try to strike him, but he slaps my arms away. I try to knee him in the groin, but he throws me back against the wall, lifts me and thrusts his knee between my legs. I gasp at the forceful contact of his knee slamming into my pussy. The blow shocks me, but it's not enough to hurt me. My heart is thundering, my blood is pumping, and the scent of sweaty male flesh is pounding through my head.

I slam my fists against his shoulders with all my strength, then I grip his hair so tight that I can feel some of the strands tear from his head. I kiss him back, pouring all of my anger into the kiss.

My unexpected response lights a new fire in Wolfe. Our kiss takes on a decidedly erotic turn as he pulls away far enough to run his mouth down the side of my neck, sinking his teeth in deep enough to mark me. At this point I can barely breathe as the air rushes in and out of me in short gasps. Desire floods through me as I cling to him, alternately trying to push him away and pull him closer.

I fight him for supremacy, finally shoving against the wall hard enough to force him to stumble back. With me in his arms he's off balance. I take advantage, twisting in his grip and wrapping my legs around his, thumping my heels into the back of his knees.

He buckles and together we fall, slamming against the floor next to the hole. With a thunderous crack, the boards break beneath us and we go plummeting into the basement of the hotel. Broken floorboards, dust and vines fall through with us.

I let out a short sharp scream as we fall. We hit something soft enough to cushion the fall, bouncing together and then rolling off. I land heavily on top of Wolfe. Shocked, I blink into the dusty air and look over, realizing that we fell onto a pile of old mattresses.

"Good aim," I murmur, my voice cracking with a cough. I looked down at Wolfe. "You hurt?"

"Not bad enough."

I frown at him. "Bad enough for what?"

He flips me onto my back so fast the room spins crazily around me and I'm left blinking up at the bright hole that we've made in the hotel floor. "Not hurt bad enough that I can't fuck you."

"Fuck me?" I gasp.

Instead of answering, he shows me. He reaches down between us, grips the laces of my leather pants and tears them open. My body shudders at the impact of the tearing cloth, but at this point I'm so ready to feel him inside me, that I help him by kicking them off my legs. While I get rid of my pants, he reaches down to his own laces, untying them and pulling himself free.

I lean up on my elbows, squinting in the dusty darkness, trying to see his cock. I felt it pressed against me before and know that, given his sheer size, it must be enormous, but I'd like to at least see it once before it makes its way into my body. I'm doomed to disappointment though; both the surrounding darkness and Wolfe thwart me.

He climbs back over top of me, grips my ponytail in one hand, and yanks my head back at the same time as he pulls my legs open. He wraps an arm around my back, lifts me up and rolls us until I'm poised directly above him.

My heart hammers in fear and anticipation. I thank god that our fight upstairs made me wet for him, or he would split me in two as he slams me down onto his engorged cock. Still, the pressure is agony as he forces his way up inside my body. I scream out and beat him with my fists while he holds me against his body so tight that I can feel my ribs creaking.

"You motherfucker, let me up!" I demand, tears springing to my eyes from the pain.

He ignores me, burying his head in my shoulder as I continue to beat and pull at him, yanking his hair and scratching the skin around his neck. He murmurs in my ear, trying to reassure me, telling me that it'll stop hurting soon.

"I'm not a virgin, you monster cock fucker!" I shout at him. "Sex isn't supposed to hurt this much."

Finally, he grips me by the ponytail again, pulls my head back and lifts his head to look at me. "You haven't had sex in over a year and I'm a big fucking man. It was always going to hurt. Shut up and settle down or it won't be good for you."

Arrogant fuck!

I sniff angrily, swiping at the tears threatening to spill. "You're such an asshole." But he's right, the pain is starting to ebb, the pressure giving way to tiny sparks of pleasure, lighting a fire through my body.

He starts to move me, gripping my hips and forcing me to undulate on top of him, my pussy clinging tightly to his engorged cock. I swear I can feel every vein and every ridge he has packed in there.

He continues to rock me, back and forth, back and forth, the tension vibrating through his arms. I know that he wants to pick me up and slam me down onto him, to fuck me for all he's worth. According to him, he's been waiting a long time for this. I'm amazed at his control. He must be doing this for me, so that I experience as much pleasure as him without too much pain.

This thought allows me to give up my control, to wrap my arms around his shoulders and relax – to feel. I moan against his neck, giving in to the desire to lick him, to draw his masculine taste into my mouth. I like it so much that I wiggle a little closer and go in for more, running my lips and tongue from his ear down his neck to his shoulder where I sink my teeth in and bite down.

He groans and clutches me even harder, making my pussy spasm around him. A few more strokes and I'm right on the edge, ready to come for him, ready to come on the man who has dictated so many years of my life.

The coiled tension gives way in an explosion of pleasure as an orgasm rips through me. His fingers dig hard into my hips and ass as he continues to use my body to stroke himself to his own edge. Seconds later he follows me over, tipping his head back far enough that I have complete access to his throat as he comes. I sink my teeth in hard enough to draw blood as he shoots hot spurts of semen deep into my body.

He shouts again and brings his hand up to cup the back of my head. I think he's going to yank me away from his flesh. Instead, he pushes me closer, pushing my teeth even deeper into his skin. If he doesn't stop, I'm going to scar him. He doesn't seem to care though and the moment goes on and on. Me biting him, while our bodies explode in unison, waves of pleasure washing over me and on to him, then back again.

Hearts thundering, he finally lets go of my head and I'm able to detach myself from his throat. I lean back just enough to stare at his face in bewilderment. My own face must reflect an expression of utter shock. I can't believe we just did that. I can't believe we fell through the floor of the hotel and then fucked it out.

I would laugh and make a joke, but the expression on Wolfe's face stops me. Stops me completely. He's gazing at me with a combination of utter devotion, fierce protectiveness and... love.

TWENTY-NINE
WOLFE

She scrambles away from me as though the bats of hell are after her, leaping to her feet and staring at me accusingly, breaking the moment.

I'm not surprised and I'm not hurt by her reaction. I knew that Skye would take time to come around, that it would be a long road to our union. I'm surprised that we've made it this far so quickly. It's been just under two months since her arrival in Sanctuary and we've made more progress than I thought possible.

"Where are my pants?" she says, almost to herself as she searches for them on the floor.

I reach for them and hand them over. She snatches them from me and hisses, "Don't touch me."

I don't say anything. I'll give her time to calm down and sort this new development out in her head. She'll have to come around to my way of thinking, but I'm willing to give her some time to do that. Now that we've established intimacy between us, I have no intention of allowing our relationship to slide back into a safe zone for her. She'll have to suck it up and learn to live with me as a constant in her life.

I push myself up and stretch, arms over my head, muscles crackling. My body feels incredible, energized, sated. I feel like I can take on anything. Now would be a good time for a horde of Primitives to show up. But first, we have to figure out how to get out of this basement.

I'm about to suggest that we start searching in the darkness for another exit, when one of the men shouts down to us. "Everything okay? We heard screaming."

"If this is your response time to Skye's screams, then we'll be discussing your ability to protect her." I gaze steadily up at the face of Kingston as he peeks over the edge.

"Put your fucking dick back in your pants," Skye hisses at me, low enough that only I can hear.

I shrug and tuck myself away, relacing the leather and straightening my shirt. I double check that all of my weapons are still strapped on. Skye does the same while Kingston fetches a rope.

Skye doesn't have the upper body strength to climb out herself, so I help her up onto the rope and hold her steady from the bottom as Kingston pulls. She reaches out with one hand to grip the edge of the gaping hole which crumbles under her fingertips. She loses her grip and nearly lets go of the rope as she swings wildly.

"Grab the beam, not the rotting boards," I growl up at her.

"This isn't as easy as it looks!" she yells back.

My lips twist in a smirk. Feisty as always, even after falling through the floor of the hotel and getting thoroughly fucked by a man she professes to hate.

When my turn comes, I climb the rope with some help from Kingston, who groans in protest as he's forced to bear my weight. I reach for a loadbearing beam, now exposed from our fall through the floor, and drag myself through the hole. I sit on the edge and glance around, making sure Skye is nearby.

She's standing behind Kingston, holding onto the rope. She must've helped him haul me back up. She can't despise me that much. When she realizes what I'm thinking, she drops the rope as though it's scorching hot and steps back, her eyes narrowing on my face. She opens her mouth to say something scathing but a shout from outside draws our attention.

"Incoming!"

All three of us are experienced soldiers and our weapons are out within seconds. "Kingston, you and I will take posts by the door. Skye, you stand back and take out any that make it past us."

Skye pouts. "You aren't going to leave any for me though."

"Just do it," I growl at her.

Her bloodthirstiness might be a turn on, but I need her to listen in moments of potential emergency. Without another word, she falls back, assuming a battle position. Legs spread and braced, one slightly in front of the other so she can launch herself into an attack if need be. Her gun hand is up, protecting her chest, while her knife hand stays low. Her eyes are trained on the door. Pride fills me as I look at her. I taught this woman everything she knows about fighting Primitives and it's clear that she took my advice to heart.

Kingston and I take position on either side of the main door, which is cracked open just enough for me to see into the street. Our people are battling a horde of primitives 20 to 30 strong. So far as I can tell there are no losses on our side, but my men are good fighters and know how to keep their heads down while taking out the enemy.

One of my men leaps onto the hotel steps as a group of five Primitives circle him, pushing him back. He lets out a savage growl and shoots the nearest one in the head. A spray of blood arcs over top of him and splatters across the door. He throws himself into the attack, picking up a screaming, writhing Primitive and throwing it at two of others, shoving them back into the street and then following them. He did his job, luring them to the hotel.

I let out a whistle, drawing the attention of the three who had fallen on their dead comrade, tearing at his flesh with their teeth. A disgusting practice that I can't understand. They don't attack and eat each other while they're alive, but the second one of them expires, it becomes fresh meat.

At my whistle a female's head whips around, her dirty black hair flying around her face and slapping her thin cheek, which is pierced through with nails. She lurches to her feet and lunges at us. I make it easy for her. I kick the door wide open and allow her to hurl herself inside.

"Take her alive," I shout to Kingston.

The female is small. Though she looks feisty, a common characteristic of Primitives, she won't be able to put up the strength of an adult male zombie.

Kingston slams his blade into her shoulder, severing the joint and pinning her to the vined wall behind her. She lets out a scream of fury and reaches out in an attempt to scratch any part of him she can get. He knocks her arms aside and throws a bag over her head, complying with the process of capture that I'd outlined to all the men. Immobilize them, cover their faces so they can't bite, secure the limbs. He does the last part with ease, able to dodge her flying hands easier now that she can't see. One down, two to go.

"Wolfe, throw one my way!"

I actually laugh out loud as Skye begs me to let her fight a Primitive. There's a kind of pure joy in fighting side-by-side with my woman in a battle we chose, rather than one we are forced to endure.

Skye gets what she wants when the next two Primitives come hurtling through the door. I'm able to wrap an arm around the neck of one who immediately attempts to sink his teeth into my forearm. He's thwarted though, since I'm wearing a leather wrist cuff. I use his own weapon against him by thrusting my arm further into his face and forcing his mouth wide open. His arms flail but he doesn't land any blows. I drag a hood from my belt and shove it over his head, pulling my arm away in time to cover his mouth completely before tying it off at his neck. Then I yank his arms behind him and rapidly tie them tightly together.

When I finish, I toss him toward Kingston. "Secure this one."

I turn to see how Skye is faring with the one that got past me. This one looks more cunning than the others. He's circling her, attempting to get behind her so he can bite her neck while she's defenseless. Skye is too smart to fall for his basic plan and makes sure that her back is against the wall, her sharp knife at the ready and her gun out. I can see the tension thrumming through her arm as she forces her finger off the trigger. She badly wants to kill this Primitive, her blood thirst alive and strong, but good sense prevails. We're on a mission to take them alive, whether we like it or not.

I cross my arms over my chest and watch as she plays cat and mouse with the Primitive, allowing him to lunge at her before dancing away from his outstretched arms. Her moves are beautiful, like a wild mountain cat dancing in then lunging away as she stalks her prey. It makes me hard and I want to fuck her all over again the moment we're done here.

Finally, the Primitive makes a mistake and steps too close to the crumbling floor. With a shriek he goes through the wood and plunges into the basement. Skye throws me a grin that's so wide and bright I'm momentarily stunned. She shoves away from the wall and leaps after the Primitive, aiming for the pile of mattresses below.

"Skye," I shout after her as she plunges through the dark hole.

I hate that I can't see her. Hate that she's now playing her cat and mouse game in the dark. We have no idea if zombie eyes can see better in the dark, but I've long suspected this to be is true, which puts my woman at a disadvantage.

Without a second thought, I step through the hole and drop into the basement. Once again, I land on something soft, but it's not the pile of mattresses I was hoping for. An old moldy couch breaks with a deafening crack as I land directly in the middle. I topple backwards, losing sight of Skye and the zombie.

"Motherfucker," I growl, shoving myself quickly to my feet and whipping my head around to find Skye.

"I'm not hauling your heavy ass out of here again," she says calmly through the dust filled shadows.

I look to my left and squint. I'm able to just barely make out the outline of her sitting on top of the prone Primitive. Her knife is sticking out of its back, but the hood is securely in place and the Primitive's hands are tied behind it. She has secured her zombie. Whether it's alive or not remains to be determined.

I shout up to Kingston to grab someone for backup to help get us out of the basement...again. Seconds later a rope is dangled down. Skye places her booted foot in the center of the Primitive's back and yanks her knife out. It lets out an angry scream telling me that it's definitely still alive and kicking. She wipes and sheaths her knife and together we drag the Primitive to the rope and secure it. The Primitive is dragged back up through the hole and I can hear a slight scuffle as it's thrown into the corner with the other two.

The rope is dangled back into the hole and I hand it to Skye who wraps it around her waist and shouts up at the men to start pulling. Skye disappears and then it's my turn once more. Once we're out of the hole I glance around. I can still hear fighting coming from the street, so I shout through the door, "Time to finish, boys. We got our three."

A whoop of delight goes up from my men as the fighting takes on a decidedly sinister and more deadly turn. Within minutes, the rest of the horde are taken care of.

Skye comes to stand beside me on the front steps of the crumbling hotel. I glance down at her. She's covered in blood and there are scratches on her neck and the side of her face, but she looks completely satisfied. The soft glow of the setting sun lights her up, making her look like a deadly ethereal goddess.

I can't help myself, I grab her shoulder, turn her on the spot, wrap my arms around her and lay a kiss on her in front of everyone, humans and Primitives alike. She gasps into my mouth and stiffens, but she doesn't push me away. Instead, she clutches my leather vest and drags me closer, kissing me back, the adrenaline of the kill rushing through her veins. Fighting is like fucking: exhilarating and satisfying all at the same time.

I lift my head and stare down at her. I would tear this world apart for her. I would put it back together again for her. The power this woman has over me is unparalleled and dangerous, yet I wouldn't want it any other way.

"Let's go home."

THIRTY

We return to the city in subdued silence. Well, not exactly silence. One of the Primitives we captured is tied up in the trunk of the car. It's making an unholy amount of noise. Banging on the trunk, letting out bellows of rage through the hood we wrapped around its head.

"You want some jerky?" Skye asks, her tone bored.

I nod and reach for it. I'm not particularly hungry, but this woman has never offered me anything before, let alone sustenance. With her, I'll take anything and everything I can get. Today, the zombie fight has put her in a good mood. Made her forget how angry she was over our sexual encounter.

It's now past midnight and we're looking at a few more hours of driving. The night is clear and the road is illuminated by a bright moon. The two cars behind us follow close. None of us have working lights, so they rely on the lead vehicle to guide them safely across the countryside toward Sanctuary.

As we approach the city gates, sometime after two in

the morning, I say to Skye, "Your things will be moved from the harem."

I keep my eyes on the road so I don't see the expression on her face, though her words and tone are enough. "Why would I move out of the harem? Am I getting my own place in the city?"

"I think you know better than that," I say dryly. "You will be moved to the Warlord's chambers."

"Absolutely not!" she snaps, so sharply that the Primitive in the trunk hears her and responds with a series of bangs and screams.

"Regardless, you will be moved."

"I won't move, Wolfe," she argues angrily. "I want my own space. Just because you fucked me once doesn't mean I'm going to lay down and take it whenever you want it."

Fury ripples through me at her words and I savour the energy. Only this woman can make me feel emotion. This is part of the reason I believe that I am deeply in love with her. No other human I have met has managed to make me feel a damn thing, let alone the kind of anger she can pull from me. Though I will admit that there are days when I wonder if my life would be easier if she hadn't come into it.

Without looking at her, I reach over to capture her wrist in a tight grip. "You will not describe our physical affection for each other in such terms."

She falls silent for a few seconds and then lets out a sharp laugh which receives an answering bang from the trunk. She sends a glare over her shoulder. "That's rich coming from you. A man who can barely string three words together. I don't care how you want me to describe sex, I will do and say as I please."

"Skye." I say her name warningly. "Despite what you

think, you answer to me, and if you continue down this path, there will be consequences to that bitchy attitude."

"What consequences?" she demands. "You promised you wouldn't hurt me."

"Didn't promise I wouldn't hurt anyone else," I say darkly, taking the familiar path through the darkened streets to the Sanctuary palace. "I can do plenty of damage to you without touching you."

She gasps and yanks her wrist away from me. "So you think it's okay to hurt me mentally, even if you won't lay a hand on me physically? You're an abusive asshole, Wolfe."

I close my eyes for a brief moment and then open them to concentrate on the road. The last thing we need to do is wreck the vehicle this close to home. "I'm done talking about this."

She doesn't say anything for a few seconds and I think she's finally done speaking her mind, but then she pipes up just as we drive into the underground garage. "That's because you can't string more than three words together."

I let her snarky comments slide. Mostly because I think it's a good sign that she continues to fight me, no matter how ineffectual she is. She doesn't realize that she'll never win against me, because she has no idea how determined I am to keep her in my life. Nothing else matters to me. I will happily lay down my life, slaughter entire hordes and claim cities for her. The day she discovers this is the day she becomes an incredibly dangerous person.

We hand our zombie friend over to the palace guards and instruct them to take all three Primitives to Dr. Summers's lab. A secure room was built into the lab for them. Likely, Dr. Summers is up waiting for the delivery.

Skye and I climb the palace stairs, floor after floor toward the top. When we reach the second to top floor, which houses the harem, Skye attempts to dart past me to go through the door. I grab hold of her arm before she makes it and continue up the stairs. She stumbles behind me, catches herself and then grudgingly continues to ascend.

"I'm not staying with you, Wolfe. Forcing me to live with you in the Warlord's chambers is too much. I won't do it." She ruins the forcefulness of her words by yawning widely.

I ignore her, continuing up until we reach the Warlord's floor. I push the stairway door open and continue down the hall until we reach the entrance. I let her go once we're safely inside and the doors are locked behind us. Skye immediately whirls around and attempts to wrench the door back open but discovers that it's locked from the inside as well as the outside.

"Let me out," she snaps at me.

"No."

I walk past her through the chambers and into the solarium. I intend to continue through to the private chambers, but she catches hold of my arm and attempts to swing me around. When I don't immediately comply, she whirls herself in front of me and glares.

"If you don't let me out, I will set this place on fire. Just like I did the harem."

I take a step away from her and rub the bridge of my nose. Goddamn, I'm tired. It's been a long few days. Satisfying and productive. In just 48 hours I managed to complete the mission of capturing live zombies as well as furthering my relationship with Skye. Though I'm happy that we've taken a big step in our physical relationship, I'm beginning to wonder at the wisdom of keeping her in the Warlord's chambers. Truly, I keep this place devoid of people and clutter so that I can have peace. Skye is anything but peaceful.

Yet, even angry, I love having her near. I look down at her, sinking into the glory of her angry profile. Her long, dark auburn hair flows in waves over her shoulders, touching the leather and the more feminine garments beneath. Everything about her is so achingly beautiful I wonder how she wasn't captured long before Silas got his hands on her. I reach out to touch her, taking hold of her shoulders.

"Not everything needs to be a war between us." I dig my fingers into her shoulder blades for emphasis, kneading her muscles, but also squeezing more tightly than necessary to get my point across.

She shakes her head dismally and keeps her eyes averted as she says, "I think it does."

"Why?"

She shrugs my hands away and steps back. She begins pacing the floor, away from me toward the solarium garden, then around the tables and back toward me. I'm gratified that she's not trying to physically avoid me.

"We're way too different to be together," she says, almost to herself, still pacing. "Killing runs through your veins, it's who you are, it's what you do. I need a better life than that, a stable one. I want things. Things you can't give me."

"What things," I demand. She clearly hasn't come to know me well enough if she thinks there's anything I won't do for her.

"Things like babies," she snaps, whirling around to glare at me with her arms crossed protectively over her chest. "Just look at you, you can't have babies!"

Now she's starting to piss me off. "If I'm understanding the fundamentals correctly, I damn well can have babies."

She throws her hands up in annoyance. "You know what I mean. It's not that you can't – it's that you shouldn't."

"Why shouldn't I?"

"Because you'll be a terrible father. You're impatient, you're dangerous and you hardly speak. Children need to be spoken to."

"And you see children in your future?" I ask her.

"Yes... no... I don't know. But I'd like the option... maybe."

"You're searching for reasons why we shouldn't be together," I say to her quietly. "You need to readjust your thinking."

She whirls around and points a finger at me. "No, you need to readjust your thinking and let me out of here. I didn't agree to this, I didn't agree to any of this."

I take several long, measured steps toward her, slowly backing her up until her ass hits the edge of the solarium table. She reaches behind herself and grips it so hard that her knuckles turn white. Like it's a lifeline.

"I won't allow you to leave," I tell her, my eyes caressing every inch of her though I don't touch her. "This is your life now."

"I don't accept that," she says, a chill to her voice.

"Then our battle will continue," I say.

Her grey eyes take on a pained expression, but she nods. "It has to."

"That's where you're wrong. The war is in here." I tap her chest with my middle and forefinger, then I tap her temple. "And in here."

"What's that supposed to mean?" she whispers, blinking rapidly and refusing to look at my face.

I consider not answering. I hate answering questions people already know the answer to. But when it comes to Skye, I'm willing to give her that little extra. "It means, you're torn in different directions. Part of you wants to be with your sister in another Sanctuary. But you won't be happy there, which is why you accepted the assignment to distribute the vaccine." I fall silent for a few seconds, giving her time to absorb my first point before I continue. "Another part of you wishes you could climb into the grave with your dead husband." She opens her mouth to disagree with me, but I continue, "And the rest of you wants me as badly as I want you, but can't reconcile that desire with my previous two points. If you decide to settle down and stay with me in Sanctuary, then you'll be giving up the ghost of your husband and the possibility of living in the same place as your only living family."

Tears spring to her eyes, creating a jewellike gleam that mesmerizes me. The tears tell me that I'm correct in my assessment. Before she can argue or break down completely, I take her arm in a gentle grip.

"Let's eat, then we can sleep."

"I'm not hungry," she mumbles, but shuffles her feet in an effort to keep up with me when I start walking.

"Eat anyway, you'll need your strength."

"For what?" she asks curiously. "Are we going zombie hunting again?"

I'm relieved to hear a hint of humour return to her voice. As much as I love and desire this woman, I despise seeing the muddled confusion in her. The depression. The grief that she's spent a lifetime battling. I want to hold her close and keep her safe forever. But I can't keep her safe from herself. Until she realizes that she needs to heal, I will protect her and give her all the time she needs.

"Not zombie hunting, but you'll need energy for the coming battle."

"Battle?" she asks incredulously.

"Battle," I reiterate seriously. "Because unless you intend to come to my bed easily, I anticipate one hell of a fight."

Like the flip of a switch, her mood turns rapidly to anger and she pulls away from my grip. "If you think I'll willingly share a bed with you, you better prepare yourself for disappointment."

"Just remember, for every hit you land, I will take a kiss in reparation."

She gives me the finger and storms away, then realizes she's heading toward a dead-end hallway. She halts in her tracks, lets out a huff of annoyance, turns on her heel and stomps past me toward the dining hall. I smile after her, eyes on her swaying hips. She might not be peace and serenity, but she's mine and I'm keeping her.

THIRTY-ONE
SKYE

My first night in the Warlord's chambers does not go quite as expected. After our evening meal together, I try to leave again. Without a word, Wolfe picks me up, tosses me over his shoulder, slaps my ass much harder than necessary and strides toward the Warlord's bedchamber.

He tosses me onto his bed but doesn't watch to see if I land okay. Instead, he turns away from me and immediately begins stripping off his clothes. Assuming that he intends to have sex with me, I yank my knife from my belt and hold it out in front of me. I'd told him our last encounter was a one-time deal. If he so much as touches me, I'll stab him until he understands.

He continues to ignore me as he washes up in a bowl of warm sudsy water that had been left on the table beside the window. The same bowl where he washed my hands a few weeks ago.

Once he finishes, he dries his hands and walks naked to the bed. I finally get a good view of his monster cock and it damn near drives me off the bed. He put that thing inside me – no wonder it hurt so much! Even flaccid it hangs down his thigh. Under my scrutiny it starts to come to life, blood slowly filling it as its true size is gradually revealed.

Wolfe says nothing about my blatant stare, the fact that his body is becoming excited or the knife I'm holding like it's my last line of defense. I move to the edge of the bed as he flips the blanket back, lies down, drags the bedding across his lower body and falls asleep completely nude, his engorged cock tenting the blanket.

Feeling ridiculous, I slowly lower my arm and sheath the knife. I can tell by his deep, even snores that Wolfe is well and truly asleep. His face has softened, though soft is not a word one could apply to Wolfe. His complete lack of expression gives him a slightly more boyish look. I almost want to reach out and trace the scar that crosses over his eye. I want to lift the eyepatch to see what's beneath. I wonder if he's sleeping with it on because I'm here or if he never takes it off. Somehow, I suspect that no matter how gruesome the sight, it won't change the way I feel about Wolfe.

To be honest, I don't know exactly how I do feel about Wolfe. I can't honestly say I hate him, but he still makes me angrier than any other person I've ever met. Besides maybe Talon, the Outsider who sold me to Santa Fe Sanctuary in the first place. I'd had my revenge though, shooting him right between the eyes when he attempted to do the same with my sister.

I slide off the bed and walk as quietly as possible to the water basin, my eyes on Wolfe. He doesn't even twitch. One arm is dangling off the side of the bed, the other bent at the elbow and stretched to curve around his head. Even in sleep his bicep bulges impressively.

I begin to strip off my own clothes, wrinkling my nose as

they fall to the floor and a dirty metallic smell wafts up. I'd forgotten about the Primitive blood splattered across my outfit. When we got back from the hunt, we come straight up here and ate without stopping to wash or change. I strip until I'm naked, confident that Wolfe won't wake up. Even if he does, he seems exhausted enough that he probably won't do anything about my nudity.

I dip the sponge sitting next to the bowl into the water. It's cloudy with the dirt that came off Wolfe, but it's not unusable. I wash my face first, then my armpits, genitals and limbs. Feeling much better, I rifle through a clothes chest, searching for something appropriate to wear to bed. If Wolfe plans on trapping me here, then I can help myself to whatever I find in the Warlord's chambers.

I come up with a soft shirt that looks as though it used to be white, but through age and hard wear has faded to an almost see-through off-white colour. I pull it over my head and decide that it'll work just fine. The huge shirt gapes around my breasts, but it goes down to my knees, which is enough coverage.

I crawl into the bed on the other side from Wolfe and wiggle under the covers. As I lie down and my eyes drift shut, the last thought I have is that the Warlord's bed is extremely comfortable. I should have it moved to the harem where I can enjoy it in peace. I fall asleep with a sigh of contentment on my lips.

Less than an hour later Wolfe and I are woken up by a thunderous banging sound. I sit up with a gasp and reach for the gun that I always keep beside the bed. I glance over at Wolfe, who's blinking blearily into the darkness, holding a knife in one hand and his gun in the other. We look at each other for a few seconds and then Wolfe leaps from the bed, every trace of sleep gone as he strides naked from the room.

Not wanting to be left out, I hurry after him, my gun still clutched tightly against my side. I stay at his back as he approaches the main doors of the Warlord's chambers. He glances at me before reaching high over his head and grabbing a key from the top of the door. I raise my eyebrow at him. Not a great hiding spot, I would've eventually figured out to look there.

He unlocks the door and jerks it open, uncaring that he's completely nude as he faces Kingston and Hannah.

"Hannah?" I say her name in confusion. She doesn't live in the palace anymore; what is she doing at the Warlord's door? Her eyes are red-rimmed and haunted. I glance sharply at Wolfe to see if this is a new development or if she often stops by unexpectedly in the middle of the night.

From the look on Wolfe's face, he doesn't have any clue why she's there either. I let out a sigh of relief and then silently chastise myself for my stupid jealousy. Why, oh why, do I always have to do things the hard way? Even falling in love feels like a fight to the death.

"Get dressed," Hannah says briskly, her voice slightly muffled as though she has a cold. "We need you down at the laboratory."

Wolfe doesn't say anything but continues to glare at the intruders as though contemplating disposing of them so we can go back to bed. I touch his arm and decide I better chime in. "We'll be ready in five minutes."

I reach out to close the door and then hurry back to the bedchamber. Wolfe trails behind me.

"This better be good," he growls, scrubbing a hand over his face and rolling his shoulders back until they crack.

Exhaustion is hitting him hard and he's as grumpy as I've ever seen him.

"There's no point in questioning Hannah's summons. She wouldn't be here unless something very big was happening. I learned that early in my career as a harem girl. Hannah is serenity personified, so if she's shaken, then there's something to be shook about."

"Don't call yourself that." Wolfe's lip lifts in disgust.

"What?" I ask, throwing him a look over my shoulder as I drag my leather pants on underneath his giant shirt. Instead of changing the shirt, I tuck the tails into the pants and reach for my leather vest.

"Harem girl."

I'm starting to get annoyed at Wolfe's demands over what I should and shouldn't call myself and what I should and shouldn't say. Earlier he told me not to be crude about our physical relationship. Now he's telling me not to call myself a harem girl. There are a few things this man needs to understand about me.

"I'm not being derogatory toward myself when I use that term," I explain to him, my voice sharp with annoyance. "I learned from my time in the harem that the women there had a great deal of power if they knew how to harness and use it. I'm proud of the growth I experienced in the harem. Some of those lessons are still with me. When I say harem girl, I say it with pride."

At first, Wolfe says nothing. He seems to process my words. I expect him to argue with me, to insist that his word is law and I can no longer use that term. Part of me thinks it's because the reminder of my time in the harem is a reminder that I was once married to the Warlord of this palace.

He surprises me though by agreeing. "It takes a lot of

strength to embrace a role that must've been difficult for you. I admire your perseverance in the harem, just as I admire you now."

I'm taken aback by his words and I stop what I'm doing to look at him, searching his face for humour. As always, I only see his usual deadly blank expression. I don't think he's just talking about my time in the harem, but also his intention that I become Warlord. The role he wishes I would accept and embrace.

"I'm ready," I say quietly.

Together we leave the palace, choosing to walk instead of taking a vehicle since the laboratory is only a ten-minute walk away. Hannah and Kingston meet us on the street and walk with us. The streets are silent, bathed in the murky glow of a crescent moon.

"What's going on?" Wolfe asks, his voice hard.

Hannah shakes her head. "You need to see for yourselves. I might be wrong... I hope I'm wrong."

"About what?" I ask.

"You'll see in a minute."

Now I'm deeply curious and concerned. Hannah isn't usually this reticent. Though she's changed over the past year, her experiences with the Primitive attacks on Santa Fe having left deep scars, I hadn't noticed a major change in her personality that would lead her to act coy with us.

Dr. Summers meets us at the door of the laboratory. Her face is pale and drawn and she's clutching a notebook.

As we walk into the laboratory with her, I whisper, "You look tired. You didn't need to start work tonight. You could've waited till tomorrow."

She gives me a wan smile. "I probably should have, but I guess I feel it's my duty to get to work on this right away. I was still working anyway, when my Primitive packages arrived. I had a rush of sick patients needing to see me."

I look at her sharply. "More than normal?"

She thinks about it and then shrugs. "I'm not sure. It could be anything, from a mild cold, to well-water poisoning, to flu. I need to do more research."

A shudder goes through me. The flu is an enemy almost bigger than the Primitive pandemic. Flu will wipe us out just as fast. Too many of us have seen that nightmare unfold in other Sanctuary cities. An echo of my sister's words during the radio call hits me and I make a mental note to talk to Wolfe about the possibility of flu in our Sanctuary.

Before we can say anything else, Dr. Summers points toward the back wall. A solid sheet of shatterproof glass has been installed and on the other side the three zombies we captured. One is sitting huddled in the corner, his stringy hair clinging to his head and shoulders as he rocks back and forth. Another paces the room, letting out shrieks of anger that are muffled by the glass. The third zombie is standing directly in front of the glass, her eerie gaze zeroing in on us and following our every move. She looks hungry.

Dr. Summers waves us toward the glass, and as we approach, the female zombie's eyes light up and her lips peel back in a grimace. Strings of saliva drip off her sharpened teeth, down her chin and onto the floor.

I stare at her teeth as I draw closer, realizing that they've been sharpened unnaturally. She must've done it to herself at some point, which means she must've realized that sharper teeth would help her hunt better. Higher-level thinking. Exactly as we suspected them capable of.

"Her teeth," I say, amazement in my voice.

"I know!" Dr. Summers says excitedly, switching from completely drained to excited about her new project. "This is a very exciting new development. The other two have had the same thing done to their teeth, which means that they must communicate in some way to pass on the knowledge of how to hunt."

"Is this why we're here?" Wolfe asks, his grumpy voice making it clear we didn't need to be woken up for this.

Hannah speaks up. "No. You're here to examine one of the Primitives."

"Which one?" Wolfe demands.

Hannah points to the male sitting in the corner rocking. "That one." Her hand is shaking, and she quickly steps away from the glass, as though unable to stand such close proximity to the Primitives.

I look closely at the huddled form, taking in his size and shape. He's not a large creature, but not small either. Somewhat frail looking from what I can tell. His arms are long and thin and so are his legs. His clothes hang in dirty rags over his limbs.

I glance over at Hannah. "What am I looking at?"

"His face," she whispers.

We can't see the zombie's face from the way he's sitting with his head tipped forward against his knees. Wolfe bangs on the glass. All three zombies immediately look toward us, their eyes sharpening and their lips pulling back automatically. The zombie in the corner lurches to his feet, becoming aware that there are humans nearby. Wolfe bangs on the glass again and the zombie plunges toward us, slamming his hands into the thick glass and shrieking.

Both Hannah and Dr. Summers jump away from the glass, but Wolfe and I remain. In fact, I step even closer to the glass, taking in each and every feature of the zombie. Its nose seems to have been scraped clear off, only two breathing holes left in his face. Something, a piece of wood, or metal, has been jabbed through his cheek and jaw. His neck has been pierced, too. He's so covered in filth it takes me a moment to realize that he looks familiar.

I lift my hands to the glass and squint at him, searching every feature, trying to get past the damage done after he would've turned, to see the man beneath. Finally, it hits me, and I let out a loud gasp.

"Silas!"

THIRTY-TWO

"It can't be," I whisper to myself.

Yet, as my eyes trace the ravaged features of the snarling, hideous creature on the other side of the glass, his familiarity is undeniable.

"It's him." Hannah comes to stand next to me, so close that our shoulders touch.

I glance at her face and realize she's experiencing the same emotions as I am. Our husband, a man who we both thought dead, has come back from the grave. The moment is heart wrenching, but there's a glimmer of hope. He's been brought here as a Primitive so that our Sanctuary can work on a potential cure.

"How is this possible?" I glance at Dr. Summers. "He had a neuroblastoma, a tumor that would have been fatal within weeks of the attacks if the Primitives hadn't gotten him. How is it possible that he's still alive?"

Dr. Summers shakes her head and gives me a steady look. "We have almost no understanding of Primitive physiology. Perhaps his tumor shrunk on its own. Or, more likely, something about the Turn either stopped the tumor in its tracks or killed it entirely. Tumors are made up of live cells and when a body goes through the Turn, it essentially dies. This is why humans like to borrow from legend and call them zombies. The living dead."

I continue to look steadily at the face of a husband I thought dead as he slams his fist angrily into the glass and snarls at me, determined to murder and eat me where I stand. This is not the Silas I remember.

"If we can somehow treat him, what would it mean? Would he still have a tumor?"

Before Dr. Summers can answer Wolfe says sharply, "It."

I glance over at him startled. "What?"

Though Wolfe's expression is smooth, I can feel the tension in his body. His gaze is steady on mine. "This is not Silas. This is not a man. This is a zombie."

Heat rises to my face and I bite my tongue so I don't snap at him. I remind myself that Wolfe wants to take me for his wife. He wants me to become Warlord of this Sanctuary, to rule over it with him at my side. In his mind, he's painted a pretty picture of the two of us holding court over a perfectly functioning city. Having Silas back changes everything. It means I'm still married, and the original Warlord of the Santa Fe Sanctuary is once more standing before us.

I glance at Silas who has now fallen into an almost trancelike state. His head is tilted to the side and slightly forward, his long greasy hair flopping in his face, his shoulders down and his hands at his sides. My husband but also not. I can barely wrap my mind around what this means.

"I hate to crash any hopes you might have," Dr. Summers says quietly, stepping up to me and Hannah and touching each of us on the shoulder. She knows that we are the two in this room that are affected most by Silas's sudden appearance. "But this man is not your husband. Warlord Silas died a long time ago and the possibility of bringing him back is extraordinarily slim. I asked for you to bring me live Primitives to study. It was never my intention to cure the subjects that you brought me, but to use them while I search for a treatment."

"But those two things don't have to be mutually exclusive." This from Hannah, whose face is twisted in grief. An answering grief rises up, piercing my heart with a sharp pain. "Why can't you use him for study and still keep him alive? Once the cure is found... you could..."

Her voice trails off as tears start to leak from her eyes. She lifts a hand and touches it over the glass where Silas's face is on the other side.

Silas jerks to life and slams himself against the window, his face hitting with such force that his cheek bursts open and blood pours down his face. Hannah cries out and jumps back. I envelop her in my arms as she hits me and I hold her while she cries.

Dr. Summers doesn't answer Hannah's question. She doesn't need to. The likelihood of us being able to change Silas back to his original condition, zombie free and tumor free, is an impossible dream. It won't happen. Perhaps it will take Hannah time to see the logic.

"We should go," I say over top of Hannah's head, my gaze meeting Wolfe's. "We're just upsetting him, causing him to hurt himself."

Wolfe's gaze becomes glacial. Probably at my repeated use of the word him instead of it. I don't care, I refuse to call Silas by anything other than his name.

"I'll be back tomorrow," I say to Dr. Summers.

Wolfe shakes his head, wraps his hand around my arm

and tugs me against his side, out of Hannah's embrace. "From now on, you'll stay out of the lab."

"Don't be ridiculous," I say sharply, frowning up at Wolfe. "I'll need to speak with Dr. Summers about her project on a regular basis."

"You will not come here again." Wolfe's voice is hard and final as he tugs me from the lab without a backwards glance at any of the others. I'm shocked that he's allowing jealousy to cloud his good sense. It's not like him.

As we walk swiftly back toward the palace, the light of dawn begins to make its way across the landscape. I shake my head to clear it and breathe in the fresh early morning air. Dew, dust and a combination of concrete and nature.

"Are you jealous of a zombie?" I ask Wolfe, an edge of humour in my voice. He's very rarely unreasonable, so it seems funny to me that he knows full well my presence is required in the lab and he's attempting to refuse me entry. It's my job to okay the flow of supplies, labour and research. Dr. Summers needs me to be available to her.

"You humanized it."

Wolfe doesn't answer my question, but I understand what he's saying. In my eyes, that zombie is my husband, not a dead creature who will be sacrificed in our pursuit of the cure.

Instead of arguing with Wolfe, I ask him, "If I had been bitten a year ago and you found me living as a zombie, what would you do? If I was capable of turning, I mean. Would you kill me?"

Wolfe takes my questions very seriously. He stops in his tracks and turns me around to face him, reaching to grip my head and tilt it up to his. His expression is fierce, his eye narrowed on my face. He doesn't say anything at first but looks down at me as though attempting to form an answer based on what he sees in my face.

Finally, he says, "No, I wouldn't kill you."

Now I'm curious. We're no longer talking about Silas, because I know that, if given the chance, Wolfe would probably remove the Silas zombie permanently.

"What would you do with me?" I whisper.

His breathing becomes heavier, his hands tightening on my face. "I would do everything in my power to keep you alive until a cure was found."

I'm surprised by his answer. Wolfe doesn't believe that a cure is possible and only tolerates the presence of the lab in our Sanctuary. Yet, for me, he would wait for a cure. The concept would be romantic if it weren't for the fact that I'd have to be a zombie in this scenario.

"Yet, you won't allow hope for a cure for Silas."

He stands silent for a long moment, then says in a grim voice, "I'm not in love with Silas."

My heart freezes in my chest. We're standing in the middle of the road, surrounded by buildings overgrown with shrubbery, the early light of dawn peeking over the mountains to shine down on us. Wolfe has just confessed his love and I have no idea what to do with it. Of course, I'm in love with him too. I have been for a long time. Probably far longer than I'm willing to admit to either him or myself. But I'm not ready to repeat the words back to him. I've only ever spoken them to my family. Not even to Silas. As much as I'd cared for him, I'd never been sure that I actually loved him, so the words had remained locked up inside.

I can't return his beautiful gut-wrenching words of love. Not yet. But I'm curious about something else. "What would you do if I died before a cure was found?"

Of course, the point is moot, because I can't turn into a

Primitive. The bite doesn't affect me. My blood contains a special agent that prevents me from catching *Necrotitis Primeval*. Still, I want to know what he would do if I died.

This time Wolfe speaks without pause. "I would hunt down every person or Primitive responsible for your death and then I would kill myself."

"No," I gasp, a sharp pain hitting me. Sharper than what I'd felt when I was looking at Silas in the lab. "You can't kill yourself. Not ever. Don't ever say that again."

I don't know why it's so important to me, and I'm not ready to look too closely at my feelings for this man. But the feelings exist whether I want to examine them or not. I can't deal with the thought of Wolfe dying. His strength, his determination, his protectiveness... gone.

"Promise me you'll never hurt yourself because of me," I demand, swiping angrily at my tears.

Still gripping my face, he bends to me and molds his lips to mine in a desperate kiss. There is no passion, no romance to it, just survival.

Without another word he takes me back to the palace.

THIRTY-THREE

"Hit me."

We all look at Hannah, whose expression is a combination of deadly serious and excited. Tabitha sighs deeply and rolls her eyes. "You have to wait your turn."

My lips twitch at the crestfallen look on Hannah's face. She tosses her cards down with a huff, crosses her arms and waits impatiently for her turn. Even if she's slightly annoyed that it's not her turn, it's good to see Hannah having fun again. She's been far too quiet and serious since I moved back to Sanctuary. The past year has taken its toll on her.

It's taken a toll on all of us. My gaze travels the table, lingering on the faces of the women who have been diligently helping me put Sanctuary back together again. We're a ragtag group, different ages, sexual orientations and races, but we're damn good at what we do.

"I got shit for cards," Christine sighs, and drops her hand on the table dramatically.

I smirk into my drink before taking a healthy sip of the corn wine Christine brought for the group. It's actually pretty good. It tastes like honey, and after two glasses, I'm starting to feel a little tipsy.

"Bullshit," Tabitha counters without looking up. "Christy has the best poker face. She'll bury us all."

I laugh and when my turn comes, I toss a card on the discard pile and hit the table. Dolly, our dealer this round, tosses me another card. Holding it close to my chest I peek at it. It's a five of spades. I've now got a pair of fives, a par of jacks and an ace. Two pair. I glance around again, trying to determine who has what. Anita folded at the beginning of the game and is leaning back in her chair, a hand rolled cigar in her mouth and a pleasant expression on her face.

"Your turn, Hannah," Dolly says, looking expectantly at Hannah, who's sitting on my left.

"No, thanks," Hannah chirps, clinging to her cards.

"No, thanks, what?" Tabitha growls in annoyance, her patience thinning with the people who are new to the game.

Hannah looks at Tabitha, taken aback and slightly offended by her tone. Tabitha sticks her tongue out and we all laugh at the exchange.

"No thanks, I don't want any more cards," Hannah says primly.

"But you just asked for another one before Skye's turn!" Tabitha explodes throwing up her arms.

"I did not," Hannah says, now completely offended.

It takes Dolly a minute to speak, she's laughing so hard, but finally she straightens out the misunderstanding. "The term 'hit me' means you want another card."

"Oooooh," Hannah says, smacking her head. Then she says brightly, "Hit me."

Tabitha snaps something about grabbing snacks, shoves her chair back and leaves the room. Hannah watches her retreating back with a bewildered expression. "What did I do?"

Christine reaches out to pat her hand. "Nothing, sweetie. She's been in a perpetual bad mood since she was born. She's fine, really. Anger is how she expresses love. Now, let me see what you have there."

Christine moves her chair closer to Hannah and the two women bend to examine the cards. Dolly opens her mouth, probably to decry them for cheating. I shake my head at her and wink. The game is supposed to be a friendly release after a long week. We've all been putting in our best efforts to create and implement programs designed to pull the city together. Tabitha and Anita have been working together to create inner city greenhouses. Anita designs the buildings while Tabitha plans the gardens and hires staff. Anita has also been working with Wolfe on strengthening the city fortifications. Dolly has been making daily trips out to the water treatment plant to work on the automated systems, many of which stopped working decades ago. Whenever I see her, she's usually frustrated and weary. However, the construction of several new ground wells has been successful and fresh water now flows into the city, which takes some of the pressure off Dolly to get the treatment plant online any time soon.

Hannah and Christine have done a truly excellent job of designing educational programs that will be functional and practical. So far, they've opened one school, hired five citizens to help teach and gathered more than 80 children to attend. They're working on putting together similar programs at three other locations spread across the city. I've heard from several grateful parents that their children are already starting to exhibit better behaviour due to the supervision and direction given at school.

In comparison to what these women have been doing, my job seems easy. I supervise all of the city projects, travelling out to the various job sites, giving advice and providing direction and supplies when asked. There is only one project I've been avoiding, partially because the Warlord has demanded I keep my distance, and also because I'm not brave enough to enter Dr. Summers's lab knowing Silas is inside.

As though I've conjured her with my thoughts, the door bangs open and Dr. Summers rushes in. She peels off a scarf, wrapped three times around her neck, a jacket and a sweater before plopping down into Tabitha's vacant chair. I laugh at the amount of clothing she's wearing. It's the middle of summer and she's acting like it's about to snow. Having spent my early years in the north, I know what true cold feels like.

She turns excitedly to me and says, "I think we're on the verge of a breakthrough in the lab. It's been so valuable being able to observe live Primitive subjects. And my new assistant is a complete godsend. He listens to everything I say without challenging me. He may not have a strong background in medicine, but he's making up for it with hard work and persistence."

I take another sip of my drink and nod my approval. "What kind of breakthrough?"

She glances around, sees the wine bottle and snatches it up. Anita slides a glass over to her and Dr. Summers pours herself a drink. She takes a long sip and daintily wipes her mouth with the edge of her scarf. She turns to me, a grin playing around her lips. "We've managed to isolate the antibody that causes *Necrotitis Primeval* and have reengineered the current vaccine to be more stable, so it won't react quite as harshly when introduced to Primitive physiology. This might actually work as a viable treatment."

I stare at her, completely at sea with her explanation. "Uh huh."

She laughs and turns her body so she's facing me directly as she speaks. "Based on the results of what happened to your sister's friend when she was given blood that was immune to the virus, we know that it is possible to reverse the effects of *Necrotitis Primeval*. The main problem is that the reversal is extremely hard on the subject's body, which ultimately leads to massive organ failure and death. So, what we've done is take the antibody found in your blood and make a diluted version of the vaccine and bolster it with a few other components. We're hoping if we give several small doses, rather than one large dose, the Primitive's body will be able to recover over time."

"You are so smart," Dolly says in awe. "Like mind-blowingly smart."

Dr. Summers smiles at Dolly and shakes her head. "I'm a good doctor, but I could never do the things that you do with technology. It seems like magic to me when you take an old computer system and bring it back to life."

Before Dr. Summers can continue, Hannah interrupts, "Will you be able to cure Silas?"

A heavy silence falls on the room, and even Tabitha doesn't say anything as she walks back in with a bowl filled with freshly baked potato chips.

Dr. Summers's gaze turns sympathetic. "What we're creating isn't exactly a cure in the purest sense of the word. It's extremely rare to actually cure a viral infection. Even the common cold doesn't have a cure and scientists have been trying to get rid of it for centuries. By introducing the antibody, created with Skye's blood, we're essentially boosting the white blood cells' ability to fight back. Attempting to send the virus into retreat."

"But what will this mean for Silas?" Hannah persists. "Will he ever be human again?"

We all look at Hannah, at the desperation written on her face. We all feel the same. Maybe not for Silas, but every person in the room has lost a loved one to the virus. If we can have even a glimmer of hope toward bringing them back, we'll cling to it with both hands.

Dr. Summers speaks as gently as possible as she tries to give Hannah the most realistic answer. "The truth is, I don't know. We're making Silas as comfortable as possible, given the circumstances. We'll experiment on the other two Primitives, tweak the treatment until it's perfect, then we'll treat the former Warlord. Even if he survives the transition, we won't know what we'll be facing. Will he still have a neuroblastoma? Maybe, but we don't know. If he still has a tumor, will it be treatable? Again, maybe, but we don't know. At the moment there just isn't enough information to give you the answers you need. Then we have to think of the psychological and behavioral impact of Turning and then spending a year as a Primitive. It's highly unlikely he'll be the same man, even if we can turn him back."

I silently praise Dr. Summers for her compassion. She's doing the best she can with the information she has, and she wants to celebrate the victories and successes she's achieving. But she understands how much this information means to the wives of our former Warlord. When Hannah opens her mouth again, I cut her off.

"Thank you for explaining everything to us, Dr. Summers. We're very grateful for the research you're conducting." I reach out to squeeze her arm and Dr. Summers smiles at me gratefully. "What we really want to know though, is how do you go about making a zombie comfortable? I'm picturing couches, game boards and zombie socials."

Everyone laughs, including Hannah, and some of the tension eases. Tabitha sets the snack down on the table and plops herself into her chair. "Who's dealing?" She looks around at all the women as she attempts to get the poker game back on track. Her gaze lands on the doctor. "You in, Doc?"

I push my chair away from the table. "She can take my place. I need to get back to the palace."

They tease me on my way out, but they're gentle. None of them are willing to step over the line with the Warlord's woman. I don't blame them. Even I'm wondering where the line is with Wolfe. Have I crossed it already? Should I keep pushing or should I settle down and accept my time with him. One year ago, I would have fought him tooth and nail. Now... now... I want to fight just for the stimulation of it. I want to prod and push him. The see where his edge is. See what he'll do when I shove him right over.

It hits me that if I'm willing to tease the Warlord, to poke at his eternal control as I find my place in his life, then I'm comfortable with him. I feel secure under his care. I don't believe he'll ever hurt me.

I step out of the house and draw in a deep breath of air, savouring the scent of the cool evening with a hint of rain that has yet to fall. I look around for my bodyguards, but instead of Kingston and Denny, Wolfe steps out of the shadows.

THIRTY-FOUR

I gape at him for a moment and then a silly grin spreads across my face. I can't help myself. I'm genuinely happy to see him. He stiffens as he watches me. I'm not surprised at his reaction. I almost never smile, certainly not at him. Yet, I feel good and I want to share that feeling.

"Are you here to walk me back to the palace?" I ask, my voice husky.

He shakes his head, but reaches for my arm, pulling me to his side. "I have something to show you."

I'm feeling good enough that I don't question him as he escorts me to his vehicle, holding the door open. I'm wearing my long leather skirt with a white shirt and leather vest. As always, I'm armed to the teeth.

Wolfe drives straight for the city limits and is waved through the massive gates. I finally ask the burning question, "Where're we going, Warlord?"

Without looking at me he replies, "Not far."

He drives the dirt road around the city, toward the mountains. I gape in awe as we reach the base of the Santa

Fe mountain range, currently lit up to a beautiful orange and red glow from the dying sun behind us. I turn to look at Wolfe, watching his profile as we drive straight into the mountains, following the bumpy broken road that's been here since before the Great Fall.

Unless we're hunting, it's rare for humans to go into the mountains. Though zombies prefer not to travel through mountains, the hordes will sometimes hide out in them, especially toward the base of the range. This gives them cover as they organize themselves for attacks.

Besides the Primitives, Outsiders are known to make their homes in the mountains. Far more cover than the desert. A thrill rushes down my spine as I realize that Wolfe is taking me to a place that could be considered dangerous. This is one thing that I like about him, he's never shied away from introducing me to danger. He loves the part of me that seeks and embraces hazardous situations. And while I'm sure he doesn't want to see me get hurt, he trusts me to handle myself.

We drive higher and higher, farther and farther from Sanctuary, until he reaches a cliff face jutting out from the side of the mountain. As Wolfe pulls the car to a complete stop at the edge of the cliff, I'm able to see down the sheer side of the mountain and right into our Sanctuary.

Without waiting for him, I push my door open and jump out of the car, eager for the glorious view. The edge of the cliff draws me, and my feet move almost of their own volition. I leave my car door open as the awesome beauty of the Santa Fe Valley stretches out below me. From this height, the city looks small, but beautiful. The greenery that has been slowly creeping through all of civilization looks like an emerald blanket from this height, crawling up the fortified city walls and into the city itself. Below our feet is a jumble of human ingenuity mixed with the nature that is slowly taking back its planet.

"Our kingdom." Wolfe comes to stand behind me, speaking quietly.

I shake my head. "Sanctuary belongs to everyone."

Wolfe doesn't argue with my small rebuke but continues to stand with me looking at our city. Standing together, side by side, my shoulder touching his arm, we watch as the sun slowly drops beneath the horizon in the west. We'll need to leave soon, before we're completely out of light and unable to drive, but the sheer beauty of our slice of the world spread out at our feet is impossible to walk away from.

"Thank you for bringing me here," I whisper.

Wolfe does something unexpected. He moves behind me, wrapping his arms around my waist and tugging me back until I'm pressed against his chest. His chin rests just next to the side of my head. Though he's not a comfortable man to be around, I feel safe and secure in his arms. I don't pull away.

After several long minutes, I sigh deeply and tilt my head back to look at him. "We should get back to the city, shouldn't we?"

He looks down at me, his clear golden eye saying the words that neither of us wants to speak out loud. Our Sanctuary is a massive undertaking of repairs, organization, effort and sheer grit. Most days, the effort is rewarding. Some days, it's an overwhelming burden. If we could stay in this moment forever, we would. Separated from our Sanctuary but watching over it like the guardians we have become.

"Do you want to go back?" he asks, running his hand

down the back of my head, sifting his thick fingers through my hair as he speaks.

I shake my head. Truthfully, I don't want to go back. Not yet.

"I will give you anything that you want. Even if it means standing on this mountain all night."

My lips tilt up in a sad smile and I shake my head. "We can't stay here forever. For one thing, the predators will get us."

Wolfe lets out a dry chuckle. "I'm the worst predator out here."

I look at him and then let out a laugh. "You have a point. I guess I can take care of myself pretty good too."

His eye glows as he looks down at me. "Then we stay, if you want to stay."

He pulls away from me and I'm immediately cold without him. He heads back to the vehicle, opening the trunk and reaching inside. I watch with curiosity as he drags a few packs out and tosses them in the dirt. He slams the lid down and reaches for the packs, striding back toward me.

I realize as he gets closer that he's holding a bundle of blankets, a bottle filled with some kind of drink and a basket that's likely holding food.

Hands on my hips I tilt my head. "You planned this, didn't you?"

Without looking up at me, he reaches down to shake out the blankets on the hard ground, next to the edge of the cliff. "I plan everything."

Can't fault the man for his logic. He certainly does plan everything, right down to my kidnapping. "Do you think that we should set up camp so close to the edge of a cliff?" I point out, raising my brow at the two packs spread out side by side.

He shrugs. "You're going to want to see Sanctuary once it's full dark." He pats the blanket, encouraging me to sit. "If it looks like you're rolling toward the edge, I'll chain you to my side."

I sink down next to him and give him a sassy grin. "Is that a promise?"

A full belly-laugh bursts from him and I jump in shock. I've never heard so much amusement spill from his lips. He is so perfect when he laughs, absolutely beautiful. He steals my breath.

As if realizing that the moment has shifted into something else, he stares at me, a look of intense longing on his jagged scarred features.

In the past several days, since we brought the zombies back into Sanctuary, I have slept in the Warlord's chambers, but the Warlord hasn't touched me. I'm not sure exactly why, but I suspect he's trying to give me space and time as I settle into the role he has chosen for me.

I'm a fighter, and he expects me to fight. I wear my emotions on my sleeve. If one part of me is angry about one thing, the rest of me is angry about everything else. Maybe not the mature way of dealing with things, but it's always worked for me. He kidnapped me and I haven't been able to let that go. Not enough that I can objectively look at the life he's mapping out at my feet and wholeheartedly accept it.

But the past several weeks, working side by side with Wolfe, I've seen just how much we can accomplish together. I'm not ready to become Warlord, as he insists I must, but I'm starting to see the wisdom in our match. He is the calm to my wild. I am the emotion to his lack thereof. We complement each other in a way that I've never been able to see before. Or maybe I never wanted to see it because I was the wife of another man.

Now, everything has changed, and I must change with it. I reach for him, touching his bearded chin and running my hands up the livid scars that bisect his face. He stiffens, but he doesn't stop me. As if my fingers have a will of their own, they drift toward the simple black patch that covers his sightless eye. Without asking permission, I gently move it up, looking at his face without the covering.

It should be a gruesome sight, but it's not. This is Wolfe and every part of him is becoming important to me, including the scarred flesh around his blankly staring eye. The damaged eye is white, devoid of colour and expression. He blinks and I realize that a deep scowl is tugging his brows down over his eyes. I lift my other hand and gently run my fingers over his eyebrows, trying to smooth his expression. Trying to show him through touch that he doesn't disgust me.

I go up onto my knees and shuffle closer to him, still holding his face in my hands. I lean over and press my lips to his. The first kiss that I've initiated with him.

At first, he does nothing but sit tensely next to me, accepting my touch but not returning it. I begin to wonder if I've made a mistake, if I'm overstepping. But I decide if he doesn't like me touching him like this, then he'll just have to suck it up, because I'm enjoying myself.

Seconds later, his arm sneaks out, snaps around my waist and drags me to him. My chest mashes against his and my lips hover over his without touching. Our breaths mingle as the world around us fades away. There is only the two of us, sitting on a mountainside, a gentle breeze washing over us, binding us together.

We stare at each other, more connected than we've ever been. I don't want this moment to end and I'm suddenly fiercely glad that he planned this overnight trip. He chose this spot on the edge of the cliff. Wildly dangerous and wildly beautiful.

Then our lips meet and our souls merge in a moment of sheer heat and love.

THIRTY-FIVE
WOLFE

When her fingers stop on my eyepatch, hovering over top, I freeze at her touch. I am not a self-conscious man, nor am I particularly vain. I know what I look like. The man with the sort of face that makes women and children cross the road to avoid him. I am at peace with my scarred visage, yet I despise the idea of Skye seeing me at my worst. Seeing my vulnerability.

She peels the eyepatch back and stares at me, her face unreadable. I'm tempted to shove her away and replace the eyepatch, but when she says nothing I begin to relax. I know that it's not a pleasant sight, but her face reveals nothing. No compassion, no pity, no disgust.

She grips my face and touches her lips to mine. Any concerns I have are gone as my cock grows hard and the blood pounds in my veins. All she has to do is look at me and I want to throw her up against the nearest wall and take her with the savage energy I feel every time she's near.

I didn't bring her up this mountain to fuck her. I wanted to show her our empire, every tree, rock and building that will belong to us in this alliance we have created. But with one touch, one glance, she has me. All I can think about is tearing her clothes away and shoving my cock so far inside her that she'll never be the same again.

I grip her hard around the waist, pull her into my body and kiss her back. Her lips open beneath mine giving me access to the perfect, erotic recesses of her mouth. Fuck, that mouth.

I take a fistful of her hair and pull her back a few inches, staring down at her, my empty eye still on display. She doesn't flinch, she doesn't move. Her breathes comes out in quick little rushes, sending a heated trail across my cheek as I look back at her.

"I'm going to fuck you."

A slow smile spreads across her lips. "I thought you'd never ask."

She jerks in my arms, trying to press her lips against mine once more, but I continue to hold her in place, my fingers wrapped in her silky hair. I want this control. I need this control. Every part of my life is planned, right down to the last detail. Eliminates surprises.

If anyone is going to convince me to take a chance, it'll be this woman. But not right now. I need to control her, show my future Warlord that she belongs to me, heart, body, and soul. Despite being such a powerful woman, she belongs to me completely.

"Not asking," I growl, leaning into her, my lips brushing her ear.

She shivers beneath my hands. "Then get on with it."

Her challenge spurs me to action. Instead of pressing my lips to hers though, as she expects, I drag her back by the hair, throwing her down on the bedding. She lets out a squeak and I can see that she has to visibly hold herself back from attacking me. The warrior in her strong and always on the edge.

I yank at the laces on her pants, dragging the leather down her hips and revealing her long smooth legs. Her pants stop at her boots, too big and heavy for me to get the leather off. I pull her feet up one leg at a time untying the laces on her boots, my gaze never leaving hers.

Her eyes tell me everything I need to know. She wants me and she wants it rough. Her eyes burn with need, the stormy grey deepening to cobalt as her pupils dilate.

I yank the boots from her feet and toss them over my shoulder. Her pants are next. She lifts her arms to help me as I grip the hem of her shirt and drag it over her head, leaving her naked and sprawled out on the bedding.

Her hair is a beautiful dark halo above her head, shining a deep red in the light of the dying sun. She is more lovely in this moment than I have ever seen her. Perhaps it's because we've already known each other in a physical sense that her appeal now has more hold on me than ever.

She sits up and flings her arms around my shoulders, climbing into my lap and pressing her bare knees against my sides, gripping me with an impressive strength that has my cock straining so hard against my pants that I'm sure I'll burst the seams.

I hold her up by the ass, plastering her naked body against me, enjoying every contour as she writhes on top of me. She is both soft and hard where there's muscle but also womanly curves. I devour her lips in a ruthless kiss that she not only accepts but gives back in equal measure. She bites down on my lip so hard that I feel a streak of pain.

I dig my fingers into the rounded globes of her ass, sliding them down the crack, touching her tiny asshole and then moving my fingers further, gliding them through the wet folds of her vagina.

I'm dizzy with need, all of the blood rushing from my head to my groin. I stroke my fingers through her pussy a few times until she's moaning into my mouth, her sharp teeth biting down on my lip. I doubt that she's aware of what she's doing.

She flings her head back and lets out a little shriek, shattering in my arms as she comes just from the touch of my fingers gliding gently across her wet pussy, flicking the hardened nub of her clit.

As she melts in my arms, I wrap my hand around her neck and pull her backwards off my lap. She flails and then catches herself, but before she has time to settle, I flip her over onto her hands and knees. She lets out a yelp, but then thrusts her hips back into mine, silently begging for my cock.

I quickly take my clothes off and fling them behind me, aiming for the pile of her clothes, but not really caring where they land. They can go over the cliff for all I care. Now I'm as naked as she is.

I grip her waist, dragging her back against me and impaling her on my cock, letting out a ferocious growl as the tight clasp of her pussy sinks onto me. She shrieks as she's forced to take more cock than her tight pussy is used to. Her passage pulses around me, alternately easing its grip and then clinging. She wiggles her ass against my hips and I grip her hard, digging my fingers into her soft flesh.

"If you don't stop moving this'll be over in seconds," I grunt.

She flings her head back to look at me, her hair flying in an arc, a mischievous grin playing around her lips. "That's a *you* problem, Warlord."

She's going to have to pay for that remark.

I lean back far enough to slap her ass, bringing my hand down hard against her flesh. It bounces and a satisfying red mark in the shape of my fingerprints is left behind. She lets out a shriek and lunges forward toward the edge of the cliff, but I wrap an arm around her waist and hold her still.

"Motherfucker, that fucking hurt!"

I grip her hair in my fist and drag her head back, placing my lips against her ear. "Got any more smart-ass comments for me?"

She stays silent for a few seconds and I think maybe she's learned her lesson, then she answers, "Is this going to take all night? I really do need to get some rest."

I throw my head back and laugh, my second carefree laugh of the evening. It startles her, but then she quickly joins in. Hell, the laughter has startled me as well. This right here is why I love her. Even when she's helpless beneath me, impaled on my cock and about to take more, she still manages to give attitude. I hope she never loses it.

"Yes, this is going to take all night." I drop my lips to the back of her shoulder and kiss her gently as I surge inside her, slamming my hips into her ass.

She shrieks and wiggles trying to find a more comfortable position, but my hold is too tight. I don't want her comfortable. I want her hurting for me so bad that she's a begging weeping mess.

I slam my hips into her, over and over, hitting her cervix with my cock and drawing screams of pain and pleasure from her. Even if I wanted to slow down, wanted to ensure her comfort, I'm past the point of reason. This woman has spent years teasing me. She didn't do it on purpose, but her mere presence was a constant reminder that the only thing on the planet I wanted for myself was the one thing I couldn't have.

Risking her hate wasn't worth it. Until now. Until Skye reached the point that she can accept me for who I am. And accept herself.

She stretches her hands out across the ground in front of her, moaning in ecstasy and undulating her hips enticingly as I continue to bury my cock in her silken passage. She's so wet now that I glide easily in and out. I reach around to touch her clit, strumming my finger against it.

"I need to come. I'm going to come!" she shouts, panting like she's running a race.

I take a fistful of her hair and drag her head back until she's forced to go up on her knees, my cock still inside her. I hold her against my shoulder and drop my lips to her cheek. "Open your eyes, look at your kingdom."

I can't see her face, but I know the moment she opens her eyes, obeying me. Her head tilts down and she gazes at the city far below, gas lamps and fires lighting up the night like tiny fireflies laid out in a blanket across the city. Our haven tucked away safely for the night.

"Come for me," I growl in her ear, rubbing her clit hard enough that she tries to close her legs. I force them open, force her to take everything I'm giving her.

Her body tenses and as she reaches for the orgasm, I thrust up inside her while pinching her clit hard between my finger and thumb. She flings her head back against my shoulder and screams, her voice echoing off the mountainside. Her pussy spasms against my cock, gripping me so hard that she forces me over my own orgasmic edge.

As Skye melts in my arms, her orgasm continuing to ripple through her, I thrust one more time before shooting my seed up inside her. I silently beg my sperm to find their way home, to create the life that will bind her to me, bind us to each other.

As we both come down from the high of our shared orgasms, I lay her down on the bedding and wrap myself around her, stroking her face and tilting her chin so that she can watch the city lights. She sighs contentedly and wiggles back against me, pressing her ass against my flagging cock.

"I thought you said we were gonna fuck all night?" she says quietly, a hint of mischief in her voice.

I lean over and kiss her temple, trailing my lips to her ear and shoving my tongue inside. She gasps and shudders beneath me while I hold her down and explore this new erogenous zone. When she's a moaning, melting mess beneath me I tip her face up to mine. "We're not done yet."

I wake up before Wolfe's heavy hand can even touch my shoulder. I reach for my weapons, no words between us as he does the same. We're both still naked, but that can't be helped. The immediate problem is more pressing than scrambling for clothes.

We're lucky. Since there's a cliff to our backs the enemy can't completely surround us, but that's the extent of our luck. If we don't watch our footing, we could easily go over the side in what appears to be an inevitable battle with an unknown enemy, judging from the shadowy forms moving through the darkness, surrounding our car.

If we hadn't been asleep, if we'd been awake and alert, we might've been able to gain the upper hand. As it is, neither of us are wearing protective gear. I flash Wolfe a grin, this is going to be fun. His lips stretch in some semblance of a smile and his eye gleams in the darkness. He feels the same.

A voice shouts at us, confirming what I'd already suspected. The people surrounding our small encampment aren't Primitives.

"Give us the woman and we'll let you go."

Wolfe looks at me sharply, a frown dragging his brows down. "Outsiders," he grunts with disgust.

I've always thought that Wolfe's disdain toward Outsiders was funny. He's just as dark, dangerous and morally grey as any Outsider I've ever met, yet he seems to despise them. I suspect it has to do with my arrival in Sanctuary the first time around, when I was the prisoner of a vicious Outsider.

"No mercy," Wolfe says to me.

"No mercy," I whisper back.

Rule one when it comes to war, mercy will get you killed. Aim to take out your enemy with swift precision so there's no one left to come after you.

Before the Outsiders can shout at us again, I answer back, "Why don't you come over here and get me."

My words have the desired effect as several men leap out of the shadows surrounding the vehicle and lunge toward us. Their attack plan seems to be to overwhelm us with numbers. If they knew how many zombies Wolfe and I have killed between the two of us, they'd come up with a better strategy.

Wolfe and I leap to our feet and start shooting. I immediately put a bullet through the head of the man nearest me. He's standing close enough to the edge of the cliff that his body topples over the side.

Wolfe grabs my arm and drags me back, bending his body protectively over mine as guns go off all around us. I flinch, but nothing hits me. I realize right away that they don't want to kill me.

Slave traders. Having been sold once before, I now have added incentive to kill every man in this group. There's nothing lower in my opinion than a man willing to sell another human being into sexual slavery so he can gain a little coin and maybe a few supplies.

With the realization that they won't hurt me comes a surge of power. I wrench my arm from Wolfe's grasp and leap in front of him, protecting him with my naked body. He growls at me to stay back, but I don't. Instead, I hurl myself into the fray, grinning like a woman about to eat her favourite treat, and start slashing anyone stupid enough to think they can put hands on me.

The element of surprise is now on my side as men rarely think that women can fight and fight well. I duck under the guard of one man and plunge my long straight knife into his stomach at the same time as bringing my gun up to his chin and pulling the trigger. Blood splatters across my body. The force of the blast pushes him backward and my knife is free once more. I slash it around in time to catch someone in the arm. It cuts right to the bone and he screams in agony as I swing my leg up between his legs, crushing his balls and dropping him to the ground.

Someone lets out a roar that echoes off the cliffs around us, making us all freeze and sending goosebumps up my arms. When I glance over my shoulder, I realize it's Wolfe, letting out a battle cry before leaping on the men nearest him. Both are dead within the blink of an eye, their bodies hitting the dirt at Wolfe's feet. I can see their blood gleaming against his skin in the moonlight.

The man on the ground at my feet swings a rifle around and takes aim at Wolfe. I let out a screech of anger and leap on him, knocking the gun aside and aiming my knife for his ribs, he grunts as it slides easily between two ribs, buried in his side. I bring my gun up, intent on ending his life, but he's better than that. With a swipe he knocks me away from him and I go flying into the side of Wolfe's vehicle. I hit hard enough that the breath rushes out of me and I fall onto my hands and knees. A bullet whizzes past my head, slamming into the hood of the vehicle.

Wolfe's angry bellow reverberates off the mountainside, once more making every man in the group freeze in fear.

Clever. I believe he's drawing attention to himself, encouraging the men to attack him instead of me. As they turn toward him, I leap to my feet, scooping my gun up and shooting one in the back of the head. Idiot. Never turn your back on a woman with a gun.

"Retreat!" someone shouts into the darkness and just as quickly as they came, every man in the group disappears, leaving their dead behind.

I stand, my knife in one hand and my gun in the other, my limbs steady as I contemplate the dead bodies littered across the ground. Eight. Nine including the man who went over the cliff. And at least another dozen fled into the darkness. Had they been serious about killing us both, we wouldn't have been able to withstand a coordinated attack from that many. Their desire to keep me alive saved our lives.

Wolfe grabs hold of me and swings me around to face him. I look up at him startled, but the crazed look in his eye is enough to keep me silent as he runs his hands over my body. I shiver in the chill night as he touches me, not from the cold but from the heat already building within.

It doesn't matter that both of our naked bodies are splattered in blood, that we were just attacked and the ground where we made love only a few hours earlier is now littered in the bodies of the dead. I still want him.

"I'm not hurt," I say quietly. "The blood is theirs."

He grips the back of my head and looks down at me, his expression fierce. Not worry, but pride. An answering glow flares to life within me. We are warriors. We have each other's backs. We kill without mercy.

"Let's go." He grips my hand and pulled me toward the car.

"Our stuff." I turn back toward our little encampment, but he continues pulling me with him.

"Leave it," he growls, opening the door and shoving me in.

I silently agree with him as the door slams shut. We're only leaving behind a few blankets and some leftover food. We're better off getting out of here in case the Outsiders are able to go for reinforcements. Or if they change their minds about capturing me and decide to come back and kill us both.

As Wolfe slides into the car, I turn to ask him, "Why didn't they steal the car?"

He shakes his head and turns the ignition. He floors the car backwards and then throws it into drive and we begin to hurtle down the mountainside. The drive is utterly terrifying since we're doing it in the dark with no headlights. I momentarily forget that I asked Wolfe a question until he answers.

"They only wanted you, not the car."

I nod my head. "They underestimated us."

I turn my gaze to Wolfe, travelling his body and taking in his magnificence. Completely naked, covered in blood, he is utterly breathtaking. The hard slabs of muscle are partially hidden in the dark interior of the car, but I can see enough in the moonlight filtering through the windows. He is truly an incredible man, bigger than life. Almost a god.

"They underestimated us," he confirms. "Thought I'd be an easy kill and you'd be easy prey."

I bare my teeth in a grin and let out a laugh. "They were

wrong." Wolfe chuckles and a pleasant camaraderie settles over us as our adrenaline from the fight begins to ebb. "Do you think they intended to sell me as a slave?"

A new kind of tension fills the car as we're forced to think of memories that are best left buried in the past. The memory of when I was brought to Santa Fe and sold to its Warlord. That initial interaction with Wolfe feels different now in retrospect. I'd hated everyone and everything that had anything to do with my kidnapping and sale. I'd especially despised Wolfe. He'd been the twisted ugly face of my sale and placement into the harem. It didn't matter that I was to become the bride of the Warlord at the Warlord's orders; Wolfe was the one my hatred settled on.

But now, I recall those memories with new eyes. The look on Wolfe's face when I was presented at the palace, the way he treated my captor with deadly disdain. I remember the way he looked at Silas as though he wanted nothing more than to gut his Warlord with the long, curved knife strapped to his belt. I recall those brief spurts of curiosity I'd had as I wondered why the second-in-command of the Santa Fe Sanctuary hated his boss so much.

"Yeah, probably," Wolfe confirms. "But just in case, we're doubling your guard in the city and I prefer you not go beyond the walls."

I direct a frown out of my window into the night. He's taking the attack on us far more seriously than he should. They tried and they failed, losing a significant amount of men in the process. They're not going to try again. Still, I know what it's like to argue with Wolfe. About as productive as having a conversation with a wall.

Instead, I ask, "How long will I be guarded?"

"Until I'm positive you'll be safe."

I frown at him. "I'm safe now. They're not going to come

after me. Even if they somehow got into Sanctuary, how would they find me? I'm just one person, not important enough to go to that kind of trouble for."

Even in the darkness of the car I can see his scowl. He knows my logic is sound, but his desire for my safety outweighs that. "Doesn't mean they won't try. Until I know that they've all been killed or are no longer in the area, you will be guarded."

Still, I try to argue my way out of a heavier guard. "If they watch the city hoping to get their hands on me, they won't hang around for long. They'll see that we're well fortified. I have work to do, I can't remain trapped inside the city walls with a contingent of guards following me around everywhere."

"This conversation is over," Wolfe says, his voice harsh.

I fall silent, staring at the road ahead. Despite his coolness during the fight, and the grin he'd sent me as he realized that we were about to take on the Outsiders together, it's clear the attack has rattled him. I know he's not worried for himself, which means he's worried about me. He didn't like that they were after me in particular.

"Hell of a way to talk to your future Warlord," I can't help but mumble.

His eyes remain on the road, but I can tell from the shifting shadows around his mouth that he's trying not to smile. "Accept the role of Warlord and we'll talk about giving you more freedom."

I stick my tongue out at him and complain, "I call bullshit. Even if I was Warlord, you'd still smother me in protection."

He says nothing. He doesn't need to. We both know I'm right.

THIRTY-SEVEN

I look around at my city council, which has expanded from the last time we met. It now includes three men: Wolfe, Kingston and Dorian Milkstone, a ninety-four-year old historian. I'm exhausted but satisfied. It's been one week since Wolfe and I spent that night on the cliff. One week since the attack by the Outsiders, and we're no closer to understanding who they are and why they targeted us.

I personally think it was a crime of opportunity. They saw a naked woman, young enough to have children, pretty enough to catch the eye of a Warlord, and they attacked us. I've put the incident behind me despite the presence of increased security. Wolfe doesn't agree with my assessment. He thinks the Outsiders were after more than just a woman to sell. He believes they wouldn't have attacked with so much force and such ferocity if they weren't after me in particular.

I think he's wrong, but I'm not in charge of security and he has insisted on a detail of at least five men with me every-where I go. Their constant presence has hindered my progress in the city, but not by much.

"How are things at the water treatment plant?" I turn to speak to Anita.

Anita has finished her work on the wall, helping Wolfe to secure it with the best possible materials available and an improved structure. She is now working out at the plant with Dolly. The two of them work together with a team of people from the city, rebuilding and attempting to get a water supply that will last our city well into the future.

As I watch her, Anita runs a tired hand over her face. I sympathize, I feel as tired as she looks.

"This is going to have to be a long-term project," she says, shaking her head. "If I had to guess, the treatment plant was one of the first places to be abandoned when Santa Fe came under attack during the Great Fall. It's been abandoned since... I don't know?"

She looks around the table to see if anyone can answer her question.

Dorian pipes up. "The city fell to Primitives in 2026. The plant was likely abandoned around the same time."

Dorian was in Santa Fe during the Great Fall. He'd abandoned the city with other survivors when it became clear that the area could no longer sustain them. However, a few years later, they were encouraged to come back by a Warlord who touted his strength and ability to both protect and provide for the inhabitants.

Anita nods and looks at me. "Then it's most likely been abandoned for the past 50 years. Dolly's having a heck of a time bringing the computer system back online. It would help if we could use hydroelectricity."

We all laugh at the joke. The water treatment plant is also connected to a dam. If they were both functioning properly, we would have hydroelectricity. We need one for the other.

"Keep working," I tell the two women. "Let me know if you need anything. Getting a stable water source is one of the most important things we can do for the city. Whatever supplies, manpower, management you need, just ask for it."

I can't help myself, I glance to the right, looking to Wolfe. He gives me a slight nod and I feel a sense of both achievement and shame. He has put me in this position and has made it clear that it's mine to do with as I please, yet I still have the desire for his approval.

I refocus my gaze on the group in front of me and turn my attention to the doctor. "Dr. Summers, how is the situation in the city?"

Like almost everyone else at the table, Dr. Summers looks exhausted, only she has a very good reason. On top of her work with the live zombies, she's also battling a flu bug that has hit our city. At first, we thought we could contain it, isolating the few individuals who were sick. However, it's become clear that there's a long incubation period with no symptoms, which means that there are infected people walking among us.

She shakes her head. "Not good," she says grimly. She lifts her eyes to meet mine and I can see the concern. "The sick are multiplying, and we can't seem to contain the virus. I'm positive that it's not new, that it's the same flu virus that swept the continent several years ago. But that doesn't mean that we're any closer to knowing how to deal with it."

My heart wrenches in pain at her words. Every person at this table would have been affected by that virus. It spread rapidly from Sanctuary to Sanctuary, despite low travel rates among citizens. Many people died, weakening city defenses and leaving them open for Primitive attacks. In one such attack on the Las Vegas Sanctuary, I'd been bitten and separated from my family.

"What..." My voice is high and worried so I reach for my water glass, taking a gulp and steadying my nerves before I continue, "What can we do?"

Though I'm scared, I am still their leader.

As if sensing my resolve, a light of hope flares to life in Dr. Summers's eyes and she sounds stronger when she says, "We'll need a real hospital. My clinic is going to be overwhelmed soon and the hospital will be better able to separate patients sick with the flu."

I glance around the table. "Does anyone have any ideas on what we can use for a hospital?"

"The old school in the western quadrant could be converted into a hospital," Dorian says.

"We're in the process of reopening a school there," Christine says to him and then meets my eyes. "I'd rather not have to come up with a new building in that section of the city for school."

I nod. "Of course. Any other suggestions?"

A few more ideas are tossed around and all are rejected. We need a building that's stable enough and large enough to hold many people. It needs to be centrally located but not in a heavily populated area.

"There's a warehouse a couple blocks from the city gates, easy to get to, on the main road, but out of the way enough that we can make it a permanent hospital. It's sturdy and well-built. Right now we're using it to house wall supplies, but those can be easily moved."

All eyes turn to Wolfe. This is the first time he's spoken in one of our council meetings. A glow of pride wells up in me as he makes an effort to engage in city planning. So far all I've seen Wolfe care about is security, security and more security. My security, the city security, the wall security, the countryside security. But he rarely engages in other city programs.

Dr. Summers gives him a slight smile and nods toward me. "That'll work perfectly. With your permission I'd like to get to work tomorrow. Get the hospital up and running before we have too many more cases of this flu."

"Yes, we need to get on this right away. I'll have Kingston assign some people to you." My gaze moves to Kingston, who's sitting on the other end of the table. I've started asking him to sit in on council meetings because he often has excellent suggestions and he seems to have his finger on the pulse of the city at all times.

"I'll see to it," he says, his voice deep and steady.

I look around the table. "Is there anything else we need to discuss?"

When no one says anything, I dismiss them. Once everyone leaves, only Wolfe and I are left. He pushes away from the table, his chair scraping heavily against the floor as he lifts his big body. He stretches and rolls his shoulders, cracking them.

"Come, our meal should be ready and I'm hungry."

I smile and gather up the papers in front of me, tucking them away in my folder. I've started having to keep everything organized on paper because it won't stay in my head. There's a lot involved in running a city.

Together, we climb the stairs to the Warlord's chambers. Despite the problems that we've been dealing with over the past few hours, a sense of peace settles over me.

I examine that feeling as we walk side-by-side. Wolfe pushes open the main door to the Warlord's chambers, holding it for me as I walk ahead of him. He places his broad hand on my back as we walk toward the bedchamber, where we'll wash up before we eat.

Home.

It strikes me why I'm so content. I feel like this is... home. Despite the city problems, despite everything, this place feels like a place that I belong.

As he pulls away from me, I watch Wolfe strip off his shirt and bend over the water bowl, scooping it up to scrub over his face and chest. The water drips down his torso, soaking the waistband of his pants, catching on the trail of hair at his groin and sparkling like tiny jewels in the light coming through the window. I watch, completely mesmerized.

Wolfe is my home.

The air is sucked out of the room as I come to this realization and a wave of dizziness hits me. I've known this man for more than seven years, but I didn't *know* him until now.

I was so busy fighting him, myself, and my grief, that I didn't see who he was. I never saw the strength, the integrity and the honesty that makes this man. He thinks of himself as a bad man, a villain, a ravenous wolf. He's not. He's the most unselfish person I know. He gives everything he has to make me happy and comfortable.

He knows me better than I know myself. That's why he left me in Tucson, because he knew that I needed time to grieve, time to stop being angry at the world, time to find my own strength. He did what he knew was best for my well-being, even if I couldn't see his sacrifice at the time.

"Your turn," he tells me as he wipes his face and chest with the towel.

I reach out and tug the towel from his hands. He lets me take it and I toss it aside. I step into him, wrapping my arms around his waist and tilting my face up to look at him.

"I love you, Wolfe."

I feel calm, at peace, completely sure of myself.

He's frozen under my fingertips, but I give him time, knowing that this is what he's wanted for a very long time. Finally, he moves, sliding his hand up to my head and cupping the back of it, holding me to him.

"Be very sure, Skye."

I nod and smile at him, but I don't repeat myself. I'm taking a page out of Wolfe's book. He knows I meant what I said, I don't have to repeat myself.

He swoops down and kisses me, telling me with his body how much he loves me in return.

THIRTY-EIGHT

As I step out of the palace, I look up at the beautiful azure sky with a sigh of contentment. I glance sideways at Kingston. "Pretty fucking awesome, isn't it?"

"What's that?" he asks with a scowl, squinting maliciously at the sky. Kingston isn't a morning person any more than I am. The only reason I'm even half-way cordial this particular morning is because I'm in love.

"Everything," I say brightly, handing my teacup to the nearest guard. I'm surrounded by five of them, they may as well be useful since there're no threats in sight.

As much as I want to balk at the added security Wolfe has placed on me, he's made sure that my work won't be hindered by the presence of his security. They do as I order without question, only checking in with Wolfe once they've seen me settled in my destination.

Though I'm no longer allowed outside the city walls, I make sure that there's a solid protection detail for Dolly and Anita at the water refinery plant. The plant itself is far more vulnerable than anything within the city walls and I want to be sure the Outsiders don't get an opportunity to snatch the two women or cause damage to the equipment.

Wolfe and I have fallen into an easy partnership. In my wildest imagination, I would never have expected this. Not my place in the city, nor Wolfe's, nor our relationship with each other. Yet, it feels right. Almost perfect.

There's only one thing holding me back from truly embracing the things that Wolfe is pushing me toward. Claiming the position of Warlord. Becoming Wolfe's wife.

The fact that my husband still lives. It's this that has directed my steps toward Dr. Summers's lab on a bright summer morning. I need to confront and accept my past so I can move on with my future. The doctor greets me brightly as I enter her lab.

I wave and say, "I hope I'm not interrupting."

"Not at all," she says without looking up from her position in front of a microscope, a plethora of notes spread out on the table in front of her.

I walk slowly toward the zombie prison, my eyes searching for Silas. Once more, he's huddled in the corner, his dirty long hair obscuring his face. I knock on the glass, drawing the attention of the two inside. The third is strapped to a table nearby, her gaze now also on me. As she strains to get up and attack, the two imprisoned Primitives lurch toward me, screaming and hitting the glass. I move to stand in front of the man.... the Primitive.... who used to be my husband. As I look into Silas's eyes, I can positively say that I see nothing of the man I once knew in the dead gaze staring back at me.

"Is he usually like this?" I turn to direct my question to Dr. Summers.

"Like what?" she asks absently, not looking at me.

I look at Silas again, his stringy hair plastered to his face, head and neck. His lips pulled back in a feral grin. His skin sallow and dark with bruising. He's been punctured in several places on his body, bits of metal shoved through the openings. His missing nose is an awful sight. I'm not sure if he's done this to himself or if other Primitives did this to him, but the effect is gruesome and sickening.

He stands in front of me, listless but alert, as though he'll attack anyone who goes in. I forget my original question, instead asking, "Don't they get infections from stabbing themselves with dirty, rusted objects?"

Dr. Summers finally looks up from her workstation. "*Necrotitis Primeval* deadens the skin, a little like leprosy. Yet somehow it doesn't rot and fall off. It's a horrific disease, one that defies medicine as we knew it at the beginning of the 21st century, and we haven't come much farther since then." She comes to stand next to me, her professionally cool gaze on our former Warlord. "For some reason, the virus mostly freezes us humans in the exact growth phase of our lives when we were bitten. Zombies don't seem to grow older, but we don't have a lot of empirical evidence either way, since studying them is incredibly difficult."

I didn't know that, but I suppose it makes sense. Even the mythology of zombie-ism agrees, zombies are dead reanimated people.

"Come with me," Dr. Summers murmurs, waving me over to a steel table where the female zombie is strapped down.

I approach cautiously, looking down. Now that I'm closer to her, I can see that she's young. Quite young. Probably not even out of her teens when she was turned. Empathy rises up, though I try to push it down. She's here for experimental purposes, nothing more. I can't see her as having been human once.

Dr. Summers takes the stethoscope from around her neck and with a questioning look places the earpieces in my ears when I give her a nod. She takes the other end of the stethoscope and places it against the Primitive's chest.

At first, I hear nothing. I look at the doctor questioningly, thinking that she's showing me that zombies have no heartbeat. I wouldn't be surprised by this. But then, I hear it. A single heartbeat. I hold my breath, believing that I misheard, my brows furrowing as I wait. Then it comes again, one more heartbeat. My eyes lift to Dr. Summers's and she nods. She pulls the earpieces from my head.

"We've always believed that zombies don't age, that they remain frozen from the moment they're bitten. But now, I don't think that's true anymore. I think they do age, just incredibly slowly. As though the virus slows their metabolism down, almost to a halt. Yet they're somehow still able to function."

"But then, how are they able to move so quickly?"

"Pure adrenaline," she says, her crystal blue gaze on the female laid out before us. The Primitive's clothes are in tatters, hanging off her emaciated frame. Her bones are visible through a thin layer of skin. Unlike Silas, she's been punctured all over, including her arms and legs. "The constant adrenaline rushes as they hunt shortens their lives significantly. So even though growth and aging slow down, the effect the virus has on the human body is devastating. I believe it's why your friend's organs shut down after she was turned human again."

I try to wrap my head around everything the doctor is saying, but it's so fantastic, so out of the realm of everything I know, it's hard to imagine. Zombies are living creatures. It's easier to think of them as completely dead. That way when I kill them, slide my blade into them and put a bullet in their heads, I'm just making sure the dead stay dead.

I turn my gaze to Silas, helpless as the memories of who he was flood through me. Silas, the quietly confident man who gradually won me over. He took the love I eventually felt for him, delicately wrapped it up, and cradled it close to his own heart. Despite many of the things he did wrong both in the city and with the women of the harem, I can't hate him.

"What about him?" I ask, drifting back to touch the glass over his face. "Have you studied him yet?"

"Not much," Dr. Summers admits from behind me. "I don't want to do anything too invasive with him. If there's one that we're going to try to save, it'll be him, which means I can't harm him as I experiment."

A shudder ripples through me as I realize what she's saying. She will have to harm the others in order to get the answers she needs. I don't know why this bothers me, considering I've spent so much time killing them. But those kills, they were self-preservation. I was being attacked. This is different. Strapping them down, cutting them open, experimenting on them. It feels wrong.

Yet, I know that we need a cure. Or as close to a cure as we can get. Until that happens, humanity will never be safe. These few will have to be sacrificed in order to help create a new world.

Hand still on the glass, eyes locked with Silas's dead gaze, I say, "He's not my husband anymore. He's no longer the Warlord." I turn to Dr. Summers, giving her a level look. "Do what you have to do to get the answers you need."

She absorbs my words and then nods, her eyes dropping to the ground. I can tell her in the brief rounding of her shoulders, the heavy air about her, that she is not as unaffected by all this as she seems.

I reach out and wrap my hand around her arm, holding her for a second. "You can do this. You've already blown my expectations away. You will go down in history as the woman who cured *Necrotitis Primeval*."

I deliberately use the word 'woman' to emphasize her astounding accomplishment. In a world run by violent men, without the proper technologies, she has somehow managed to rise up to confront a virus that has crippled our entire planet.

Her shoulders stiffen and she raises her chin, giving me a sharp nod and stepping away, breaking my grip on her arm. "I'll do whatever it takes."

I glance at Silas, biting my lip. I don't regret the decision I've made, but knowing that when I walk away from the lab it might be the last time I see him is a hard pill to swallow. "Can I... can I touch him?"

I shake my head at myself. I'm as good as the Warlord and here I'm asking for permission. Dr. Summers opens her mouth, probably to deny my request, so I repeat myself, rewording the phrase. "I want to see him." I turn to Kingston and Denny, who entered the lab with me and are now standing by the door watching our exchange. "I need you two to secure him please."

No one denies me, no one tries to stop me. They put the female zombie back inside the glass cage before attempting to lure Silas to the door so he can be recaptured and strapped down for my inspection.

When they finally wrestle him into a chair, we quickly strap his arms and legs, then pull back his head up with another leather strap. Dr. Summers insists on covering his mouth with a leather mask, so his bite is rendered ineffectual if he manages to get teeth on any of us.

"Please leave." I give the command without looking. I only have eyes for Silas in this moment.

"Skye..." Dr. Summers begins to argue.

I shake my head. "Please go. I won't be long and then he's all yours."

I hear them shuffle out, though I don't turn around to watch. I know my time is limited; one of the guards will be radioing Wolfe about this. Once the door closes behind them, I reach out to take Silas's hand. His fingers immediately curve into sharp broken claws as he attempts to dig his nails into my flesh. I readjust my hold, determined to keep touching him. Even though zombie Silas wants me dead, I still want him to feel the comfort of my touch.

"A lot has happened since I last saw you." Tears immediately fill my eyes, though I try to dash them away. "I fled the city like you wanted me to. I went with Wolfe and a bunch of other survivors to the Tucson Sanctuary where we were set up on the outskirts of the city. Except we were followed to the Sanctuary and had to endure constant attacks. It was awful."

I know he can't hear me. Not really. But I imagine that my voice is calming him. His unblinking gaze remains on my face and I hope that some small part of what I'm saying is getting through.

"I saw my sister there. She has a baby now and seems happy with her husband. Hannah is doing well too. Do you remember Hannah?" I shake my head at myself. "Stupid," I mutter. If even a small part of his brain has been preserved then he'll remember Hannah, his longest held and most caring wife. The rest of him, the zombie parts, know nothing of any of us. "Hannah has been helping to create educational programs for the children living in the city. You would be proud of her. She's still our sweet Hannah, but she's grown quite a backbone. One made out of solid steel."

Death and destruction will do that to a person. I'm a much tougher woman than I used to be. A warrior now. I don't tell him this though. If any part of him understands what I'm saying, I don't need him knowing how many zombies I've killed in the past year. His Primitive side might take offence.

"I'm with Wolfe now." I force the words out through a tight throat. I swipe at the tears dripping down my face. "I love you Silas, a part of me will always love you. My heart shattered when I was forced to leave you behind. I would have given anything to die at your side. But it's time for me to move on. This past year has taught me just how short our lives are, and I need to take advantage of the years I have left. Try to be happy. You know what I mean?"

Of course he doesn't know what I mean. I'm not going to get anything from him, so I decide to finish this. Sever the connection still holding us together and step into the future with my new love.

"Please don't hate me," I whisper, closing my eyes and allowing grief to settle over me. I just need a few minutes to allow the memories free rein, then I'll pull myself together and walk away, leaving him to the experiments.

"What the fuck are you doing?"

The roar comes from behind me, startling me. I twist around on my knees to find Wolfe stalking toward me, his face twisted in rage, his muscles bunched, his fists ready.

I know he's not coming for me, so I leap to my feet and throw myself across Silas, knowing if I don't calm Wolfe down, he'll kill my former husband. He can't do that; we need Silas too much.

"Wolfe, stop!"

I've never seen him like this, blinded by rage. He's a killer, yes, but he's always in control. This is different. This is personal.

He blindly shoves me out of the way and I topple to the side. I immediately twist around to look as he sends his fist flying into Silas's face. Silas's chair flies backward, shattering against the bench. Silas falls to the floor in a limp heap, unmoving.

"What have you done?" I shout, hurling myself at Silas.

"Don't touch him!"

Just as I reach out to touch Silas, he lunges from the floor and leaps on top of me, his unnaturally strong hands gripping my limbs as his face descends to mine. His sharp teeth pierce the mask and dig into the delicate skin at my neck.

THIRTY-NINE

The mask saves me from having my throat torn out by my zombie husband. For one frozen second we stare into each other's eyes, my grey ones sad, his red streaked brown ones crazed. There's no trace of the Silas I knew in the face above mine.

Then our moment is over. Silas is torn from my prone body and thrown across the lab. I flinch as I hear his body take out several tables. Glass smashes to the floor.

I roll onto my side to check the damage and to see if Silas is still alive, but Wolfe is on top of me, kneeling over me, his hands everywhere as he checks for injury. His expression is thunderous, nearly as out of control as when he first entered the lab.

"Wolfe..." I try to appeal to him, but he slaps my hand away and surges to his feet, turning back toward Silas.

I climb stiffly to my feet as well, holding onto the table for support. I look around frantically and see Silas is still lying in a heap on the opposite side of the lab, Wolfe rapidly closing the distance between them, his hand on the hilt of his gun.

"Wolfe!" I scream.

He doesn't flinch and he doesn't stop. He pulls his gun out of the holster at his hip and holds it on Silas as he approaches.

I hurl myself across the lab as fast as I can possibly move and fling myself in between them before Wolfe can pull the trigger. I see his finger twitch on the weapon, but he pulls back as soon as he realizes who he'll hit.

"Get out of my way," he snarls.

I can sense movement behind me and realize that Silas is still alive and attempting to get up. Dammit, I don't want to keep my back turned to a zombie, but I have to stop Wolfe.

"No," I say sharply. "Your reason for killing him is wrong."

"He's already dead." Wolfe reaches out, grips my arm and drags me out of the way.

Relief surges through me for a split second now that I no longer have my back to a zombie. But a new fear arises, the one that I can't stop Wolfe no matter what I say or do. I have to try though, for the sake of everything we're trying to accomplish in this lab. For Silas's sake. For the sake of my budding relationship. Silas doesn't deserve to be put down by his former second-in-command, the new Warlord of the Sanctuary that Silas gave so much of his life to.

I clutch Wolfe's arm, digging my nails into his skin in an attempt to draw his attention. He doesn't shift focus for even a second though.

"Wolfe, if you kill him now it'll be revenge. This is not a mercy killing. This is not because he hurt me. This is purely because you want my husband out of the way." I soften my voice and my grip on his arm. "Please, don't kill him. This isn't you. You don't kill innocents and you don't kill without reason."

Finally, he drops his gaze to me, his face smoothing into an expressionless mask. "If you think that, then you don't know me."

Anger surges through my body at his words. This is the first time Wolfe has ever lied to me and it makes me unreasonably furious. I yank my hand away from his arm.

"That's a lie. If you killed without reason, then that man who attacked you on the wall would be dead. I would be dead. Instead of teaching me how to fight you would've left me to the zombies. You've saved countless people, all of them innocent. So don't you stand there and tell me that you're a badass merciless killer with no sense of remorse or regret." I point at zombie Silas who has now lurched to his knees and is attempting to regain his footing. We need to end this conversation quickly before he becomes dangerous again. "If you murder Silas now, you will regret it. I'll make sure of it."

Wolfe stares at me, never looking away for a single second as Silas finally regains his footing and starts looking around, his crazed eyes searching for the prey he'd lost sight of. To Wolfe's credit, he doesn't seem even remotely concerned that there's a zombie alive and well only a few feet away from us.

"He's no innocent," Wolfe says, his voice hard, his expression disappointed as he looks at me. I've put that look there, but I don't understand why. Or what I've done.

Without looking, Wolfe reaches out and takes hold of Silas zombie by the back of the neck.

"No!" I shout, thinking that he intends to finish Silas.

I'm wrong though. Wolfe drags the struggling Primitive over to the glass walled cage, opens the door and throws him in. He slams the door shut and locks it. For a minute all three zombies go wild, screaming, banging, attacking each other and themselves.

I look away, unable to watch as Silas beats the smaller female zombie who is curled in a ball on the floor.

Wolfe stalks back over to me, grips me by the neck and drags me up onto my toes, his gaze boring into mine. "Even before he was turned, Silas was never innocent."

I don't have time to argue as Wolfe grips my arm so hard I think it might bruise and drags me from the lab. He doesn't stop to speak to Dr. Summers or her assistant as we move rapidly toward his vehicle. He shoves me inside and then goes around to his side. It speaks to how angry he is that he doesn't insist I buckle my seatbelt or do it for me.

We make it back to the palace in record time due to the insane speed Wolfe insists on driving. He drags me up flight after flight of stairs, uncaring that I can barely keep up. I'm in damn good shape, but this man, when angered, can probably climb mountains without losing his breath.

When we reach the Warlord's chambers, he continues without stopping until we reach the bedchamber. Over the past few weeks all of my stuff from the harem has been moved in and the space is much less austere. My patchwork quilt, made by Hannah four years ago, is spread out on the bed. A tiny glass bird my sister gave me is sitting on the table next to the wash bowl. Wolfe doesn't seem to mind the feminine touches, if he even notices.

Finally, he drops my arm and steps away from me. But when he turns to look at me, I take a step back, fearing for myself even more than when Silas jumped on me and buried his teeth in my neck.

"What the fuck you were doing in the lab?" he demands.

My gaze drops to his fists, both clenched and shaking in

anger. He wants to punch something, and I hope to god it's not me. One punch to the head with those massive fists and I could easily be finished.

Still, I straighten my spine and speak with dignity. "I was saying goodbye to the man who used to be my husband, before he probably dies under experimentation. Now you tell me, what the fuck were you doing in the lab? We went to a lot of effort to bring those live zombies in and you damn near killed one."

Fury flashes across his face and I take another quick step back. Perhaps I should moderate my tone, but I've never been one to back down from a fight, and Wolfe declared war in that lab.

"Don't pretend that you care about Primitives all of a sudden," he growls. "You wanted to see your husband."

"He's not my husband anymore!" I yell furiously.

He points at me and shouts, "*Exactly!*"

The room shatters with the force of his shout and a ripple of fear goes down my spine.

"Then what's your problem?" I yell back at him. "We both agree, he's not my husband anymore!"

Wolfe lunges at me before I have time to step away, grips me by the back of the head and drags me into his body. I'm forced to go up on my toes or risk being strangled by his hold. I reach up and grab him by his thick leather vest and cling, like a desert shrub shaking against a boulder. I may be a warrior to be reckoned with, but without weapons, against a man the size and skill of Wolfe, I don't stand a chance.

"You belong to me." The words are said with such conviction that there can be no doubt.

"I know!" I bare my teeth at him, showing my own anger, as ineffectual as it might be.

"You've always belonged to me." His eye is a laser

focused on my face. As everything else fades, we're left with each other, our emotions, our perfectly fucked up love.

"Then why didn't you claim me a long time ago?" I allow him to hear the hurt in my voice as I speak the words I never dared to say when I didn't want him to know how badly he'd hurt me when he left. I try not to allow the tears to come, but I know that a sheen now covers my eyes. "All those years ago when I was brought to the Sanctuary, you acted like you hated me. Like I was a nuisance. You treated me like a problem instead of someone you might actually care about. And then, a year ago, you let me go. Instead of claiming me as you say you want to do, you let me go."

Hurt colours every word coming out of my mouth and I can see the effect of them reflected on his face as his own hurt rises. Then he does something unexpected, something I never thought to hear from him. He admits he was wrong.

"I should have," he says quietly, his grip becoming less painful.

"Should have what?" I ask, confused.

"Should have claimed you when that Outsider brought you here to sell. I should've put a bullet in his head and immediately claimed you. Should've overthrown the Warlord, taken the city and reigned over its inhabitants with you as my queen."

My heart hammers in my chest as I remember those moments all those years ago when I was first brought to Sanctuary, the tension in his body, the look in his eyes. I didn't recognize it then, couldn't possibly have known what he was thinking. But now... now I realize, I changed the entire course of his future when I'd been brought into Sanctuary.

"Why didn't you?" I whisper.

He answers right away, surprising me again. "Because

you weren't ready for me and I sure as fuck wasn't ready for you."

Before I can question him further his lips crash down over mine, sealing our moment of truth in a kiss. He holds himself that way, his lips pressed to mine, not taking it further but simply allowing the moment to unfold.

It's not until I try to pull away, try to take a breath that he finally snaps and devours me. His lips take mine in a harsh, all-consuming kiss. His teeth sink into my lip, tugging until I open my mouth then his tongue thrusts inside, conquering the territory within.

His hands are everywhere, and before I know it my leather jacket, my shirt and my pants lay in a pool on the floor. He lifts me naked against his own leather clad body and strides with me to the bed where we fall together.

I reach for him, burying my hands in the tangles of his hair and dragging his head down to mine, anchoring myself to him as I kiss him back, showing him with my actions instead of my words how much he has always meant to me. I pour the turbulence of our relationship into every second of that kiss as he reaches between our bodies and unlaces his pants.

I lift my hips and in one smooth move he surges inside. I fling my head back and gasp as I'm stretched to the hilt. He wraps an arm underneath my neck and holds me against his body as tight as he possibly can as he thrusts savagely against me, slamming his hips into mine over and over.

Our coupling is both erotic and painful. I'm going to have bruises to show for this, but it's worth it. With each thrust I fly higher and higher, dizzy from lack of breath, exhilarated from the things he's told me. This is much more than sex, it's the intertwining of our souls in a passionate, angry, loving explosion of ecstasy.

As I fly off the cliff into the arms of my orgasm, he follows directly behind, his hips slamming into me one last time as he buries himself as deep as he'll go, touching my womb and shooting his seed inside me. As his warmth bathes me, I close my eyes and inhale his wildly masculine scent, a feeling of well-being settling over me as I drift in contentment.

FORTY

"You look exhausted. Is there anything I can do to help?"

I'm standing next to Dr. Summers at the entrance of the new hospital. Within a week we've managed to get it up and running, but we've barely had time to breathe as new patients swamp the hospital.

She shakes her head, puts her hand on my arm and pulls me back outside into the fresh air and sunshine. My escort of soldiers is standing with us. Dr. Summers unhooks her mask from her ear and pulls it down, taking a deep breath and closing her eyes.

I remain silent, giving her the time she needs to recover.

She opens her eyes and looks at me. I'm worried about the dullness of her gaze, the lines of tiredness in her face that weren't there before, and the slight slump to her shoulders. She is overwhelmed by the illness gripping our city, but she's our first and best line of defense so I have to keep asking more from her, even though I desperately want to send her home to sleep.

"There are over fifty patients in this hospital. I lost two today and one yesterday. We've lost a total of 16 people since the flu started. This thing isn't slowing down." She stretches her arms over her head and then back, rolling her shoulders as she eases the tension in her body. "Most are either very young or very old, but even healthy adults are getting hit hard by this."

I pause for a moment, gathering my thoughts. I need to make sure that I'm asking the right questions, giving the doctor what she needs to make the best possible choices in this grim situation.

"Do you think this is the same flu that ripped through the sanctuaries 15 years ago?"

She nods her head. "I think so, though I don't know for sure. I was still learning medicine back then and wouldn't know how to recognize different viruses under a microscope."

"Fair enough," I answer. I step to the side, pulling the doctor with me as a family arrives at the hospital and goes through the entrance, one of them looking gravely ill. "It has all the hallmarks of the flu that took out the Las Vegas Sanctuary while I was living there is a teenager."

She nods but doesn't say anything. Either she's too tired or there's nothing left to say. The origins of this flu are important, but we might never understand where it came from. Our resources are best concentrated on mitigating the damage.

"I want you to be completely honest with me," I tell her, giving her a stern look to emphasize my comment. "Would you say things are getting dire in our Sanctuary?"

Without giving it thought she nods her head. "I was lucky enough to be living on the east coast during the last flu epidemic. We didn't get it as bad as you did out here in the west, but I can tell you from my knowledge of infectious diseases that this is going downhill quickly."

Though the news is grim, this is what I needed to hear. "Tell me what we need to do."

Her gaze meets mine for an intense moment and then she looks away, staring out at the city. "You won't like it."

"Let me decide that. I need all of the information so I can make the best decisions for the Sanctuary that I can. You're the expert, I'll do what I can to abide by any advice you give me."

Her eyes fill with tears and she nods, swallowing visibly before answering. "I needed to hear that," she whispers. "I need to know that the future leader of this Sanctuary has its citizens best interests at heart. I'll tell you what needs to happen, and you can decide what you'll do."

"Go ahead," I tell her.

She looks at me, her gaze serious. "You need to post a citywide order telling everyone to stay home, then impose a curfew. The only ones that are exempt are people who have permission directly from the Warlord. You'll need to come up with a system for your citizens to let you know when they need supplies. Have your security forces drop the supplies off and leave. No contact between households. Anyone who's sick must be immediately isolated. And finally, no one in and out of the city."

My mouth goes dry as she speaks and I nearly shake my head automatically. What she's proposing goes counter to everything I believe in. This country, this continent and this world have fallen. There are a select few of us who survived the apocalypse. It's our duty, our right to fight for our freedom, our right to survive as a species. If I enact the changes that she's proposing, I'll be taking away those freedoms.

But freedom means nothing if we're all dead.

After several moments of thought, I say, "I'll make sure it gets done."

"Thank you," she tells me, her sincere gratitude clear in those two words. She pulls her mask back over her face and turns to go back into the hospital.

I stop her. "Have you managed to make any progress at the lab?"

She glances back at me and gives a slight nod. "I've been going to the lab in the evenings, and my assistant works during the day when I have to be at the hospital. For obvious reasons our progress has slowed, but we're getting there." A kernel of hope has entered her voice and my heart leaps in response. "I think we'll have a treatment soon, Skye."

I twist my lips in a smile, thank her and wave her back into the hospital. I turn back to my escort, glancing at Kingston in particular. He has become my righthand man, my second-in-command. Some days I wonder what I ever did without him.

"What's next on my agenda?" I ask him, half joking. It drives him nuts when I treat him like a secretary, yet we both know how indispensable he's become to me.

He ignores my teasing and looks down at me, his dark eyes serious. "I think we should go back to the palace."

I shake my head at him. "We have more stops planned. Hannah is going to meet me at the new school for an inspection and then I'm going to go to the wall to see if Wolfe needs anything."

"I think we need to go back to the palace," he insists.

I frown. "Why?"

His gaze is steady on mine, but I can feel the tension in the air. Finally, he says, "No more hospital visits."

It finally dawns on me what he's so upset about. He doesn't want me near the flu-stricken hospital or out in the city where I can meet citizens who might be sick. I appreciate his protectiveness, but I can't stop doing my job. The city needs me, and I must make myself available.

I reach out to touch his arm. "I understand your concern and I promise to be very careful. I'll even wear a mask when we come to the hospital, but I have to go where I'm needed."

He shakes his head. "No, you don't."

Now I'm starting to get annoyed. This man works for me, not the other way around. "It doesn't matter what you think, we will continue with my agenda for the day."

He looks at me with a straight face and I can see the hesitation in his eyes. "I'm afraid I'm going to have to disagree. Your safety is more important than your desire to tour the city. You are going back to the palace immediately, Skye."

I open my mouth to argue with him, but he takes my arm in a tight grip and pulls me toward the vehicle. His men falling in around us. I frown at them. This is a coordinated plan, and I know exactly who's to blame.

Wolfe.

We get into the lead vehicle, Kingston sliding into the driver's seat while I take the passenger seat. The rest of our escort get into the vehicle behind us. "Tell me, Kingston, were you given permission to defy my orders?"

At first, he doesn't answer so I add, "It's in your best interests to tell me now what the standing order is so I take out my anger out on the correct person."

He seems to see the wisdom in my words. "Warlord Wolfe has made it very clear that your health must come above anything else, including your direct orders."

"And whose decision was it that I should be removed from my duties when the illness in the city became critical?" I demand, my voice rising in annoyance.

"The Warlord and I have agreed that if you become at-risk for catching an illness, you are to be returned to the palace immediately."

"When I become Warlord..." I start to say and then stop myself. I haven't agreed to become Warlord, yet here I am, acting as though it's inevitable.

We remain silent for the rest of the trip to the palace. As Kingston drives into the underground garage, he finally murmurs, "He cares about you. More than he'll ever say. If anything were to happen to you..."

He trails off, but he's said enough. Those few sentences have diffused my anger. Wolfe loves me more than logic or reason and this is why he's trumped my orders when it comes to my health and safety. I don't agree with him, but I understand him. Finally, I understand Wolfe.

"Thank you, Kingston," I say calmly, letting myself out of the vehicle. "I'll see myself up to the Warlord's chambers. Please let Wolfe know where to find me."

It's a mark of our mutual respect and how far we've come as a team that he nods and turns away, striding from the garage to find his Warlord. He trusts me enough not to escort me and I care about him too much to break my word to him. I stride over to the stairwell and start the climb up 30 stories to the top.

FORTY-ONE
WOLFE

"Warlord, Miss Skye is waiting for you in your chambers."

Kingston bows his head toward me as I pass him in the hall. I grunt my acknowledgement and continue on my way, but his voice stops me.

"Sir... I'm not sure it's my place to say anything..." He hesitates, his tone uncomfortable.

I raise a brow and turn to look at him. It's not like Kingston to be so tentative. He's one of our top warriors and I've been pleased by his service to my woman. Whatever he's trying to say must be about Skye. She's about the only person that can disconcert a man like Kingston.

"Either spit it out or let me get on with it. I'm tired, dirty and eager to see my woman."

He clears his throat and says, "I am completely loyal to Skye. She's a good person, in her heart and in her actions. As such, I will be her devoted servant until she no longer needs my service."

I listen to his words and nod. "I'm pleased to hear it." Though I have to fight a bolt of jealousy telling me now would be a good time to find out what his intestines look like.

Both Skye and I have been so busy lately that she ends up spending more time with her personal bodyguard then she does with me, her husband. Well, her soon-to-be husband. Though I know that there's nothing to be jealous of, I still dislike that this man gets to do for her on a daily basis everything that I want to do.

"Is there more?" I demand.

He stares at me hard, clearly indecisive. I would be amused if I didn't badly want to leave his presence for the much more pleasant company of another.

He nods his head sharply as though coming to a decision. "She's in a bad mood. You should probably watch out."

I try to think of what I might've done to her since I saw her last, which was this morning in our bedchamber as we each got ready for the day. I can think of nothing that might've pissed her off.

"I've navigated her moods in the past, I think I'll be fine." I turn to walk away.

"I told her she has to stay in the palace," he rushes to stay. "The illness in the city has grown rampant, the doctor is concerned. She's recommending a citywide lockdown."

Now I understand what Kingston is trying to tell me. "Thank you for the warning."

"Yes sir, I wouldn't let my worst enemy walk in on her blind when she's..." He lets his words trail off as he realizes he might be overstepping.

I smother a chuckle. He's right, it would be downright cruel to let anyone walk in on Skye after she's been told that she must abide by rules she didn't set herself. I was the one to tell Kingston that everything Skye demands goes, except when it affects her health.

"I appreciate the warning," I tell him, then turn and walk away.

With Kingston's words in mind, I open the door to the Warlord's chamber a little more cautiously than I normally would. I don't necessarily fear Skye, but I prefer not to get stabbed, shot, or bashed in the head with something heavy before I get a chance to talk to her.

My hesitation is unwarranted though, as she's not lying in wait with a plethora of weapons to sharpen on my hide. I find her standing next to the open bedroom window, gazing out across the city. She's deep in thought and I realize that she hasn't heard me come in.

"Skye." I call her name and she turns her head to look at me.

Light from the early evening sun sets fire to her hair, the waves falling across her shoulders in a multitude of colours.

"You're home." Her simple words root me to the spot.

This is the first time she has referred to her place at my side as home. The moment is significant and lost on neither of us. She's trying to tell me something, though I'm not sure exactly what.

She walks toward me, away from the window. I realize she's wearing nothing more than a robe draped over her shoulders and crisscrossed in front, giving brief glimpses of her nude body as she walks. As she approaches me, she allows the robe to slide slowly down her shoulders, catching at her elbows then falling to her wrists, revealing her breasts. For a couple of breathtaking seconds, she holds it closed over her stomach before allowing it to drop completely.

Skye is stunning no matter what she's wearing, but nude is when she truly shines. Every curve of her body is shaped to perfection, as though built for the touch of my hands and the worship of my lips. She is muscle and sinew, womanly curves and graceful movements. She is mine.

Before I can reach for her, her walk turns into a run and she leaps at me, jumping up into my arms and swinging her legs around to grip my hips. I drop my hands to catch her so that she doesn't fall and hurt herself.

Before I can say anything, she loops her arms around my neck and drags my face down to hers, thrusting her tongue aggressively into my mouth. Every thought in my head flees as that perfect small tongue darts in and out in a devil's dance. Skye is attempting to seduce me, and I am her willing victim.

I clutch her tightly, pressing her curves against my body and sliding her bare pussy over the rapidly growing bulge in my leather pants. I hold her up, kissing her back with the voracious appetite of a man gone too long without his favourite treat.

I swing her around and push her against the wall, slamming my hand into the concrete behind her back to make sure that she's protected from the roughness. She gasps into my mouth and I take the opportunity to thrust my tongue deep into hers, sweeping her mouth with as much if not more aggression than she'd shown me. She clings to me tightly as I treat her to the tempest that constantly swirls within.

Finally, she breaks the kiss and tips her head back against the wall. I drop my lips to her neck, devouring her sweetness as she attempts to catch her breath.

"Wolfe," she says breathlessly. "We need to talk."

Ah, now we can get to the root of this seduction.

"Should've talked before you jumped on me and rubbed that naked little pussy all over my crotch." I drop my hand to her ass and squeeze hard until she's squirming against me, then I slide my fingers down her crack and let them linger against her pussy, now dripping wet and soaking my hand.

"I need you to let up on the security. I can't do my job if I have a dozen men trailing me everywhere."

I give her ass another hard squeeze and then bring my hand back around to the front to loosen the ties on my pants. She squirms, pressing her wet little pussy against my knuckles, trying to make herself come as she tries to negotiate her security detail. Cute, but ineffectual. I take my hand away and she groans in disappointment.

"Is that all?" I demand, pulling my cock from my pants. She immediately tightens her legs around my hips and attempts to push my cock towards her entrance. I hold back.

"You can't keep me locked up in the palace. You told me to get the city in order and I'm doing it. I can't do it if I can't go out into the city."

Her voice is surprisingly steady considering how needy her body is. She's thrusting her hips against me and yanking at my hair so hard it feels like she's pulling it out by the roots.

"Find a way," I tell her. "We aren't negotiating your safety."

She growls at me, uses the strength in her arms and legs to drag herself up my body and poise herself above my throbbing cock. I'm impressed by her athleticism. I drop my hands to her hips and hold her still, not allowing her to sink down.

"Do *you* intend to remain locked up in the palace?" she demands. "Because you're just as important to the city as I am. Your life must also be preserved. If this flu is so threatening that I must remain in isolation, then so must you."

Though her body is begging for mine, her words are serious, and her stormy grey eyes are hard with purpose.

"You're too precious to risk," I tell her. "My life is a shield for yours. The city isn't strong enough yet to hold under attack. I will not rest until every defense is in place to protect you."

Her eyes soften and she nods. "I thought so. I feel the same, Wolfe. I won't rest until there's fresh water for you to drink, education for our children, food in our bellies, and a safe place to recover if we become ill. You must allow me to continue my work, for the sake of our family."

I stare at her, watching her features, reading her. She means every word. This place is our home. I am her home. Together we are creating a home for the people we care about, including our future children.

I nod and give her what she's been waiting to hear. "You may continue work if you take every possible precaution. You do not go where there's known illness, you'll wear a mask, and you will report often."

"And my security detail?" she pushes.

I graze my thumb across her cheek, marveling at the softness of her skin. "Your security detail remains as is."

She sighs and wiggles against me. "Good enough."

She drags my head down to hers and kisses me, her tongue lingering against the seam of my lips before thrusting inside, meeting mine aggressively in a dance that sends a shower of sparks down my spine to settle heavily in my groin.

I drag her body down onto my cock, savouring the incredibly tight squeeze of her pussy as it takes everything I have to give, inch by inch. We cling to each other, Skye pressed against the wall as I thrust my hips up, fucking the only woman I've cared about, the last pussy I'll ever touch.

She can do little more than cling to me and take my aggressive thrusts as I slam into her over and over. Sweat drips off my forehead and lands in a droplet on her lips. Her tongue darts out to catch the salty wetness and her head tips back against the wall, her eyes closing and her face twisting into an expression of ecstasy, as though she has tasted the nectar of the gods.

This woman is my everything, my equal, my superior. I will stop at nothing to keep her.

She squirms on top of me and digs her nails into my shoulder. I can tell that she's reaching for the height of her orgasm and I pound into her even harder, squeezing the flesh of her rounded ass hard under my fingertips. There'll be marks, but she loves it.

She lets out a scream and her pussy clasps me so tight that it feels as though she'll break me in two. I have no choice but to follow her into the chaos of my own orgasm. I grit my teeth as my balls grow tight and a rush of pleasure slams through me. Hot semen gushes into her, easing my brutal thrusts.

Before I can collapse under the weight of the lethargic pleasure rushing over me, I stumble to the bed, setting her down and then dropping beside her. I fling a heavy arm across her belly, making sure that she can't go anywhere.

"You used sex as a weapon," I grunt.

She rolls against me and grips my hair in her fist, yanking my head back until I'm looking at her. She drops a kiss against my lips and touches my beard. "I'll use anything as a weapon, so long as I get my own way."

I roll on top of her and pin her to the bed, dragging her arms over her head and holding her wrists with one hand. With the other I reach down and pinch her nipple hard enough to make her cry out and squirm against me.

"I think I like this whole sex as a weapon thing."

She lets out a laugh, both ringing and sweet. "You would."

I smother any more words in a kiss.

FORTY-TWO

SKYE

The first thing I see when I wake up is a naked cock. I blink and then squint at it. Yup, there is a big, fat, veined, semi-hard cock inches from my face. I'd like to enjoy the view, but I decide I better make sure that it's actually attached to the man I'm supposed to be in bed with.

My eyes travel up his flat stomach, tracing the trail of hair and the chiseled muscles of his abdomen. I've only ever seen one man with a stomach like that. Thank goodness, the cock and the stomach belong to the same man, the man I slept with last night. I roll onto my back and blink up at him, a sleepy smile hovering around my lips.

He looks serious, but he always looks serious so I don't take it personally. I reach out to touch him and he takes my hand in his, wrapping his big hand around mine until he's enveloped it completely. Then he does something completely unexpected; he sinks to his knees next to the bed.

I roll onto my side, frowning at him. I reach out with my other hand to touch his face, lightly running my fingers over his eyepatch before smoothing the wrinkles from between his brows. I want to smooth the seriousness away. This bedroom, filled with light, sitting on top of our tower, is our sanctuary. Our sanctuary away from Sanctuary. This is where we come to be us, to be together. Seriousness and frowns have no place here.

I open my mouth to ask him what's the matter, but he speaks first.

"Marry me."

His words are simple. So simple that it takes a moment for them to sink in. I'm shocked and I scramble to sit up, staring at his face. Still completely serious.

I stare at him, my heart pounding, my head spinning. I don't know why I'm having such a visceral reaction to his words. I don't know if I'm scared or exhilarated. He's told me before that we'll be married, that I didn't have a choice. But this feels different.

Marry Wolfe. It seems like a dream but maybe a nightmare at the same time. He's so brutal, harsh, and often selfish in his care of others. Except with me. Then he's so unselfish that it almost hurts, because I know that I don't deserve that kind of devotion.

He doesn't repeat himself. He never repeats himself. He knows I heard him and he waits for an answer.

There's only one answer I can give him. "Yes."

Without another word, he stands and walks to his pile of clothes on the chest at the end of the bed. He bends to get dressed as though we didn't just have one of the most intense moments of both of our lives.

I don't know what to say. Should I ask him when the wedding will be? Ask him how many guests to invite, or what kind of feast we should prepare? I want to tell him that I'd like my sister to attend, but his movements are so mechanical and economical, as though nothing has happened, that I keep my mouth shut.

Did I just imagine him asking me to marry him?

I did not.

Still, I do nothing but watch as he finishes dressing, bends over to kiss me on the head and then walks away, leaving the Warlord's chambers.

"I guess I'm getting married," I say to no one in particular.

I slide off the bed and start searching for my own clothes. I dress for a day in the city, assuming that Wolfe will let Kingston know that I am now allowed to leave the palace. I choose a pair of jeans, tight enough that I can strap weapons to my thighs. I wear a sleeveless shirt and a light jacket over top. I'm not anticipating any zombie action so don't need my leather.

Fifteen minutes later I leave the Warlord's chambers, wandering through the dining room where I grab an apple and a tea before heading out the door. Kingston meets me in the hallway and without a word hands me a mask. I grin and take it from him, juggling my breakfast with my new safety procedure.

Our day touring the city goes smoothly and I bow to Kingston's advice on where to go and how to handle myself around people. He doesn't want me near crowds and he prefers that I stay away from the hospital for now. Though it's in my nature to be reckless, my new situation in life has given me hope. I don't think I ever really wanted to die, but at the same time I wasn't taking extra measures to preserve my life. I had no one to preserve it for. My life was better used in the service of a vaccination and hopefully, eventually, a treatment to the Primitive virus.

Now that I have Wolfe, now that we're settling down

together and creating a home, the thought of children and a future seems far more within reach than it ever did before. I want to cling onto the shining picture in my mind of a family and a home, and never let it go.

So, I allow Kingston to dictate our time in the city, allow him to smother me in protection. If this is what it'll take to keep me safe and to give Wolfe peace of mind, then I'm willing to accept it. I can be a reckless bitch sometimes, but I can also recognize the value in continued breathing.

We're just about to wrap up our day, entering the palace underground parking. I'm deep in discussion with Kingston about the rest of the week's activities, when a guard comes rushing toward us. Kingston steps in front of me, his hand dropping to the gun on his belt. We both recognize Denny at the same time and relax.

Denny is no longer my full-time guard, but still occasionally rotates to my detail. He has served the city well and has earned his place in the palace.

"Miss Skye, I must speak to you right away!" he says breathlessly as though he's been running.

"Yes," I tell him as he comes to a halt in front of us. "Is everything okay?"

He shakes his head. "No, we have an emergency at the water treatment plant. An accident, one of the women. She's been hurt, she needs a doctor right away."

"Who is it? Dolly or Anita?" I demand. "Has she been brought into the city?"

He shakes his head. "I don't know which one, but one of them has been hurt badly. She's too injured to move. We need to take the doctor out to her."

"Of course," I say briskly and then turn to Kingston. "Go to the hospital and pick up Dr. Summers. Meet us at the treatment plant."

Kingston hesitates, clearly torn between his duty to me, the Warlord's orders to never let me out of his sight, and his desire to protect one of the most important citizens of our sanctuary. We can't afford to lose either Dolly or Anita, their knowledge is too valuable.

Eventually, he bows to my wisdom, nods and turns away. I call after him, "We'll meet you out there."

"Take your guard," he shouts back before disappearing.

I look at the men surrounding us and say, "Follow us. I'll go with Denny."

I don't wait to see if they listen, but rush out of the palace, Denny on my heels. I look around for a vehicle. "Which one?"

He points at a rusty car that looks as though it shouldn't be roadworthy. I frown at it. Wolfe is very good at making sure that all of the palace security has access to solid, well maintained vehicles. This one looks as though it's on its last tire. Maybe Denny got the short straw today and had to take whatever was left over. I don't question him, sliding into the passenger seat while he goes around to the other side.

He turns the ignition and we speed off together toward the city gates. I glance behind me, but I don't see the guard car. I briefly wonder if I should tell Denny to wait for it, but decide not to. It's more important to get out to the treatment plant and see to the women than it is to wait for my guard.

I wave at the security on the gates and they open the doors allowing us to drive through. Denny guns it and we fly through the desert toward the treatment plant.

FORTY-THREE

When we arrive at the plant, there's no one in sight. I'm confused, as I had guards posted at both the gates, the doors and inside the facility. I don't wait to find out what happened to them though. I follow Denny from the car and inside the building.

"Which way?" I shout to him, now feeling panicked by the darkness inside the building and the eerie silence.

"This way," he yells back and takes off down a hallway, toward the back of the plant.

It must be Anita who's been injured. Dolly would be up in the control room with the computer system. But Anita works in the main area of the plant itself, trying to rebuild the crumbling infrastructure.

I fly through the halls, chasing after Denny. His pace is only increasing my panic. He wouldn't be running so fast if Anita wasn't gravely injured. Only as I round the last corner and follow through the door onto the facility floor do I realize I've made a very stupid mistake.

Standing next to one of the massive treatment tanks is a group of ragtag men. They're a rough group, clothes dirty and ill-fitting, hair wild. Big and mean-looking. Most have beards, all have a plethora of weapons pointed straight at us. I reach for my own weapons and attempt to dive back through the door, but Denny catches my arm.

I immediately go into self-defense mode and strike his arm hard in the bicep with my fist, deadening it. He drops his hand but brings his other fist up and slams it into the side of my head. Blackness engulfs my vision and I drop to the floor. I'm only unconscious for a few seconds, but it's enough that the surrounding men are able to take my weapons from me.

I groan in pain as I'm dragged to my feet by a huge man. He holds me up and stares down at me, his expression both fierce and satisfied. I recognize him. He was on the side of the mountain the night Wolfe and I were attacked. He was bellowing at the other Outsiders. Must be their leader.

"What the fuck do you want?" I snarl at him.

He ignores me and reaches for his pocket, pulling something shiny from the interior. He tosses it to Denny who catches it. I think it might be an old turn of the century watch or something else that holds little value. Money has no meaning in Sanctuary, but people still trade goods and services. There are some who still treasure gold and other precious metals, despite their holding little value anymore.

"There'll be more where that came from when we get the other woman." His voice is deep and raw, as though he spends most of his time shouting and tearing up his throat.

"What other woman?" I demand.

They're talking about a specific woman and I can only think they must mean one of my friends. They're all highly skilled and would make excellent commodities to an Outsider willing to peddle in flesh.

Again, the Outsider ignores me.

"Let's go," he snaps at his men.

I'm dragged through the facility to an exit and then out into the open. The sky is cloudy and it looks like we might have rain, a somewhat rare event for our Sanctuary. I look around and catch sight of three vehicles, all in rough shape, all similar to the one Denny had been driving. Is Denny an Outsider or is he just working with them? I'm confused and frightened, but also completely and utterly pissed off. The second I get my hands on a weapon, these men are fucking done.

The door to the nearest vehicle is yanked open and I'm shoved inside. I grip the edge of the seat, slowing my descent, and frantically search the vehicle for a weapon. Instead of a weapon I see the terrified pale face of a person I recognize. Scarlett. My mouth falls open in shock and I allow myself to be shoved completely into the back seat of the car, where I fall against her. She catches me and helps me sit up.

When I find my voice, I immediately demand, "What are you doing here?"

She shakes her head frantically and stares in horror as the Outsider rounds the vehicle to get into the driver's seat. Another Outsider takes the passenger seat.

I grip her chin and force her to look at me. "I don't give a fuck if they're listening. Talk to me, right fucking now! What are you doing here, where's Deacon?"

Her eyes fill with tears and she shakes her head again. Before she even says the word, I already know. "Dead, I think."

My heart is crushed as the last year rushes through my memory. Deacon and I were friends. We had a relationship based on mutual respect and an understanding that the vaccination we were carrying was the single most important thing we could do with our lives. Now he's gone, Scarlett is sitting in the back of an Outsider car and I have no idea what happened to the rest of my vaccination team.

I'm about to demand more information, when the car takes off so fast I'm flung backwards into my seat. Scarlett grips my arm and pretends to fall against me, tipping her head into my neck. She speaks fast, her voice low but clear. "They grabbed us before we made it far from Sanctuary. They killed everyone except me."

"Why didn't they kill you too?" I demand in a suspicious whisper.

Her eyes grow dim and haunted and I realize why they kept her alive. My stomach churns and I blink away the burning tears of fury. I nod my head, telling her I understand.

"I t-told them I could help them find you, so they let me come along." Her eyes fill with tears and I pat her arm. There was no way for her to help me. Scarlett is a lover, not a fighter. She learned to fight when she had to but she's never had the killer instinct that runs through my veins.

"Why do they want me?" I ask.

She opens her mouth to answer, but the leader answers instead, looking at me through the mirror with his dead gaze. "You are the Blood Saviour. You will buy us anything we could possibly desire when we find a buyer willing to pay."

I narrow my eyes in a glare. "What the fuck are you talking about?"

He lets out a bark of humourless laughter. "You are Skye, the woman whose blood will cure the world. Every Sanctuary across the continent is talking about you. It was only a matter of time before we picked up your trail."

I'm stunned by his words, but the more I think about it,

the more he makes sense. It was inevitable that Sanctuaries who are allied with each other would share the knowledge of a woman and her team of warriors, travelling from Sanctuary to Sanctuary, distributing a vaccine. I just hadn't realized anyone would care enough to come hunting for me.

Their mistake.

We travel across the landscape at speeds so fast I feel positive the junker of a car we're in will fall apart beneath us, but we somehow manage to make it to the mountains. The Outsiders must have set up some kind of home base.

We follow the twists and turns of an old, cracked, overgrown road until we reach an encampment. I count men as we pull up. Twelve total, with another six in the cars behind us. Wolfe and I must've made a dent in their population when they attacked us on the mountainside.

Before we can exit the car, I bend over, clutching at my head, pretending dizziness from the punch I took from Denny. I quickly pull a knife from inside my shoe where they forgot to look for a weapon. As I straighten, crying out in pain for added effect, I shove it into my shirt, where the cold steel presses comfortingly against my skin. Scarlett is staring at me with wide eyes, having seen my action. I squeeze her hand reassuringly.

As we're pulled from the car, I turn to face our host, the leader of the Outsiders. I allow him to see my fury, but I carefully calculate my words. "My husband the Warlord will find you, and when he does, he'll kill you all."

He laughs and shoves me so hard that I trip and fall to the dirt at his feet. I curl into a ball, concealing the gun I'd pulled off his belt. I have no idea if it's loaded, but I have no choice but to assume it is.

"Your husband will be a dead man if he shows up here.

We've learned since our last run-in with you two. We'll be ready."

I roll my eyes. He clearly hasn't learned a damn thing if he thinks I'm going to wait for Wolfe before I turn this party into a bloodbath.

I crawl to my knees, groaning in pain and curling my arms into my stomach. Scarlett drops next to me, her face creased in concern. I pull her against me in a hug and growl in her ear, "You need to run as fast as you can."

I pull back and look at her face. She looks worried, but not surprised. She knows what I'm all about. She makes a show of sliding her hand against my waist and helping me to my feet. She blocks me from view as I plunge a hand into my shirt and drag the knife from the folds.

I nod at her and whisper, "Now, run."

She gives me a desperate look. "They'll kill you!"

"No, they won't. I'm too valuable."

She bites her lip and finally nods, releasing me and turning away.

I shove her and shout, "Run!"

She doesn't pause, but streaks through the mountain clearing into the trees. Shouts rise up around us, as confusion sets in. I turn to the man who orchestrated my kidnapping and grin at him as he swings his gaze from Scarlett's retreating back to me.

"What the fuck are you – ?"

His words are cut off as I slam my knife into his belly and swing the gun up. His eyes widen as I pull the trigger.

To be continued...

ALSO BY NIKITA SLATER

If you enjoyed this book, check out some other works by #1 International Bestselling Author, Nikita Slater. More titles are always in progress, so check back often to see what's new!

Angels & Assassins Series

Book One – The Assassin's Wife

The Queens Series

Book One – Scarred Queen

Book Two - Queen's Move

Book Three - Born a Queen

Book Four - The Red Queen (Coming 2021)

Alejandro's Prey (a novella)

Fire & Vice Series

Book One – Prisoner of Fortune

Book Two – Fight or Flight

Book Three – King's Command

Book Four – Savage Vendetta

Book Five – Fear in Her Eyes

Book Six – Bound by Blood

Book Seven – In His Sights

Book Eight - Burning Beauty

Book Nine - Chasing Ecstasy (Coming soon!)

The Driven Hearts Series

Book One - Driven by Desire

Book Two - Thieving Hearts

Book Three - Capturing Victory

Novella - The Princess and Her Mercenary

The Sanctuary Series

Book One - Sanctuary's Warlord

Book Two - Sanctuary on Fire

Book Three - The Last Sanctuary

Book Four - The Road to Wolfe

Book Five - Skye's Sanctuary (COMING SOON!)

Standalone books

Because You're Mine

Mine to Keep (a novella)

Luna & Andres

Loving Vincent

Loving Jared

Stalked

After Dark

In collaboration with Jasmin Quinn

Collared: A Dark Captive Romance

Safeword: A Dark Romance

Chained: A Mafia Marriage Romance

Good Girl: A Captive BDSM Romance

Hostile Takeover: An Enemies to Lovers Romance

Visit **nikitaslater.com** for more information

and the latest updates!

ABOUT THE AUTHOR

Nikita Slater is the International Bestselling dark romance author of the Fire & Vice series, Angels & Assassins series, The Queens series and several standalone novels. Her favourite genre is mafia romance, the bloodier the better, though she loves to write about every subject under the sun. She lives on the beautiful Canadian prairies with her son and crazy awesome dog. She has an unholy affinity for books (especially erotic romance), wine, pets and anything chocolate. Despite some of the darker themes in her books (which are pure fun and fantasy), Nikita is a staunch feminist and advocate of equal rights for all races, genders and non-gender specific persons. When she isn't writing, dreaming about writing or talking about writing, she helps others discover a love of reading and writing through literacy and social work.

www.ingramcontent.com/pod-product-compliance
Lightning Source LLC
Chambersburg PA
CBHW060234100726
47907CB00003B/629